A TIME FOR SHADOWS

T. J. Banks

PublishingWorks, Inc.
Exeter, NH
2010

The Prologue of this novel, originally titled Dancing Toward the Light, *won 3rd Place in* ByLine's *"1st Chapter of a Novel" Contest in November 2003.*

PublishingWorks, Inc.
151 Epping Road
Exeter, NH 03833
603-778-9883

For Sales and Orders:
1-800-738-6603 or 603-772-7200

Designed by: Anna Pearlman
Cover image from Holland's Magazine, March 1918.

LCCN: 2009925344
ISBN: 1-933002-71-9
ISBN-13: 978-1-933002-71-2

Printed on recycled paper.

For Marissa, and in loving memory of my parents,
Morris and Shirley Banks.

ACKNOWLEDGMENTS

This book started one summer afternoon long ago, when my maternal grandmother, Esther Widem Shinder, told me about her beloved older brother, Max, who had died over in France at the end of the war that changed all wars. Years later, I wrote a story about it—"Esther's Soldier"—that became one of my first published pieces of fiction. But I was still haunted by a war that had ended when my own father was barely four years old.

Esther planted the roots of this story in me, and another grandmother—my late grandmother-in-law, actually, Dorothy "Fitz" Skinner—provided the inspiration for Iris: remembering Fitz, I saw the person that I wanted my heroine to become.

Many thanks go to Gary Reeves and to Dusty Rainbolt of the Cat Writer's Association (CWA) for making available to me the letters of Jennie Dunlap, a real-life American Red Cross nurse stationed in Paris near the end of WWI. Thanks, too, to Daniel J. Clark, whose recollections of France were vital in helping me re-create Iris's war-time world. I also appreciate the time that Carrie Grady of the Simsbury 1820 House and Celia Richards of the Simsbury Public Library took to share their information on conservationist Gifford Pinchot and his aunt, Antoinette Eno Wood, intriguing personalities in their own right.

I'd like to thank my publisher, Jeremy Townsend, for her incisive, insightful editing *and* for putting me through my paces, and Anna Pearlman for her cover illustration that captures the spirit of the times as well as the spirit of the book. And I've been lucky in my readers as well: Janet Moote, Cynthia Daffron, Sandra Costarella of Orphan Alley, and Rita Reynolds of *laJoie* have seen Iris and me through this story from its beginning, helping more than I can say.

Last, but certainly not least, here's to Phyllis Hobe, my late editor at *Guideposts*: we discussed the manuscript at length before her untimely death, and she was, as always, an invaluable sounding board. In almost seven years of working together on various stories, she taught me a great deal about writing, and in her own thoughtful, understated way, she left her mark on this work as well.

When I think of the War to-day, it is not as summer but always as winter; always as cold and darkness and discomfort, and an intermittent warmth of exhilarating excitement which made us irrationally exult in all three. Its permanent symbol, for me, is a candle stuck in the neck of a bottle, the tiny flame flickering in an ice-cold draught, yet creating a miniature illusion of light against an opaque infinity of blackness.

—Vera Brittain, *Testament of Youth*

PROLOGUE

The house was larger than it appeared from the outside. A white Cape, its lines simple and true, it was set back from the road a ways and half-hidden by the maples and spruces around it. Only on my second visit, when I had more time and inclination to study the place, did I see that an L-shaped addition had been attached to the back of the house, making it look like an elegant old white cat with its tail curving around its haunches.

I pushed the doorbell and waited. I thought I heard some quick-footed movements—which surprised me since the info I'd gotten from the seniors' center indicated that Iris MacCurdy was well over ninety with a bad back. I hate to admit it, but I was pretty much expecting a dried-up remnant of a woman, an identical twin to the bad fairy in "Sleeping Beauty." But the woman who came to the door held herself with a certain spirit and grace despite her back trouble. Like her house, her lines had held true over the years.

Her eyes were what caught and held me, though: they were large, blue-gray, and shimmering like abalone or labradorite, fire still flickering in them. They made me think of a line from a song I'd heard once about having crow's feet around your soul. There was sadness in them, yes, but wonder, too, as if she still hadn't gotten over the habit of being fascinated by life after all these years.

She carried a book in her hands. There was, as I soon learned, almost always a book in her hands or somewhere within reach: Mary, the physical therapist who came three mornings a week, would bring them to her from the library. Iris was always telling me about some book or lending it to me. "You *must* read this," she'd insist once we were more at home with each other. "It's a very superior book of its kind."

Right now, though, she was just an elderly shut-in that I'd volunteered to visit once a week as part of a new program at the center, and I—well, I was an out-of-work journalist who had raised being at loose ends to a new art form. The newspaper I'd been working for had recently folded, and the few short pieces I'd written on the side kept coming back with depressing regularity. Yep, from where I was standing, my career looked like one flat line. I'd signed up to help out with the shut-in program on an impulse one day when I happened to be down at the Eno Memorial, where the center was located. But, to be honest, I'd never really expected a call back. And now here I was, staring at this strange old woman with her incredibly far-seeing eyes, not knowing what to say. I quickly glanced down at the book in her thin, still-beautiful hands and said, "So, what're you reading?"

An impish smile lightened the sallow fine-boned face. "A book of vampire stories," she confided, flipping it over and showing me the cover. "You know, I've always been fascinated by vampires. And I love a good supernatural yarn." She freed one of her hands and offered it to me. "You must be Dawn Kailey. The people at the center called me yesterday to say you'd be coming this morning. They told me you're a writer. Do you ever write about vampires?"

"Oh, only the kind you're not allowed to put a stake through," I replied flippantly, shaking her hand. Her grip, like her eyes and her stance, caught me off guard: it was so much stronger than I'd expected.

She tilted her head to one side. "That's your mistake right there, Miss Kailey—you're writing about people you don't care about. How can you expect anyone else to?"

I laughed sheepishly and withdrew my hand. "Tell me, were you a teacher once, Mrs. MacCurdy?"

She laughed, too, as she ushered me into her living room. "My goodness, does it still come through after all these years? It becomes part of you after a time, I suppose." There was a long covered old-fashioned stand-up radiator underneath that window; on the radiator itself was a mix of cut-glass bowls, pitchers, and vases. The sun sifted through the lupines, foxglove, irises, and bee balm outside and onward through the glass dishes, setting loose a riot of rainbows in the room. "Can I get you anything?"

"Please don't go to any trouble. Your back—they told me—"

"My back is behaving itself today, thank you. And I don't get many chances to play hostess these days." And before I could say another word, she had disappeared into the kitchen.

I walked around the room, trying to get a better handle on this woman whose life I'd just walked in on. In the wide Victorian bookcase, authors whose names I knew from rummaging through my parents' library—Elizabeth Goudge, Margaret Campbell Barnes, Gladys Taber, Thomas B. Costain, Booth Tarkington, and both Ernest Thompson Seton and his daughter Anya—kept company with *Watership Down, Wuthering Heights, Jane Eyre,* Loren Eiseley's essays, George MacDonald's fantasy novels, and countless biographies. On the walls with their warm buttery yellow paint were a couple of embroidery pieces and several haunting watercolor landscapes.

But what really caught and held my eye was a quaint framed piece that must've been culled from some old book of flower poetry. In it, a nymph in a flowing green-patterned gown twirled green vines about her as she danced. And just below her bare feet, in the lower right-hand corner of the print, there was this bit of free verse:

"There's traveler's joy
To entwine
At our journey's end
For greeting."

At our journey's end for greeting, I murmured to myself. I liked that.

I moved on to the photographs. They covered the mantel, the bookcase, and the ornate turn-of-the-century desk with its many pigeonholes. I got up from the rocker and sauntered over to check out a grouping on the desk. As with the books, it was a quirky mix. One sepia-toned photo in particular intrigued me. It showed a very young Iris MacCurdy all togged out in a prim white pinafore apron and cap, circa 1918. Same pointed pixie-ish face (with smoother skin, of course) and same large eyes.

I was still studying it when she came back in with a tea set on a slightly faded red tin tray. She set it down on the coffee table and began to pour the tea; her hands trembled a little, though, and the tea slopped out of the teapot and puddled around the blue-and-gold lusterware teacups. "Jesu!" she said with mild irritation as I hurried over to help her set things to rights. "Excuse my clumsiness, my dear. It's these stupid, stiff fingers of mine." She held up one of her hands, and I saw a thin lacing of scars on them like the cross-hatching on old letters.

"What caused that?" I exclaimed.

"Sepsis," Iris replied matter-of-factly as she wiped up the spills with a paper napkin. "I was with the Red Cross as a nurse during the Great War. The soldiers were full of sepsis, and it was quite common for us nurses to catch it while we were dressing their wounds. The doctors would simply lance our fingers, and we'd be back in business in no time." She handed me my teacup and saucer, then settled down with hers in her recliner. "Now, let's make ourselves comfortable and have our tea, Dawn—I may call you Dawn, mayn't I?"

"If I may call you Iris." My tea and I retreated to the rocker. "And I'd love to hear your war stories. They must be incredible."

She sipped her tea. "You may certainly call me Iris. But the stories will have to wait."

"I'm sorry. Are they so painful?"

She placed the teacup and saucer back down on the tray and sat there so silently for so long, I almost thought she had forgotten me. "Painful, yes," she finally said. She ran her fingers absent-mindedly around the gold rim of her cup. "There are some things you never get over, you know. But the infection—the really terrible part of the hurt—does come out of the wounds, just as it has from my fingers here.

"No"—she shook her head—"the time's not right for the telling yet. Well, my stories have kept this long—they'll keep a bit longer, I expect." She smiled, and I caught a glimpse of the young woman in the sepia-toned photo. "So, tell me a little about yourself, Dawn."

And I did. More than a little, actually. She turned out to be a good listener, Iris MacCurdy, her magnetic eyes never leaving my face. And she didn't rush in with fussy bits of advice, plastering them on like Band-Aids, the way that so many folks did. No, she seemed to sense that I wasn't looking for her to do that—that I was doing some very necessary thinking aloud.

Then, suddenly sheepish about having blurted so much about myself to a stranger, I fielded the conversation over to her. There was nothing wrong with her memory, nothing colorless about her stories. She had met some pretty interesting characters along the way, including conservationist Gifford Pinchot on one of his frequent visits back home to Simsbury, his birthplace, and could describe them vividly.

"He was a tall, dynamic man," Iris reminisced, still talking about Pinchot. "And he had this deep ringing voice. I only met him once at an ice-cream social at Mrs. Wood's house right before I joined up with the Red Cross. She was his aunt, you know, and very conservation-minded, too: when she died in the 1930s, she left a $20,000 scholarship to the forestry department at Yale in her husband's memory. But that day, the day that I met her and Gifford Pinchot, the talk was all about the war. The U.S. had just joined up a few months before, so it was pretty much all everybody was talking about wherever you went in town.

"I was just a young school-ma'am, still pretty new in town and too shy to open my mouth much in front of such a great man." She smiled and shook her head gently—at the memory of herself back then and of an opportunity missed, I guessed. "After all, he was a friend of Theodore Roosevelt! But I remember his voice, yes, I do. And his presence—Mr. Pinchot had great presence. Of course, many people, especially in the lumber business out west, loathed him. They called him 'Gifford the First' and 'Czar Pinchot.' But I was always glad that I had the chance to meet him."

"Strange that you met him right before you went overseas," I mused, the writer in me taking over. "I mean, here you were talking"—I smiled—"or, rather, listening to a man who was dedicated to conserving nature—life itself, if you will—and next thing you knew, you were in the midst of all that slaughter. I mean, the soldiers were being reduced to moles in their trenches. And it couldn't have been much better for you nurses."

She leaned her head against the back of her chair. "No, it wasn't," she said. "We had to draw water for hundreds of patients from a single pipe, then heat it on these little camp stoves. Why, we barely had enough water for cleaning the mud and blood off the wounded, let alone for bathing ourselves. Jesu, we used to *dream* of long hot baths and fat, fluffy towels."

She chuckled softly, then lapsed into silence—communing, no doubt, with those long-dead presences that her words had summoned into the room. Not that I saw a book or a knickknack move or heard ghostly footsteps, mind you. Maybe it was just the magic of her words—for Iris MacCurdy, I was beginning to see, had the makings of a storyteller in her, too—but the energy in the room had changed. It no longer felt like we were the only ones in it.

Iris finally looked up and smiled. "I've been wandering again, haven't I? Now, let's finish up our tea, shall we?"

And there you had it: she'd closed that door to her past as nicely and neatly as she'd set out her old-fashioned eggshell-thin china on the once gaudy tray.

But I came back again and again, finding in those visits a kind of—well, *solace*. Her word-weaving held me spellbound, yes. But there was something about Iris herself—some reflective quality as pure as the white-gold light limning the trees on a winter morning—that always left me more at peace with myself than when I first walked in. I don't mean that she was a stereotypical nicey-nice old lady with all sorts of cutesy knickknacks and a house that reeked of mothballs. No—Iris, as I quickly learned, had very definite opinions, and once she made up her mind about someone or something, she never let anyone sway her on the subject.

Her house was filled with what she herself lightly referred to as "interesting clutter." I was always stumbling across a picture or a curio that I'd somehow missed before, and each one had its own story. There was, for instance, a simply but beautifully carved robin perched on a piece of driftwood, its head inquisitively cocked. "Oh, that," Iris laughed affectionately. "That's from May Prentiss—La-Joie, her name is now. We were nurses together over in France. We have a friendly competition every year over who sees the first robin, so she sent me this for my last birthday." Iris shook her head, sighing. "She's almost the last of my old friends left."

One day, I came across an old spur next to a photograph in a cheap brass frame—a sepia-toned photo of a soldier posing with a funny black kitten. The kitten was sitting on—of all things—an artillery shell. They clearly had been having a sparring match just as the picture had been taken, for the soldier had one hand slightly raised and the little animal had one inky paw hooked around it. The kitten seemed to have lighter flecks scattered throughout its coat and these absurd little crescent moons around its eyes that really did look like spectacles. The young man turning his face toward the camera was lean and taut with mocking deep-set eyes and a crooked grin.

Somehow I'd missed both items before. I picked up the spur—which, despite its age, still had a dull gleam to it, as if it had been frequently polished—and looked at Iris, my eyebrows raised.

"Oh, that." She smiled, shaking her head. "That was a gift from a very brash young man I met overseas."

"A *spur?*"

"Oh, yes." She laughed. "He was from Georgia, you see, and he told me that it was customary there to give a girl one of your spurs if you had any serious intentions." She ran her fingers along the metal. "Believe it or not, he said you didn't even think about flirting with a woman back home who was toting one of these, that's how significant it was considered."

Iris handed the spur back to me, and I laid it gently back on the top of the bookcase where I'd found it. I gestured toward the picture in the tortoiseshell frame. "Your husband was a very good-looking man."

"Yes, he was." Her smile never wavered. "But that's not my husband." Her eyes traveled up to a slightly less-old photo—judging from the clothes, that is—of a young couple, which was hanging to the left of a piece of crewel embroidery just above the mantel, then back to the young soldier's picture. "Oh, there's some similarity, I'll grant you—both were slim, dark men—but that's not my husband, Joe. And, in case you're wondering, no, it's not my brother either. I was an only child."

I raised my eyebrows.

"That," she said succinctly, "was Jerry Enright. I knew him when I was over in France. He was with the Canadian Infantry. The kitten was his battalion's mascot—a little stray they'd found in a shelled village. Jerry was fond of animals and used to write me about him. 'Hawkeye,' they called him—he seemed to have a sixth sense about where the landmines and snipers were, Jerry said, and the men all thought of him as their good-luck piece." She sighed and closed her eyes for a moment. "He must've gone missing the morning that Jerry died." She shook her head. "It was a month to the day before the Armistice was signed, can you believe it? Just a month."

I studied the man with the deep-set eyes. "So he was your"—I fumbled for the right word—"beau?"

"I suppose you might call him that. We really only knew each other a short time. But he had this way of making everyone else seem . . . well, *drab.*" She moved her hands restlessly about. "When he died"—the elegant old hands with their crisscrossing of faint scars fell limply to her sides—"the color went out of my world, and it took me a while to find it again."

My eyes happened upon still another photo—a lovely one of Iris holding a little girl with dark ringlets and wistful eyes. Iris followed my gaze. "That's my daughter, Lucy," she said briefly. "I have other pictures of her, of course, but that's always been my favorite."

"I didn't know you had any children," I murmured.

"She was, shall we say, a *surprise*." Iris smiled oddly. "She's been teaching art at the University of Edinburgh these last few years."

And that was all I heard of her dead lover—or of her daughter—that day. But it was enough to tell me that they were where a good part of her heart—and the heart of her story—lay. I would just have to bide my time to learn the rest.

We no longer had a set time for our visits: I would simply call Iris, and she would leave the door unlocked for me. Sometimes I'd find her asleep in the big recliner that seemed to ease the pain in her back, and I'd just sit there, taking in the peacefulness of the room and waiting for her to wake up.

"Why, how long have I been asleep?" she'd ask as soon as she'd opened her eyes.

"Not long," I'd assure her, and we'd pick up the threads of our last conversation wherever we'd left off from the last visit.

Late one afternoon—it was Halloween, and the October wind was gypsying through the dry leaves—Iris surprised me by bringing out a dusty pale-green bottle, a corkscrew, and two wine glasses with worn gold rims. "I don't think the only spirits should be outside," she remarked with the same mischievous look she'd worn that first day, when she'd confessed her liking for vampire stories. She handed the bottle and corkscrew over to me. "Do the honors, will you, Dawn?" She set the glasses on the table, touching them affectionately. "Joe and I got these at Eno, back when it was a movie theater. Some sort of promotional thing, I guess you'd call it these days."

I opened the bottle of cognac. It had a picture of a stag and the words "*Vieille Grande Champagne*" on the label. "'Ladies' Vintage,'" she explained as I was pouring it. She glanced up at me and smiled. "It got that name because with the men mostly off at the front, the women ended up taking over the wine-making, just as they did with nearly everything else during the war." She sipped her cognac. "Over in England, especially—you name it, the women did it. Clerking, farming, working in the munitions factories, delivering the mail—why, some of them even worked as prison guards."

"So the war freed you, too," I said. I gave the brandy a taste. It had a sweet but surprisingly subtle flavor at the same time.

"Oh, it did, it did. But what a price, my dear . . . what a hideous price." She took another sip. "You know, I read a few years ago that they've never been able to figure out exactly how many men were killed during the Great War. And, of course, many came away with chronic bronchitis or tuberculosis from being gassed or with heart disease from the sheer hell of having to live through it all." A shudder ran through her thin old body, and she shook her head. "Such a terrible bloody price tag . . . ."

"For you, too?" I queried softly. For I knew her well enough now to be able to ask her that. "How long did it take you to get over it—over him?"

She turned those large luminous eyes on me. "I never did," she replied, her voice a dull, aching whisper. "I never did." She set her wine glass back down on the table and twisted her fingers about the stem. "*My friend, you would not tell with such high zest/To children ardent for some desperate glory,/The old Lie: Dulce et decorum est/Pro patria mori.*"

"Wilfred Owen," I murmured. Iris gave me a sharp look. "War literature seminar at college," I explained hastily.

She took another, longer sip of the cognac. "I remember the first train filled with soldiers coming down from the north on its way to New Haven. It was all very hush-hush—no lights and all that—but somehow word got out, and a lot of us went down to the station to meet that train and gave the soldiers candy, gum, and cigarettes. I remember their faces, white flames against the darkness . . ."

Her voice quavered slightly. "I see them that way sometimes, you know—young and hopeful. It's better than seeing them all burned and bloodied, sides of their faces blown away, mangled by shell, missing noses, eyelids . . . it was a sculptor, you know, who came up with the idea of making masks for them to wear . . . British fellow named Derwent Wood. I knew him, too." She had finished her wine by now and was playing with the stem of her wine glass again. "I met so many people, and now less than a handful are left. This brave new world is too brave and new for me." Her mouth went up in a quirky half-smile, but her eyes remained soft and sad. "Jerry gave me this bottle of wine. That and the spur. We were supposed to share the wine when he came back from the front, but he never did."

I put down my own half-empty glass on the tray across from hers. "Tell me about Jerry," I said, knowing that this was the time.

Iris nodded, almost to herself. "Yes, I think I will . . . you can remember him for me when I go West."

"West?" I raised my eyebrows, frowning.

"That's what the soldiers used to call dying. 'I'll be going West soon,' they'd say, the ones beyond our helping. Of course, some—the ones whose faces were just about gone—helped themselves there. They couldn't bear what they saw looking back at them in other people's eyes. That's why the sisters at the hospital used to tell us it was so important not to flinch when we were tending those cases."

"That must've been hard," I murmured, "keeping it all bottled inside. I don't know if I could've done it."

Iris shook her head. "Oh, you'd be surprised," she replied firmly. "You'd be surprised what you can do when you have to, Dawn. I surprised myself continually back then."

"In a good way or a bad way?" I asked—then wanted to brain myself. *God, I sound like Glinda in "The Wizard of Oz,"* I told myself disgustedly.

"Good and bad," she said softly. I followed her wandering, wistful gaze over to Jerry's photo. "Good and bad . . ."

CHAPTER ONE

"You really must see how I've got it all laid out," a woman's voice was saying not far from the shady spot where Iris stood, sipping her lemonade and idly wondering what on earth her hostess, Antoinette Eno Wood, was talking about. "I'm very impressed with the design—it's exactly what I wanted."

"So you've gone ahead with the more formal old-fashioned flower garden design?" another woman's voice inquired politely.

"Oh, no." The first voice was dismissive, almost scornful. "I decided that formal gardens sounded too stuffy and imitative. Anyway, I've hired a very good gardener since you were here last—a bright young man who used to work for one of those wealthy old Dutch families in New York—and I'm letting him handle all that. No, what I'm talking about are my mausoleums. There are several of them atop the hill in the center cemetery."

"*Several?*" echoed the other woman. Iris tried not to choke on her lemonade.

"Why, yes," the first speaker retorted coolly. "We'll stroll over after the festivities, and I'll show them to you. I think you'll like their lines: they're classical—nothing ornate or pretentious about them, I assure you."

A regular estate, Iris thought, seeing it all in her mind's eye: the Eno and Wood mausoleums lording it over the lowlier graves and well-heeled spirits floating about, carrying their ghostly calling cards. She shook her head, glad that there was nobody close by to see the smirk she felt sure was plastered on her face. She was, after all, practically a newcomer to Simsbury, a little out-of-town schoolma'am, and she didn't want to offend Antoinette Eno Wood, a wealthy, influential widow who hobnobbed with the likes of Senator George McLean. A woman whose nephew was Gifford Pinchot, a former member of the Department of Agriculture and a crony of Theodore Roosevelt's. Iris didn't want to be teaching school in this out-of-the-way place forever; but neither did she wish to be ridden out of it on a rail so soon after finishing her first term.

She glanced around her. People were milling about Antoinette Eno Wood's comfortable shady lawns, chatting by the wooden gazebo, and otherwise enjoying the hot July day. Iris's landlady, Mrs. Banning, had explained that every Fourth of July, Mrs. Wood threw an ice-cream social for the entire town. Aside from Mrs. Wood and a few very wealthy families, most of the people in Simsbury farmed or worked in the tobacco fields or such local industries as the Ensign-Bickford plant, the nearby Tariffville Lace Co., or the silver-plating factory, also in Tariffville. A lot of them were immigrants who'd been able to purchase land very cheaply in this (literally) off-the-beaten-track Connecticut town. So this town-wide social of Mrs. Wood's was definitely a treat for them.

The social was, Iris supposed, as she strolled over to study a stand of pretty coral daylilies, a good way of meeting people, although most of them had that keeping-themselves-to-themselves manner that she'd come across in other small New England towns since she'd begun teaching. *I'd probably have to live in town a good twenty years or more to be counted as anyone who really belonged here,* she thought, bending over to sniff the daylily.

Belonging. Did anyone ever completely feel as though he or she belonged anywhere? She surely never had, Iris thought tiredly. Not for very long, at least. Orphaned at eight, she'd lived with her mother's parents. First her grandfather, then her grandmother had died; the farm had been sold to pay off their outstanding debts. Iris had been 16 then, old enough to make a living for herself.

So she'd done what hundreds of girls in her situation did: she'd started teaching, taking positions in one-room schoolhouses until she'd saved enough to put herself through teaching college. That had been three years ago, and here she was now, stuck in yet another one-room schoolhouse. Teaching didn't quite satisfy her, but it did pay her bills, and the teaching routine gave some shape and color—admittedly, not much—to her days.

Truth was, she thought, bending over to stroke a coral petal, she didn't know what would cure that restlessness, that emptiness inside her. It might be hard to have your heart set on something and not get it—she straightened up, absent-mindedly rubbing her nose as she pursued her thought—but it was infinitely worse to have your heart set on *nothing* . . . to know that nothing mattered enough to hurt for . . .

"You seem to be having some serious thoughts," a male voice said teasingly. It was a musical voice with a warm Scottish burr. "Basking in the shade and commiserating with the daylilies as you are."

Iris's head whipped around. Right by her side was a slim young man in a light summer suit—not expensive, but neatly made. He smiled at her whimsically. His manner was downright familiar, although she didn't remember ever having seen him around town before. As they stood there, staring at each other, his smile turned into an out-and-out grin. He whipped out a crisp white handkerchief.

"Er—excuse me," he said. "You might be needing this. Your"—he was choking back something that sounded suspiciously like laughter—"your war paint seems to have gone awry."

She swore she could feel a blood vessel about to burst. "War paint!" she retorted. "Listen, sir, I don't know who you think you are, but I do NOT wear rouge, do you hear me?"

"Sorry, miss," the stranger replied. The laughter left his mouth but not his large blue-gray eyes. "It's just that you happen to have this odd orangey-yellow splotch on your nose and—"

Iris gasped, putting her fingers up against her nose. When she took them away, the tips were orangey-yellow, just as the young man had said. Forgetting her manners, she tore the handkerchief from his long artistic fingers and rubbed her nose till it hurt. "It's the pollen from the daylilies," she groaned, handing back the streaky handkerchief. "Do you think anyone else noticed?"

"No, I don't," he assured her, stuffing the handkerchief back into his breast pocket. He stuck out his hand. "Joseph MacCurdy at your service, miss. You've already met my handkerchief."

She took his hand and was surprised at the strength in it. "Iris Amory," she replied. "I've been teaching at the schoolhouse on Firetown Road. Please excuse my outburst—it's just that I don't really know anyone here other than the family I've been boarding with and—"

"It's a hard town to get acquainted with folks in," he agreed. He fell into step with her as she moved away from the daylilies. "Have you been introduced to Mrs. Wood yet?"

Iris shook her head. "No." She laughed a little sheepishly. "I'm ashamed to admit it, but I'm more than a bit afraid of her. She's so imposing—just like this house of hers."

Joe laughed. "She can be a Tartar, all right," he admitted. "But she's really a very good soul, very interested in gardens and all sorts of causes. Especially conservation. She has these soirees every Sunday with folks like Reverend Winslow, Senator McLean, and her nephew there, and you should hear them go on about the forests and the parkland and the trains."

"The trains?"

"Oh, yes. The trains run from Hoskins Station into the center here, through West Simsbury, and over the mountain into Canton, and a great many cinders fall from them, kindling forest fires. All we've got hereabouts are the various town tree wardens, and they've got neither money nor proper equipment to deal with the consequences, so to speak. A fellow by the name of Goodwin was holding forth about it a couple of Sundays back."

Iris looked up at his lean face with amusement. "And what do you do, Joe MacCurdy, that you know so much about what goes on in Mrs. Wood's parlor?"

He doffed his straw hat and bowed. "You are looking, ma'am, at Mrs. Wood's latest gardener. Imported, no less."

A burble of laughter escaped Iris's lips. "So *you're* the 'bright young man from New York'!" she exclaimed. She raised an eyebrow. *"New York?* Really!"

"By way of Scotland," Joe assured her, shrugging. "I worked for a large estate in New York for a while. Very fancy folk—the *crème de la crème*, I guess you'd be calling them. Or, at least, that's how they thought of themselves. Anyway, I took this job here with Mrs. Wood. When the train left me off at the station in Weatogue, I took one look around me, grabbed the stationmaster by his coat lapels, and shook him. 'When's the next train back to New York?' I demanded. You see, the place was all mud and pretty forlorn-looking to a young fellow like myself who'd been living in the likes of New York."

"But you stayed," Iris remarked.

"Yes, I stayed," he retorted, grinning. "There wasn't another train heading to New York for a few days. By then, I'd gotten myself in hand and chanced to meet Mrs. Wood, who was in desperate need of a gardener, having driven the last one off. So it all worked out, you see. Anyway, if it's an introduction to herself you're wanting, I'm your man." He offered her his arm. "She really isn't such a bad old soul. Very liberal compared to most of these rich madams. None of the ones I ever worked with before would have let me sit in on their soirees like she has."

Iris hesitated—both at the prospect of meeting Simsbury's *grande dame* and at taking this strange young man's arm. But she *did* want to meet Antoinette Eno Wood and possibly—just possibly—her nephew, whom she'd read so much about in the papers.

As for Joe MacCurdy—well, something in his large expressive eyes called out to her, and she felt oddly at home with him. "All right," she said, taking his arm. "But mind you give me a proper introduction, Joe MacCurdy."

"We aim to please, Miss Amory," he assured her, as they wove their way through the crowd to the gazebo, where Mrs. Wood was chatting with someone whom Iris knew by sight to be Mrs. Darling, another one of the Powers That Be in town.

Not that you really noticed anyone else when Antoinette Eno Wood was holding court. She definitely had presence, Iris decided as Joe did the introductions. Something like Queen Victoria, only a whole lot handsomer. Not exactly Queen Alexandra either, but she carried herself with style and poise. The thick dark hair had only a lacing of white in it, and the dark brown eyes had spirit and luster.

After excusing herself to Mrs. Darling, who nodded graciously enough to Iris as she left, Mrs. Wood immediately turned her focus on Iris. How did she like Simsbury? With whom was she boarding? How did she find students in Simsbury compared to students in other towns where she'd taught? Finally, having exhausted all other topics, Mrs. Wood fired off the question that Iris had been dreading: "What church do you attend, Miss Amory?"

Iris gulped for air. "I don't go to church much, Mrs. Wood," she blurted, feeling as though her lungs were about to come out of her throat. *There, I've just hanged myself,* she groaned mentally. *In front of the grande dame of Simsbury society, too. Really, they'll probably run me out of town like they did the Quakers in Massachusetts. I wonder if they still brand people in these parts?*

But she had to speak truthfully. Her grandmother had been a strange old soul, not holding much with churchgoing, preferring to rely on herbs, the phases of the moon, and a number of other practices that Iris had learned not to question too closely. Once in a great while, Iris's grandfather had taken her to hear a Sunday sermon or prayer meeting, but she had found both the service and the liturgy cold and lifeless. Yet there had been times out in her grandmother's garden or the woods surrounding the farm when Iris had felt a sort of glory and power, and that had been God to her.

But she couldn't confide such feelings to just anyone. And certainly not to Antoinette Eno Wood, who probably would've been grossly insulted at being lumped together with all the "just anyones" of the world.

The aforesaid lady was frowning, and Iris began to think that the Queen Victoria comparison wasn't so farfetched after all. "But, Miss Amory, how do you expect to have any influence with the parents, let alone with your students? They'll think you heathenish."

"Come, Aunt Nettie," a tall mustached man said pleasantly, putting his hand on Mrs. Wood's shoulder. "Give the young lady a chance to catch her breath." He turned to Iris. "Gifford Pinchot. I take it that you're the new teacher and heathen in town. I'm glad to meet you. We don't get many heathens in Simsbury."

Mrs. Wood rolled her eyes. Iris, flustered, murmured something polite and inconsequential and stepped back a little to take in the conversation around her better.

It soon turned, as most talk did these days, to the fighting over in Europe. In April, the U.S. had finally entered the war against Germany, and war offices were forming all over the country. There was one in the big brick building across from the center cemetery here in town that Henry Ellsworth, Jonathan Eno, and George Pattison were in charge of. In Simsbury there was a very real cause for concern: the Ensign-Bickford plant in the heart of town was a major supplier of explosives, and the Heublein Tower on Talcott Mountain was, the War Bureau officers worried, a possible vantage point for signaling German U-boats in Long Island Sound or firing on the Colt munitions factory in Hartford.

"I understand that Henry and the others were training with General Leonard Wood up in Plattsburgh, New York," their hostess was saying. "The general, Henry told me, had been anticipating our entering the war for quite a while and felt we were terribly ill-prepared."

"What would you say to that, sir?" Joe asked Pinchot. Clearly, he felt very much at ease with the former Chief of Forestry.

Pinchot shook his head. "Is one ever prepared for war, Joe?" he asked, his thoughtful eyes troubled.

"But you're no slouch when it comes to fighting, sir," Joe remarked. "Look how you took on President Taft and Richard Ballinger about the Alaskan coal fields—on the floor of Congress, no less."

"That was different, Joe. Lives weren't involved. Well, not directly." Pinchot let his gaze drift over to the center cemetery before turning back to the younger man. "No, I'm just glad that Cornelia and I have no son old enough to fight over there."

"That's selfish, Gifford—almost as selfish as that subscription practice during the Civil War," his aunt rebuked. "What about those stories we've been hearing about the German corpse-rendering works, the crucified Canadian soldier—there was a story about that in one of the Los Angeles papers, I distinctly remember reading about it—and all those pitiful bayoneted babies over in Belgium?"

"Yellow journalism, long may she wave," he replied. "We saw it during the Spanish-American War, and it's being reborn like some hideous phoenix in this war. It's all designed to inflame public opinion against the Germans and push America into the war. You know what Clarence Darrow says, Aunt Nettie? He says that for some time now, he has been offering a large sum of money to anyone who can bring him a photo of an actual bayoneted baby and that no one's come forward with one yet."

Pinchot scuffed at the ground with his wing-tip shoe. "No, Aunt Nettie, those stories have about as much foundation as Mr. Arthur Machen's story about the ghostly English bowmen who fought at Agincourt coming to the aid of their countrymen at the front now." He kicked a pebble at his feet. "Good story, that."

"So you're a pacifist, Mr. Pinchot?" Iris finally found her voice. All this talk of war stirred something in her that she couldn't quite put a name to. It was as if she'd been trotting along on a docile old farm horse, only to have someone smack it and set it galloping wildly off on its own.

He smiled. "Oh, I'm no Jeanette Rankin, Miss Amory," he replied, referring to the Montana representative who had alienated her own party—and many others in Washington—by opposing the U.S.'s entry into the war. "But I understand her feelings on the subject, I do. I've spent most of my life trying to conserve things—land and trees—and this just goes against the grain. We *have* to fight now to help end this horror, but there will be a tremendous waste of life and effort. And as a man and a conservationist, I abhor that. You won't have mausoleums enough to hold the bodies from this war, Aunt Nettie."

"I understand that Harry Lauder's delighted that we're finally entering the fray," Joe remarked. "Of course, he's been agitating for it since he was touring the States three years ago. And now that he's lost his own son in the war, he's been campaigning like a man possessed and entertaining the Scottish troops right at the front lines. He's got his own recruiting band that travels with him at his own expense, I hear, and this small piano he had made special. There's even talk about his making one of them moving-pictures with Charlie Chaplin and using the money from it for the Harry Lauder Million Pound Fund for maimed men and Scottish soldiers and sailors."

"A brave man," Pinchot said. "We need more men—and women—like him. Still, what was it that that British nurse, Edith Cavell, said before the Germans shot her for aiding Allied troops? 'I know now that patriotism is not enough. I must have no hatred and no bitterness toward anyone.' Well, patriotism isn't enough, she was right about that. Still, I'm afraid there'll be plenty of hatred and bitterness from this blood harvest."

The hot, bright July day went cold and leaden. Time had completely stopped: the chatter and laughter of the other townspeople seemed to be coming from very far away. Iris shivered and glanced first at Joe, then at the other young men flirting and enjoying themselves at the social. *How many of them will be here next year?* she wondered, her hands trembling like aspen leaves in the wind.

Similar thoughts must have been crossing her companions' minds as well: even Mrs. Wood's face was suddenly as shadowed and pensive as that of a figure in a Rembrandt painting. You could almost see the older woman make a physical effort to pull herself back to the present moment. "Well, there's no way around it now," she said matter-of-factly, "though Lord knows, President Wilson has looked for one. So all that remains now is for us to go through it."

"All," Pinchot said cryptically.

"I suppose I'd better go talk to Mrs. Ellsworth now," Mrs. Wood went on, ignoring her nephew's last little jab. "You, too, Gifford—

she'll be expecting you and Cornelia to call on her soon, you know."
As she passed by Iris in a sweep of summer silk, she paused and said
in a low voice, "Buck up, girl, and conserve your energy. No matter
what kind of outlandish ideas you have, this country will soon be
needing you just as much as they will old Henry Ellsworth."

CHAPTER TWO

"There's a train full of soldiers coming down from the north tonight," a voice with a rolling Scottish burr murmured behind Iris in line at the post office. Joe's hand came to rest lightly on her shoulder.

"How do you know?" she whispered, staring at the Red Cross posters hanging behind the postmaster's counter. One was pretty plain: a couple of knitting needles, some tangled skeins of gray yarn, and the words "Our Boys Need Sox!" The other showed a nurse walking hand-in-hand with a heavily bandaged soldier and demanding, "WHAT are YOU doing to HELP?" Truthfully, Iris couldn't imagine how they boosted patriotic spirit—and the nurse in the last one with her doughy features and lugubrious eyes made her skin crawl—but she kept her eyes fixed on them, not wanting to give the women behind them in line any more cause for gossip than Joe probably already had by pushing past them to talk with her.

"Heard Jonathan Eno and George Pattison talking it over with Mrs. Wood this morning," he explained. "They stopped by the house—looking for a contribution to the war office, I expect. It was supposed to be all hush-hush, but I was trimming back some of the trees, and they didn't pay me any mind." Joe grinned at her. "We gardeners get all the opportunities."

12

"I can see that," she retorted, laughing in spite of herself. "Anyway, why are you telling me about it, Joe?"

He shrugged but flicked a stray side-curl away from her face. "Maybe it's because I've a weakness for chestnut-haired women," he told her, his eyes scanning her face. "Or maybe, just maybe I'm thinking it's a historic moment that neither of us should be missing out on. Either way, I'd like you there with me." He paused, his face oddly shadowed. "There's some things I'm in the process of settling. And I'd feel easier in my mind talking them over with you—if I'm not being too forward, that is."

He was smiling again. And Iris—moved by that something she couldn't put a name to but that he somehow evoked in her—touched his arm, suddenly not minding about all those curious dowagers. "I'll be there. What time should the train be passing through?"

"Eight-thirty, according to the stationmaster. I did some checking with him before I came down here. Shall I stop by Mrs. Banning's for you?"

"I'll meet you down there." Mrs. Banning was a nice down-to-earth soul, but Iris didn't want her knowing too much of her business.

"Good. I'll be seeing you at the station then." He tipped his tweed cap to her and sauntered out the door, whistling. *He's so easygoing,* she thought, half-shaking her head. Not likely that whatever he wanted to discuss was all that earth-shattering.

Still, she couldn't help wondering what those "things" he'd talked about might be. A good, sharp poke in the ribs from Mrs. Hendricks brought her back to the drab Tuesday-morning reality of the Station Street post office. The postmaster was holding out a packet of letters for her. And the nurse in the poster was staring down at her more dolefully than ever.

Iris was breathless by the time she reached the station, having run much of the way from Mrs. Banning's. The late summer afternoon afterglow was giving way to a wistful twilight, but there was still enough light to see by.

She didn't see any sign of Joe among the people who were drifting toward the station and was ready to give up on him when she turned around to find him right behind her, smiling.

"'Candle-lighting time,' my granny used to call this," he said with a reminiscent smile. "It's my favorite time for wandering around in the gardens and checking on the roses and what not—well, that and the early morning." His eyes were big and warm as they rested on her face. "It suits you, too. But, then, you've got a flower's name, so I should've known that that would be how it is."

Iris felt her cheeks burning. Joe laughed and turned the talk to something else. "Yes, if you ask me, this is definitely the time of day when the souls of the trees and flowers come alive. And when the other souls do, too, if you'd ever heard my granny talk."

"Old Country stories?" she laughed back at him. Then, suddenly remembering her own grandmother, she asked, "Do you believe in any of that, Joe?"

He looked at her coolly enough then. "I'm not saying 'yes,' and I'm not saying 'no.' But there's this room in Mrs. Wood's big mansion there that always feels cold, even when it's hot as blazes outside. They used to wake bodies in there, I'm told. You think there's not a tale or two behind that? Still, I'm not a great one for opening some doors."

"Why not?" she countered. "I didn't think there was much you'd stop at."

"Depends on the door," he replied, grinning slightly, though his eyes were serious. "But there's some doors that aren't so easy to close once you've pried them open."

Iris felt herself blushing again. She wasn't exactly sure what her feelings for Joe were—they'd known each other such a short time, after all. But they'd run into each other quite frequently since Mrs. Wood's Fourth of July ice-cream social, and he always managed to squeeze in a friendly chat. Sometimes, indeed, he did more than that: he spun it out, like the girl in the fairy tale spinning her straw into gold. And in the last couple of weeks, he'd taken her for some walks over the Drake Hill Bridge and along the Farmington River. Once, they'd seen a swan ready to take flight, its great sail-like wings uplifted.

"Like the hands of a soul in prayer," Iris had murmured, not realizing at first that she'd spoken aloud. Then she'd blushed. It had sounded so silly.

But Joe hadn't laughed. "You're an incredible person, Iris Amory, you know that?" he'd replied, leaning toward her. "You make me see things I might not have seen otherwise. I'm thinking you've got a touch of the poet about you." There'd been just the hint of a caress in the way he'd said "touch": for a dazzling second, she'd thought he'd been about to kiss her. He hadn't. But the warmth in his eyes had been a kiss in itself.

Not sure where their banter was heading now—or whether she was ready to handle it—she turned aside, glancing around her. "There are so many people here. Children, too. It's really amazing, especially"—her lips curved upward—"since it was supposed to be 'all hush-hush.'"

"News travels fast in a town the size of this. I expect Eno or Ellsworth may've let it slip to other parties along their travels this morning without meaning to, or maybe their wives did." Joe shrugged.

The dark swept in like mist coming off the sea, swallowing up what was left of the sunset. Joe's face—and, indeed, the faces of everyone else in the crowd—was reduced to ghostly flickers of light. Gradually, Iris became aware of the *clickety-clack!* of a train in the distance . . . of the screech of its brakes as it pulled into the station and rumbled to a stop. There were no lights on in any of the cars. Soon, however, the faces began appearing at the windows: pale as corpses but determined at the same time.

The children surged forward. They pressed their little offerings into the soldiers' outstretched hands—candy, gum, and cigarettes that they must've bought earlier with carefully hoarded pennies. The soldiers' stiff waxen faces relaxed, and they laughed and joked with the kids as if this was just some silly escapade they were heading out on.

Some of the bolder young women went forward and kissed the men. But Iris just stood there, a terrible sadness washing over her. It was, as Joe had said, a historic moment. *But what a terrible history in the making,* she thought. *We are seeing the end of everything we know. We are all children in the dark, and this is the nightmare to end all nightmares.*

She shivered, and Joe placed his hand on her shoulder, steadying her. "All right?" he asked.

"Somebody just walked on my grave, I guess," Iris said, trying to laugh and failing utterly. The soldiers were disentangling themselves from the young women's embraces: one freckled red-haired boy rubbed his cheek ruefully as he let go of his well-wisher, and Iris hoped especially hard that he would make it home. He was so young and good-natured-looking.

"There'll be a lot of that particular feeling going round," Joe said grimly as the train began pulling out of the depot. "Let's just hope it's not really your grave or mine." He hesitated. "I'm joining up."

Her lips parted to form a "No," but not a sound came forth. She just stared at him disbelievingly. She didn't know exactly what her feelings for him were, but he was the only friend she'd made in this town, and he was leaving. And not just for another town or state or even for his own homeland, but for the mud and blood of the front. For the large trench rats—she'd heard stories from other folks who had men fighting "over there"—and the stench of dead men and horses that all the quicklime in the world couldn't smother. Iris looked at the long, lithe lines of him ... at the blue-gray eyes that weren't laughing and flirting with her now ... and wished that they *had* kissed down by the Farmington the day they'd seen the swan.

"It won't be for a couple of weeks yet," Joe was saying. "I'll be joining up with the Yankee Division—this is my country now. But, you know, I've got a lot of kin back home who've joined up—there's a powerful lot of Scots out in those trenches—and I wouldn't want them thinking I've gone white-feather and am shirking my duty now that I've gotten Americanized. And I want to be making a difference." He spoke with a passion that she didn't remember ever having heard in his voice before, and his eyes were oddly shadowed. "You understand, don't you, Iris?"

She nodded, not trusting her voice.

"You'll write me?"

"Yes." The word came out slowly and creakingly like a motorcar being cranked. She searched about for the right thing to say and smiled faintly as she stumbled upon it. "I understand why you're do-ing this, Joe—I really do. But"—she faltered—"I wish you weren't."

"You mean that, do you?" His own voice was low. Urgent.

She did, more than she could possibly have imagined. There was this awful tug at her heart at the thought of turning some cor-ner in the center of town and not seeing him come round it. "Yes, I do mean it," she said more firmly.

His face lit up. "Well, I'm glad to hear that," he told her simply. They began moving slowly away from the railroad tracks and all the chatter. "I know it's not long we've been acquainted with each other, and we can't be making promises, what with none of us knowing where we'll be in a month's time, let alone a year's. But I like you, Iris Amory. You've got a tang that most women don't. You don't talk unless you've got something to say, and *that's* downright refreshing, it is."

"Must be that 'heathenish' upbringing of mine," she laughed, instinctively turning her face away from him.

"Oh, that's right—your old witch of a grandmother," he chuckled. Iris had told him about her grandmother during one of their walks when they were trading family histories. "Can't think how the school-board trustees missed that blot on the old family escutcheon when they were hiring you."

Iris grinned in spite of herself. "Well, I'm depending on you to keep my secret safe. After all, I wouldn't put it past some of the natives here to bring me to trial. And with my luck, rope is probably on sale down at Pattison's store."

"Not till the end of the month," Joe said, grinning back at her. "But I hear they've got a nice deal on tar and feathers. Still, it'd be a shame to spoil that pretty dress of yours. I expect they've never really had an honest-to-goodness witch around here—unless you count the poor soul who stole the communion plate from the church and drowned herself in the pond while they were chasing her."

They walked along companionably till they came to Plank Hill Road and Mrs. Banning's gate. Joe put his right hand on the latch, then paused. "So, what're you thinking now, Iris Amory?"

She lowered her eyelashes. "That I'll be seeing you, Joe Mac-Curdy."

"Aye, that you will, and soon." He reached out with his left arm and pulled her close, kissing her. She'd been kissed a few times before but never like this, his mouth all tender and searching and his teeth gently nipping her upper lip.

"There, now you've been kissed by a Scotsman," he said, letting her go. He tipped his cap to her and sauntered away, whistling. Iris stood there, the feeling he'd kindled flaming through her as she watched him disappear into the dark.

She sleepwalked through the next morning. Joe's kiss had left her unsettled: that, along with the memory of all those pasty-faced soldiers going off to the front, had kept her from falling asleep for a while. And when she had finally drifted off just before dawn, she'd dreamt of a hideous black train belching blood instead of steam, tearing up the tracks, and spitting out severed arms and legs . . . and even a head, its dark hair blood-matted, its blue-gray eyes still moving . . .

So she was glad that Mrs. Banning had taken it into her head to put up preserves that afternoon and needed her help. It was hot, sticky work for late August, but at least it didn't require much thinking. After a few hours, they had enough jars to satisfy even Mrs. Banning's housewifely heart, and Iris retired to the garden with a copy of Sarah Orne Jewett's *The Country of the Pointed Firs,* which she'd just taken out of the library.

But the book lay unopened in her lap as she sat there in her landlady's garden, the sun slanting through the leaves of the birch and fruit trees. Many of the flowers had finished their blooming, but the chrysanthemums and roses were still holding their own, and a few white bellflowers and purple harebells had opened up unexpectedly by the gate that morning. And morning-glories were weaving themselves over the gate itself, their pink, purple, and blue faces popping out mischievously from the tangle of heart-shaped leaves and vines.

Funny how much this garden with its quaint old-fashioned flowers reminded her of her grandmother's. Except, of course, there were only a few herbs in this one, nothing like the curious collection of arcane ones that her grandmother had had. Iris leaned back on the wooden bench. She could just see the old lady, her skin paper-thin and stretched over her pointed face ... her bird-claw hand touching leaves and blossoms with a gentleness she only showed her plants.

"Mugwort," she remembered the old lady murmuring. "That's for good dreams, child. Same with lady's bedstraw here. Lovage. Now that'll get rid of your freckles, and bathing in it'll bring out your true beauty. Catnip ... mix it with rose petals for a love charm. Betony makes a good tea for headaches and purifies the body. Comfrey mends cut skin, but you must make sure the infection's out first, or you'll find yourself with a world of trouble on your hands ..."

That's what this war is, Iris mused now, staring into the heart of a heavenly blue morning-glory. *A world of trouble—a big, ugly infection oozing forth and threatening to kill us all. Like the train in my nightmare.* Shaking off the memory, she got up and strolled over to the gate. She stroked the silky morning-glory petals and thought of Joe's eyes when he'd been telling her about joining up ... how their grayness had receded, leaving them as blue and vivid as the flower she was touching.

I want to be making a difference. His words played themselves over and over in Iris's head as she paced through the garden, only half-noting its late-summer loveliness. But something else was taking shape there, too—had been, she realized now, ever since Mrs. Wood's ice-cream social—and her talk with Joe last night was making it quicken inside her. She kept walking till she came to the hidden little stream cutting across the far end of the garden, where the willows grew.

Iris knelt down, dabbling her fingers in the stream. She picked up an already yellowed willow leaf lying on the ground beside her and idly, childishly flicked it into the water. She watched it bobbing, dancing along the water until it disappeared downstream. Jumping to her feet, she ran past the willow trees to a vacant lot, where the stream reappeared briefly before going completely underground.

Where the leaf had gone was, of course, anybody's guess. She had to laugh at herself, remembering how as a child hungry for the company of other children—her grandparents' farm had been very isolated—she'd done this selfsame thing, spinning adventures for her leaf and flower people. She could just see herself now, kneeling by the stream that ran past her grandparents' cow pasture, her faded lavender gingham pinafore and little hands grubby, the hunger in her satisfied for a time.

The thing growing inside her now was very different, but it needed satisfying, too, Iris thought, and that wasn't going to happen here, teaching children their multiplication tables or the geography of lands that the German war machine was trying to swallow whole. "You can no more win a war than you can an earthquake," peace-loving Jeanette Rankin had been quoted as saying in the paper. Well, maybe the representative from Montana was right about that; but they were at war nonetheless, and there were men bleeding and suffering that she might somehow be able to help.

I want to be making a difference, too, she thought, standing there, staring out at the sea of field grasses, chicory, butter-and-eggs, and Queen Anne's lace. Oh, she could knit socks or help make up sheets and bandages right here in Simsbury—she didn't dismiss the importance of those things to the war effort—but she didn't want to be on the sidelines of life anymore. And that, Iris realized with a jolt, was what she'd been doing her whole life. Holding herself back, afraid of being hurt and of having people taken from her as her parents had been. It had become her way of dealing with life, this not dealing with life.

Well, no longer, she thought, staring at the stream. She couldn't fight in the trenches, naturally, but she definitely had other options. The navy had been accepting women for clerical positions in order to free men up for the front lines. The Secretary of the Navy, Josephus Daniels, inspired by England's example—women clerks there had numbered more than 100,000 by 1916, and thousands of others had enlisted in Queen Mary's Auxiliary Army Corps (WAAC) and the Voluntary Aid Detachment (VAD)—had opened the door for her and other young women in one of his speeches. "Enroll women in the naval service as yeomen," he'd said emphatically, "and we will have the best clerical assistance the country can provide."

The Marine Corps had followed suit and started recruiting women for similar positions. A handful of women proficient in French had gone overseas to work as telephone operators with the Army Signal Corps; and a few more with training in physical and occupational therapy had enlisted as "reconstruction aides" with the Army Medical Department. There were even, Iris knew, a few women war correspondents. She could almost see herself sitting at a rickety table in some makeshift shelter, pounding away at an Underwood typewriter while the shells screeched like banshees overhead.

But none of these things is really the right one for me, Iris conceded wistfully as she walked slowly back past the willow trees and back into Mrs. Banning's homey little garden. She slumped down on the bench and picked up the library book, staring blankly at its cover. Then it all came to her in a rush. Mrs. Todd, the story's people-wise herbalist, her grandmother . . . two dissimilar women, yet both with the gift of healing. Once again, she was back in her grandmother's garden, seeing that bony hand fasten on the fuzzy stem of the self-heal and stroke its soft oval leaves. "Some folk call it all-heal," the old lady had been muttering. "Self-heal, all-heal—either name suits it, to my way of thinking. My book"—she'd kept a much-thumbed broken-spined copy of Culpeper's *Complete Herbal* on the mantel shelf in the kitchen; Iris had it among her own books now—"says it's good for inward and outward wounds. It's a quick healer, and you can mix it with other wound-herbs like comfrey."

Self-heal … all-heal … self-heal … all-heal … The words kept chasing each other around in her head till they blurred together, and all she was left with was the memory-picture of the delicate flower among the velvety leaves and of a little girl solemnly watching the old woman she was half-afraid of. Then she saw that same child, a little older, a little taller, puncturing a pus-filled wound on her grandmother's arm and binding it up after treating it with a paste made of comfrey, self-heal, and several other herbs she couldn't recall now. "You've got the gift," her guardian had said, nodding. "Golden hands. Your mother never had it, but it's found its way to you."

I'll be a nurse, Iris told herself, and an odd, warm glow settled itself down inside her. She would use "the gift" that had come to her through that old half-witch woman who had raised her. She would … Iris smiled, tapping her fingers along the spine of the novel and thinking about that awful poster she'd seen at the post office that morning—tomorrow she would go down to the war office, which was coordinating everything from war gardens to liberty loans, and she'd sign up with the Red Cross.

CHAPTER THREE

"And this is where the gas cases are," Sister Katherine Owens told Iris in a prim, precise voice. But her eyes were warm, kind, and shimmery, like a stained-glass saint's. "It's most important to keep an eye to the weather—and the windows—where they're concerned. Their lungs are already badly damaged, of course, and the slightest drop in the temperature can exacerbate the condition. We keep oxygen by their beds for them, as you can see. And then, of course, there are the eyes."

"What about the eyes?" Iris asked, thankful that she had been taken in hand by one of the English nurses. She was none too sure about her French despite the lessons that she and some of the other nurses were taking twice a week from a woman who lived near the hospital.

"They have to be bathed and treated. Remember, these poor fellows generally get it full in the face." She went around to the side of first bed. "Hand me the basin and a fresh towel, please. How are we doing today, Tommy?"

The young man in the bed—was he really eighteen? Iris wondered—grinned and groped for the older woman's hand. "Can't see worth a damn outta these eyes of mine, begging your pardon, Sister

Katherine," he replied, squeezing her red, chilblained hand. There was a Highland lilt to his voice that brought Joe to mind. "I mean, I can sorta make out shapes but not the details. I don't mean to complain none, but they're burning a bit more today. Who's the new Sister come to call?"

"Iris Amory," Sister Katherine told him. *Why, she didn't correct him,* Iris marveled. The nurses from England and other parts of the British Empire all seemed to be called "Sister," regardless of whether they were military or civilian nurses. The Red Cross nurses were simply "Nurse," far as she could tell. *Well, if Sister Katherine's not going to say anything, neither am I,* Iris decided.

She watched quietly as Sister Katherine dunked the towel into the basin and, wringing it out, began moving it lightly against the sore eyes. When she'd finished, she put the eye ointment in so deftly, he barely blinked. "And don't worry, Tommy: the sight's coming back to you far more quickly than the doctors and I anticipated. A few weeks ago, you couldn't even have made out those shapes. In a month's time, you'll have the full use of your eyes back and be wreaking havoc among all my younger nurses, I expect."

"That I will, Sister Katherine," he chuckled, giving her hand another affectionate squeeze. "That I will."

Iris trailed behind Sister Katherine, watching her chat and joke with each of the soldiers. As her grandmother would've said, this woman had "the gift," and not just in her hands: there was something peaceful and healing in her manner, and the men responded to it instinctively, their faces lighting up, even when, like Tommy, they couldn't see well enough to read hers.

Not that Sister Katherine let Iris stand there gawking while she did all the work. Nature had made the Sister a teacher and a healer both: she soon had Iris putting in the eye ointment and checking on wounds and dressings, as they made their way through the other wards.

Dealing with the wounds wasn't as awful as Iris had feared. Sometimes there was a powerful knock-you-down-to-your-knees odor, yes, but she could handle it—or even the sight of a missing arm or leg—without getting too queasy. After all, she'd been raised on a farm, and she'd seen some pretty nasty accidents with scythes, spooked horses, and the like over the years.

Still, would she ever be able to put the same kind of feeling into nursing that Sister Katherine did? It worried her, Iris had to admit. *Am I always going to have this outside-looking-in feeling, even here? Surely, I should be feeling something.*

"How do you manage it—taking care of their wounds and still managing to put a good face on things?" Iris blurted out as they left one of the wards. Then she bit her lip. There! She'd forgotten all about protocol again. Probably she shouldn't have been addressing Sister Katherine so familiarly. She'd heard that some nursing sisters and matrons were really quite touchy about rank. But the other woman seemed not to mind at all.

"It's hard not to get attached to them," she told Iris simply. "And it doesn't add that many more minutes to the rounds to say a few kind words. I mean, it's little enough to do when you think about the sacrifices they've made." She smiled. "And while we're at it, dear, I'm not much for formalities at the best of times, and these hardly qualify as that. So call me Katherine, and let's have done with all the bowing and scraping."

Iris smiled back. All at once, she felt less transplanted. The pale, almost wintry sun shone a little more brightly through the cathedral windows, bringing badly needed warmth both to her spirit and the long, drafty corridor.

The hospital had once been a seminary, she'd been told, and it had taken the local authorities a while to get into suitable shape for the incoming wounded. The walls were all whitewashed, and every door was painted an absurdly cheerful scarlet, but Iris liked it. It made the place feel less like a hospital and more . . . well, *homey*, despite the lack of running water, heat, and other amenities.

"What an interesting old building this is," Iris marveled. "It's not at all what I imagined it would be like, but it's got a lot of charm and history to it."

Katherine nodded. "I agree—there's something about the place that soothes the soul. It must be the history, as you say. For a hundred years or more, this was training camp, so to speak, for young priests. Something of their piety, their *godliness*, must linger." She glanced down at her watch and began moving down the corridor at a more business-like clip. Iris hastened after her, finding the shorter, stockier woman surprisingly hard to keep up with. "By the way, have you seen the chapel at the end of this hall?"

Iris shook her head.

"It's a really wonderful room, and the wood carvings and stained-glass windows are still in amazingly good shape, considering that it hasn't been used since the separation of church and state here in France. It's sort of a special place of mine. I go there when all of this"—she gestured toward the wards they'd left behind them—"gets to be too much to bear." She threw Iris a glance over her shoulder. "You may find yourself wanting to do likewise."

"I'm not particularly religious – or Catholic."

"Neither am I, though I used to sing in my church choir when I was about your age. But I say at times like these, we have to hold on to what we can."

She halted by a door near the end of the hallway, and, for a second, Iris thought that this must be the chapel. Katherine's tightened lips and a sudden, indefinable change in her manner told a different story, however.

"This is not like any of the other wards you've seen this morning," Katherine cautioned. "This is like nothing you've ever seen, except maybe in your nightmares."

Iris looked at her, bewildered, her own throat all at once tightening.

"These are the eyeless, the noseless, and sometimes even the faceless," Katherine continued, her voice gone low and raspy. "These are the men whose own families wouldn't be able to bear the sight of them. And the men, they know it, and there's where the heartbreak comes in." She laid one of her strong, firm, squarish hands on Iris's wrist. "You must always look them full in the face—what's left of it, that is—and smile. Smile until it feels like the damn thing's permanently etched into your own face, but *smile*. Can you remember to do that, Iris? It's terribly, terribly important."

Iris nodded.

"Good. There's a Dr. Kazanjian, who's over with the 1st Harvard Medical Unit—a dentist, I believe—who's doing some wonderful things with rebuilding jaws. They wouldn't even let him return to the States when the rest of his unit went back. And back at 3rd London General, there's an orderly, Francis Derwent Wood. He's actually a sculptor, and he's come up with these, well, *masks* for the men with the faces damaged beyond repair. We're hoping that perhaps he'll be able to come over at some point and take a look at some of our boys here. It would give them such hope."

She shook her head and, putting her hand on the doorknob, looked up at Iris. "And that's what you're here to do, too—give them hope. Not false hope, mind you, but hope that people'll be able to look at them and still see them for who they truly are." She opened the red door and slipped through like a shadow, Iris following.

Even with the warning she'd just received, she was unprepared for each gargoyle face that turned expectantly toward them as the old bandages were snipped off. She could feel her lips start to curl back like a cat's encountering a strange and frightening smell: it was only Katherine's calm, cool hand on her arm that kept her from turning tail and bolting back through that door.

One man was missing half his face; another had no lips and two tiny holes where his nose had been; and yet a third had no eyelids and would have no way of hiding from the weird mask his face had become when he left this place.

And there were the smells. The smell of flesh that had been ravaged by shell fragments. The smell of pus-filled abscesses that needed lancing. The smell of carbolic spray and other medicines that couldn't disguise either of the others.

This is hell, Iris thought, fighting the nausea that swirled about in her stomach. And her mind flew back to that Red Cross poster she'd seen back in the Simsbury post office the day that Joe had told her about his decision to enlist. The soldier being helped by the dough-faced nurse had been rugged and manly-looking despite the bandages on his forehead. *How can they tell such lies?* she wondered now. *It's nothing like that at all, at all.*

"Good morning, Arthur," Katherine said pleasantly as she sat down by one man's bedside and began clipping away at his dressings. He was missing his lower jaw. Iris tried not to stare, but all she could see was that tongue of his wagging back and forth. "How's the pain this morning?"

"Less, considerably less," he replied, trying to raise himself up on the pillow a bit. His voice was slurred, but Iris found that after a while, she could make out his words. "Who's the new recruit?"

"Iris Amory. She's fresh from the States, so I'm showing her the ropes this morning." Katherine left off from her work long enough to chafe her hand in his. "Come here, Iris. I want you to meet Arthur Henson—he's a special friend of mine."

"Aw, Sister Katherine, all the fellows here are special friends of yours." Arthur gave her the faint ghost of a smile. "Have to say, you ain't mighty particular about the company you keep."

"And I say it's because I have such excellent taste," she retorted. "Come over here with the salve and fresh bandages, Iris."

Iris came, but neither her spirit nor her feet were particularly willing. *What can I possibly say to him?* she wondered. *And how in God's name do I keep the horror out of my face and voice the way Katherine does?* Then somehow she was standing right at the cot, holding the disfigured man's hand, although she didn't remember taking it. It was, she noticed immediately, a surprisingly fine-boned hand with the kind of long tapering fingers you'd associate with a pianist or a surgeon. She looked up at the wreckage of his face and saw that what remained was fine-boned, too, and that the eyes were dark and deep-set. Why, he'd been a handsome man before this, she realized. And something welled up inside of her, more powerful than the horror and nausea she'd been feeling. It washed over her soul, drawing her to this other soul and changing her completely. She was no longer standing on the edges, looking in.

"It's a pleasure to meet you." It was all she could do to keep from shaking her head, the words sounded so inane and tea-party-ish.

The poor marred mouth arranged itself into a smile again. "Thank you for saying so, miss. You sound like you mean it."

"I do," she said, surprised to find it true.

After that, it was easier to tend to them. The trick, Iris figured, was to study each man for the feature or features that had survived the shell's onslaught. Then she could roughly reconstruct in her head what he must've looked like before. As long as she could hold on to that mental picture, she could talk to him almost as easily as she could've to Joe or any other young man whose face was still as God had made it.

That is, of course, until she came to the soldier with barely any face at all. She didn't realize it, of course, not until after Katherine had set up the folding screen around his cot and scissored away the stained bandages. Only the eyes remained in the scorched earth of his face. If this was Hell, then here was a soul that had been tormented beyond what any soul could surely be expected to endure.

"Hello, Sister," the man said to Iris. Like Arthur, he had some trouble enunciating. "My eyes are acting up today—the shrapnel scarred 'em some, I reckon—but I can still hear pretty good. And y'know, I can still smell some, even though my old honker is gone. Don't that beat all? Anyhow, that sure is a pretty scent you're wearing, if you don't mind my saying so. Is it honeysuckle?"

"Why, yes, it is," Iris said. "How did you know?"

"My ma grows it in her garden. Great hand with flowers, Ma is. Morning-glories, hollyhocks, phlox, love-in-a-mist—there ain't nothing she can't grow." He gave a weak, raspy chuckle. "Y'know, she even rooted a corsage from the big anniversary shindig that she and the old man had 'fore I come over here. Said she couldn't be sure of his giving her flowers again 'less she was all laid out in her coffin."

They both laughed awkwardly, then fell silent. "My grandmother had a garden like that," Iris told him before the silence could swallow them whole. "All herbs and old-fashioned flowers."

"You got a nice voice, Sister." He raised a half-bandaged hand toward her face. "You wouldn't think it too forward if I—?"

She surprised herself by saying, "No, not all. And then I'll clean your wounds." It was the first time that day she'd volunteered to do that for any of the men without Katherine's quiet prompting.

The callused blunt fingertips with their ragged nails were gentle on her face, and Iris found herself fighting back not nausea but tears. "Thank you, Sister. My fingers work a whole lot better than my eyes, so it helps learn folks easier." His hands fell to his sides. "Sister Katherine don't mind my doing it, although some of the other nurses gets squeamish. But you sat through it like a real trooper, Sister, and didn't flinch once."

"Iris," she said and began carefully washing the wounds on his face. Some of them were still weepy, but he didn't look hideous to her anymore. "What's your name?"

"Archie Edgerton at your service, Miss Iris."

"I don't foresee myself commanding anybody here," she laughed. She ran her fingers across his face, checking out her work. The wounds looked clean enough now: she could begin putting on the ointment and fresh bandages. "I'm still learning the trade, Archie."

"Aw, you're a natural, Sister Iris. It's in your hands—I can feel it. Sister Katherine's got it, too. Way I look at it, you either got it born in you, or you don't. And you come through with flying colors."

"Thank you." The mutilated face was fast receding under the clean linen strips: he looked more mummy than man now, with only his eyes looking out at her. She fastened the last strip in place. "How's that feel?"

"Good as new, Sister Iris," Archie replied. He reached for her hand, and she took his, holding it as if he'd been an old, old friend. "Good as new. And thanks—for not running when you seen me."

"I couldn't," she told him and realized it was true. "I just couldn't." She was aware of Katherine having come up behind her and practically purring her approval.

"That's 'cause it's not in you to run from a person or a thing, no matter how bad it is. You might've wanted to, but you didn't, and that's what counts." He squeezed her hand, then let it go. "Flying colors, Sister Iris—flying colors."

CHAPTER FOUR

Iris paused at the doorway of the linen room and peered in. Mrs. Abbott, the Englishwoman who oversaw the hospital's linen room, was setting out a Christmas Eve tea for all the nurses. The tea cloth—which was, in reality, a patchwork flannel quilt with lots of red in it—camouflaged the long ugly table and threw some of its blue-red glow against the high whitewashed walls, giving the room an almost festive look.

A regular sleighful of parcels crammed with oranges, chocolates, candy, and other goodies had just arrived from the States. Mrs. Abbott, a little red-haired woman with a china-doll face and a temper that didn't match, had told Katherine that she thought the nurses "could do with a bit o' cheering up, same as the men" and had set some things aside for "a right proper little party. Do 'em all a power o' good, I say, to just be girls and not have to be patching bodies back together for a bit."

Iris shifted her patients' chart to her left hand now and, resting the other on the doorjamb, sniffed appreciatively. Mrs. Abbott's lynx-like ears heard the sniff, and she looked up, shaking her head.

"Off with you, Miss Schoolmarm," she scolded, shooing Iris off as if she were an especially pesky chicken. "You'll get your tea at five like the others, so don't you be making big eyes at *me*. That may work with the men in the wards, but it don't sway me any more than it would Queen Victoria, God rest her soul."

Iris—who, by this time, had learned that Mrs. Abbott was really a very nice dragon once she was certain you weren't a slacker—laughed and continued down the hall. *One more ward to go*, her heart sang. *One more, and then we'll have tea and chocolates.* And letters, too. For there were letters now. Warm, homey ones from Mrs. Banning, who was clearly lonesome rattling around in her little house and who worried about Iris being all alone "over there with all those foreigners." And letters from Joe at the front that were so friendly and funny, it was almost like having him right there to talk to. He made no reference to their kiss in his letters, but his affection was evident, making her happy and nervous at the same time.

But she was settling in here, finally. Katherine had time and again steered her through—there was no going around—the difficulties of dealing with the plethora of war-time casualties. Most of the other nurses were chatty, friendly souls, more than willing to include her in the occasional picnic or even more occasional train trip up to Paris, as her roommate, May Prentiss, just had. It hadn't been simple: even with a *carnet* or an identification passbook, you had to put in an application for leave at least eight days beforehand. But it *had* been lovely: there hadn't been a flake of snow, just some frost hanging hard on the ground like ice, and walking the old cobblestone streets as they made their way from one forlorn little shop to another had made her feel as though she'd stepped into another time and place.

And there were the men. As Katherine had told her that first morning, it was impossible not to get attached to them. They were funny, brave, and grateful for the littlest thing. Of course, the Matron was always lecturing the nurses about not falling for any of their patients. "No loitering or canoodling on the grounds with them," she'd say crisply. "Not while they're patients here, at least. It's too easy to put yourself in a situation, cut off from normal life as we are here. That's not fair to you, and it's certainly not fair to them. Wait till they're convalescent, then do what you please on your own time."

It was sound advice, but naturally, a number of nurses—including May, who had taken up with a Frenchman, René LaJoie—ignored it and happily "canoodled" with the abler-bodied patients. There was a song that both soldiers and nurses played over and over on the old Regina music box that some kind soul from the States had sent over:

"There's a long, long trail a-winding
Into the land of my dreams,
Where the nightingales are singing,
And a white moon beams,
There's a long, long night of waiting
Until my dreams all come true;
Till the day when I'll be going down
That long, long trail with you."

It was a haunting sort of song, Iris had to admit, and it had a trick of stirring in her a yearning for things she couldn't put a name to. Not that she even thought of any of the men here in that way; no, she was definitely with the Matron on that one.

But she liked working with the men—tending their wounds, monitoring their progress, and hearing their stories. Why, one fellow—Lionel Cameron of the Canadian Machine Gun Corps—had swum a river in one night, then lay among the corpses littered across a battlefield for nine more hours before crawling up behind enemy lines to gain some key strategic information. Afterward, he'd swum right back to his camp again. When you heard stories like that, you couldn't help being proud of being a part of it all.

She stepped quickly into the ward, trying to ignore the faint growls coming from her stomach. She'd skipped lunch, wanting to leave room for Mrs. Abbott's special tea. Not that there had really been time to stop for a bite. A lot of casualties had come in while she and May had been gone, including one amputee.

Iris accepted amputations as a fact of life in a war-zone hospital. You had to, given the high rate of sepsis and gas gangrene. She was infinitely less philosophical—and infinitely readier to retch—when it came down to being in attendance while Dr. Pratt or Dr. Brisbane sawed through flesh and bone, and blood spurted all over her apron. The stains never did seem to come out; even worse, most of the amputations would, she learned from listening to the doctors, have to be done over later on.

Placing her tray down on a badly scuffed and scarred table that one of the older nurses had commandeered from the chapel, she picked up the chart lying there and scanned it for the newcomers: Alexander Maxwell: double amputee as a result of gas gangrene. Roger McClure: facial lacerations. George Parmalee: shoulder and stomach wounds.

Iris tucked the chart under her arm and—she was getting better at juggling things—took up her tray again. She shook her head. *Might as well get the worst over with first*, she told herself, squaring her shoulders. *At least, there's only one amputee in this batch. Buck up, as Mrs. Wood would say.*

So she bucked up and went straight over to his cot. "Hello there, Alexander." She had initially worried that addressing the men by their first names right off was too familiar, but Katherine had insisted that it made the men feel more at home. "I'm Iris Amory. I was up in Paris when you arrived the other day."

"Paris, eh?" He tried to smile but could only manage a weak grimace. "I was there once, when I first come over. Quite the city."

And it would've been for you, Iris thought compassionately.
All those French girls would've thrown themselves at you. He was a
good-looking young man with thick blond hair and features that
might've been chiseled by a sculptor. *He's like one of those illustrated
heroes out of the magazine serials. What a waste . . . what a terrible,
terrible waste . . .*

"Well, it says here that you need a dressing change. We can't risk
any infection getting by." She sat down in an old metal chair and
patted his hand. It was warm but not burning, so at least he wasn't
running a fever. And there was no "smell of death," as Dr. Pratt
called it, creeping out from under the blankets as she lifted them.
Maybe Alexander Maxwell would be one of the lucky ones—she
winced—and not have to go under the surgical saw a second time.
"I'll try to be careful undoing these old dressings."

"Oh, it's all right, Sister." He turned his head wearily to one side.
"I don't feel anything there. How could I?"

Iris paused in the midst of her unwrapping, a strip of stained
linen in one hand and scissors suspended awkwardly in the other.
"But I thought all the"—she fumbled about in her mind for a kinder
word than "amputees"—"soldiers who'd lost arms and legs did. Dr.
Pratt said so. 'Phantom limbs,' he says they're called."

"Oh, yeah, I've heard that one, too. But the only pain for me
is up here, Sister." He turned toward her, pointing to his head. A
shiver ran through his slim body. "Got a cigarette?"

"Let me finish with the dressings first, then I'll check with Sister
Katherine if it's all right for you to have one." It probably would be:
the gas cases were generally the only ones who couldn't because of
their already damaged lungs. "You know," she began hesitantly as
she returned to her unwrapping, "Dr. Brisbane was telling us that
there's a Dr. Daniel Reardon with the 1st Harvard Medical Unit
who has his patients write about their experiences on the battlefield.

It does them no end of good, he says—cuts down on their night-mares and helps them through their convalescence." She paused. "Maybe it would help you—talking about it, I mean."

"Yes—no—I don't know." His bruised and bloodied fingers picked at an edge of his blanket that had begun to unravel. Iris noted it with one part of her mind. She must remember to bring it to Mrs. Abbott's attention. Or maybe just fix it herself. With linens and blankets in such short supply, they had to mend and re-mend what they had: still, sometimes, as with the men themselves, there was only so much they could do.

One thought flowed into another, and she glanced down through lowered eyelashes at the exposed stumps that were all that remained of the young man's legs. They seemed to be healing nicely, but she'd still have to put some dressings soaked in that vile Carrel and Dakin's Hypochlorous Acid ¼% Solution on them. You never knew when a wound could go septic, killing the patient in a matter of hours.

There was enough of Alexander's thighs remaining for Iris to see that those legs had been taut and muscular; his torso was long, so she imagined that his legs had been, too. *He must've been a good athlete and a good dancer, too,* she thought, *slim and light on his feet.* She bit her lip, thinking how cruel such a phrase was now.

"You know, Sister, I believe I will," Alexander said suddenly, rais-ing himself on one elbow.

"Will what?" blurted Iris, startled out of her reverie.

"Tell you about it. You've got a listening kind of face, if you know what I mean—thoughtful but not like you'd get all mawkish and gushy with cheap, easy sympathy like some women do. A fel-low can't take too much of that." He drew his breath in sharply. "So, you ready for it, Sister? It ain't a pretty story."

Iris finished anointing his stumps with salve and straightened herself up. "Of course, I'm ready," she chided. She began to put the new dressings on. "I'm sure I've heard worse." She laid her chilblained hand on his restless one.

He clutched the offered hand. "I sure hope so, Sister—I sure hope so. It haunts me at night, when I can't sleep. I gotta tell someone . . ."

She had to listen hard then, his voice was so low and pained as he talked about lying there in the trench with his buddy, Jordan Shaw—"the best friend a guy could have in those damned trenches. Always ready with a joke when we thought we couldn't take it anymore and a real crack shot when it come to picking those trench rats, I tell you.

"It had been pretty quiet that day. Then, all of a sudden, gunfire breaks out over our heads. I hear this damn funny noise, sorta like a dog whining high and sharp, and Jordan, he's gone. Weren't no dog but a shell, see, right to the head. The shells, they sound that way, y'know. And he's bleeding all over 'cause"—his voice was tear-choked and ragged—"'cause the top of his head's gone, and he ain't even Jordan anymore, and I feel this pain slashing through my legs, and it all goes kinda dark, just like it does in the novels."

Iris squeezed his hand, trying to picture herself in his place. "You mustn't blame yourself," she soothed him. "There was no way you could've saved him."

The young man shook her hand off and began talking in a low monotone. He was so clearly back there with his dead friend in the trench, she wondered if he'd even heard her. "I was there in that damn hell-hole forever. 'Least, that's how it seemed to me. The pain in my legs was so bad, I didn't know much. Didn't even feel hungry.

"But I was powerful thirsty after a while: a fellow can go without food a whole lot longer than he can without water, y'know. It'd been raining to beat the band, so I crawled best I could over to this part of the trench that was filling up with water. I tried cupping my hands to get some, but they weren't much good to me, being stiff and sore, what with the cold and me having had to rely mostly on them for the climbing, see. So I end up lapping like a dog. It was only after I'd gotten some down my gullet"—Alexander clutched at Iris's hand again like a frightened child, and his voice rose, turning into a banshee wail—"I saw Jordan's body lying there, half ways in that hole, *rotting.*"

He was crying now, each sob sounding as if it were being ripped out of him. "I wouldn't have drunk the damn water if I'd known Jordan was in it, Sister! I would've died of thirst before I done it! Makes me feel like a goddamn ghoul!"

Iris sat there, stunned, her mind screaming at the picture his words had conjured up. She knew what she should be saying to him, of course: *You didn't know. You did what you had to. Jordan would have wanted you to live, would have been glad that there was something of him left to give . . .*

But she couldn't look at him. Nausea washed over her, and, jerking her hand away, she ran out of the room to the closest port she could think of, the linen room. She pushed past Mrs. Abbott and threw up on some freshly laundered towels till she had nothing left to throw up. And even then, the dry heaves and sweats shook her body every time the image of Alexander lying in a sodden, bloodied trench, lapping up the stagnant water mixed with the rotting remains, came back to her.

Gradually, she became aware of Mrs. Abbott's cool hands on her clammy forehead. The little woman was oddly gentle and quiet as she cleaned Iris's face: the water was ice-cold, of course—it almost always was here, especially now that it was winter—but it felt heavenly on her sweaty face.

"I'm going to walk you over to the chapel now, that's what, and let you have a good sit," Mrs. Abbott said once she had finished tidying her up. "And I'll send Sister Katherine in to you as soon as she—"

"But I've disgraced myself!" Iris blurted tearfully. "I ran out on this man—not a man, really, more like a boy, they're taking them so young now—he'd had both his legs mangled by a shell—"

"Hush, love. You're not the first, and you won't be the last," Mrs. Abbott retorted. "Now, let's get you into the chapel. It's cool and quiet in there; you'll have a chance to collect yourself."

She whisked Iris off before the younger woman could get another word out and stayed with her long enough to make sure she was "over the worst of it." Iris barely noticed her leaving. The scene kept playing itself over in her head. Alexander Maxwell had reached out to her for some kind of solace, and she'd dropped his hand and fled his bedside as if he had indeed been a ghoul. And here she'd been so pleased with herself because she'd handled Archie and the other disfigured men so well.

"'Flying colors,'" she said aloud, bitterly mimicking Archie's words of praise. They were good friends now, she and Archie, and she would have to tell him how she *had* run. And his disappointment in her would be awful, she didn't doubt it. "Flying colors, indeed! How could I have done that?"

"Done what?" The male voice was casual, almost flippant, with a definite Southern drawl. "Don't mind saying, I hope it's interesting."

Iris turned toward the chapel doorway. Lounging against it was a slim young man in a muddied uniform with—she squinted—the Canadian Militia insignia just visible. *Then, what about that accent—?* she wondered, as he ambled over to the pew where she was sitting. Talk about a puzzlement.

He sat down next to her, throwing one arm over the back of the pew. "Name's Jerry Enright, ma'am," he told her, holding out his other hand.

41

She took it and almost jumped back. There was a kind of raw energy about the man that flowed through his touch like an electrical current. "Iris Amory," she said a little unsteadily.

"Pleased to meet you, Miss Iris." Jerry turned her hand over in his and studied it. "It's a right nice little hand. Doesn't look like the murdering kind. What did it do?"

She eased her hand out of his grasp and looked downward, hoping he'd mistake it for maidenly modesty when she was actually scanning her nurse's apron for telltale vomit stains. *Oh, Jesu*—she'd already picked up one of Katherine's favorite exclamations—*there's one right on my knee!* She clamped her hand down on the offending spot. "It can't be of that much interest to you," she faltered.

"Oh, but it can," Jerry assured her. He stretched out his long legs and flexed his fingers. "I'm always up for a good story, Iris. And it looks like I'm grounded here for a while, so I figure I'd rather be sitting right here, listening to whatever you've got to say."

"First, why don't you tell me what a Southern gentleman's doing in the Canadian Infantry?"

He laughed shortly. "Means I forgot what my daddy always was telling me."

Iris smiled up at him. The nausea was receding now, thanks to the coldness of the drafty chapel. "Which was?"

"That whatever you run from becomes stronger than you are, or you sure as hell wouldn't be running from it." He reached for a cigarette out of the breast pocket of his frayed uniform and lit it with an odd lighter. Probably a shell casing. The men were always coming in with curious things they'd fashioned out of battlefield debris.

"Y'see," Jerry told her, taking a drag on the cigarette, "I got drafted down in Georgia, where my daddy's farm is. Didn't much care for the picture of myself gassed or hanging off some barbed wire or getting blown to next Sunday by a Hun shell, so I hightailed it to

Canada. Well, ma'am, it wasn't long before the Canadians found me and decided I was just what they was looking for. So here I am."

He leaned his curly dark head against the back of the pew and, taking another pull on his cigarette, practiced blowing smoke rings out. Clearly, he didn't trouble himself greatly about the propriety of smoking in a chapel. "Damn. Still a couple short of Sam Ryan." He grinned at her. He had this engaging crooked grin that made you want to be in on the joke. "Seeing who can blow the most smoke rings is a popular pastime down in the trenches—right up there with popping off the rats and picking off the nits, in yours truly's humble opinion."

"I don't think you're all that humble," she retorted. "But what are you going to do now? While you're here, I mean?"

He threw her a look that melted her right down to the bones. "Oh, I guess I'll chase you till I get caught," he said casually, then laughed. "You're blushing awfully hard."

"And you certainly know how to catch a body off guard," she replied. She put a hand up to her throat, as if that could still the trembling inside her. "Not very gentlemanly."

"No, ma'am, I'm not," he agreed meekly, though there was still laughter lurking in his voice. "That was right improper of me." He polished off the cigarette and ground it into the chapel floor. "So, if you don't mind my asking, what horrible, unwomanly thing have you done?"

Iris stared at her knee. *Might as well tell someone*, she thought, remembering her words to Alexander before—before she'd heard that horrible, horrible story. *And maybe then I can finally stop thinking about it*. "I ran out on a patient and threw up in the linen closet."

"Must've been right hard on the sheets and towels," he agreed. He reached for another cigarette, then seemed to think the better of it and pulled a creased envelope and a pen out of another pocket instead. He began doodling on the back of it, and Iris watched, fascinated as a tiny caricature of herself took shape there. "Surprised the folks in charge of linen supplies didn't have you court-martialed, it's so damn hard getting soap and water for cleaning anything hereabouts." He paused. "So, why'd you run out on that there soldier?"

Haltingly, she told him the whole story. "I don't know why it affected me so. I mean, I can handle cleaning up men who have half a face—or less—but I can't handle this." She struck one fist weakly against her open palm. "Why—why can't I handle this?"

"It's a new kind of horror, that's why." His tone was different somehow; she looked up into the deep-set brown eyes and saw a weary kind of pain in them. "And a body—or a soul—can only take so much." Another caricature—Jerry himself this time—appeared next to the one of her. "Those fellers with their faces blown away, hell, you've gotten used to them. You see them every day—you change their dressings—you wash what face they got left. You talk to them: they talk to you about the farm back home, the girl they was courting before they joined up, and how they're worrying what she'll think of them when they get shipped home again. They're real to you now.

"This other feller—this Alexander here—why, he looks pretty much the same as you and me, only his legs aren't all there. But he's carrying most of his disfigurement—that story of his—up in his head, and it's a pretty damn sickening one at that." He began fiddling with his makeshift lighter. "Ever hear folks talk about the 'bowels of compassion'?"

She nodded. Her grandfather, in his final illness, had accused her grandmother of "having no bowels of compassion." Iris had always thought he might have had a point there.

"It's a phrase my daddy bandies about a lot," Jerry continued in that easy, conversational way of his. "Always struck me as a peculiar one. I mean, why bowels? Why not heart?" He shrugged. "Well, I come over here and saw the gas gangrene cases, the men caught on barbed wire and dying by inches 'cause there's no way no how their buddies can get to them, and I threw up plenty, I tell you. Felt my insides twist and turn on me more times than I can count."

Putting his hand on her shoulder, he turned her about to face him. His eyes were still pained, but there was an almost mystical glow in them now. "But, y'know, that's how I figure compassion's gotta start: breaking you down from the inside out and taking root in the blood and the mud and this horror that's fit to swallow us all up alive."

Their gazes met and locked. All the sounds from the adjacent wards had died away, and the dusk was filling the room. It was as though they'd stepped out of time.

"You've made me feel better," Iris finally told him. Placing one hand gingerly on the back of the pew in front of them, she rose. Her legs still felt rubbery, but the clamminess and nausea were completely gone. "Thank you."

Jerry touched her hand. "Glad to oblige, ma'am." He gestured toward her skirt. "Looks like you just begun to earn your stripes there."

She followed his glance and realized that he was looking at the splotch she'd been trying so desperately to hide from him. "Guess I have," she replied, feeling her face redden again. "Well, I hope I'll be seeing you again before you go back."

"Oh, you will be." He smiled, but his smile was a preoccupied one. "I'm not going anywhere for a while—'least, that's what they're telling me." He handed her the drawing. "Here you go—you can keep it as a souvenir of our meeting."

"Thank you," Iris murmured. Sliding the drawing up her sleeve so it wouldn't get wrinkled in her pocket, she headed out the chapel door. Halfway down the hall, she almost collided into Katherine. "Iris!" the older nurse exclaimed, catching hold of her wrist. "Mrs. Abbott just told me what happened. Are you all right?"

"I am now," Iris said, passing a hand over her forehead. "The young man in there helped me. He's a Canadian soldier—well, he's really from the States, like I am, but he's with the Canadian Militia . . ."

She surprised herself with the way she blurted out her story, sparing her friend no detail about Alexander Maxwell and the chance meeting with Jerry, chattering like one of the patients when they came to after surgery and the chloroform was still on them. "He really did make me feel better. Funny how somebody I never laid eyes on before could do that, isn't it?"

"Not really," said Katherine a bit absent-mindedly. "Some folks have the gift." She frowned. "What did you say his name was again?"

"Jerry. Jerry Enright."

Katherine began flipping through the pages on her chart. "'Comfort, James.' . . . 'Diprose, Frank.' . . . Ah, here it is—'Enright, Jerry.' Knew I'd seen that name somewhere." She scanned the notes next to his name and bit her lip. "He's in for shell shock," she said quietly. "He may be a fine young man—I'm not saying that he's not—but, remember, you're dealing with someone who's, well, not quite right."

"He seemed sane enough just now while we were talking," Iris argued.

"Judging from what's written here, he's probably one of the milder cases," Katherine replied. "It's hard to tell, though: shell-shock can take so many different forms, everything from incontinence and spasms to hallucinations and full-fledged seizures. We had one fellow here a few months before you came who somehow managed to get his hands on a kitchen knife. I was near the end of my rounds one afternoon and if the chap in the bed next to his hadn't called out a warning, I'd have gone right over there and gotten filleted for my pains." She sighed, tapping her blunt-nailed fingers against her clipboard. "He's back in England now, in an asylum, poor devil."

"But you say Jerry Enright's one of the milder cases." Jerry had helped her over her shame and horror back in the chapel; the least she could do now was to stick up for him.

"'*Probably* one of the milder cases,' I believe I said. We don't know what he's seen or what demons are dancing around in that head of his, Iris, dear. All you know is that his commanding officer thought it safer to remove him from the battle lines for a time."

Iris could feel a throbbing starting up behind her left eye. "I don't believe it, Katherine—I *can't* believe it. I don't know why, but I can't."

"Maybe you're right," her friend allowed. She sighed and ran her fingers through her graying hair, knocking her nurse's cap off kilter. "God knows the doctors themselves barely understand it—they can't even make up their minds whether to call a man 'shell-shocked' or 'neurasthenic.'"

She stowed her chart under her arm and patted Iris's arm. "Do what you feel is right, dear. Your instincts are good, and you're not giddy or thoughtless like some other younger nurses. Be his friend. But remember what I said. Do you think you could possibly manage going to the tea?"

Iris shook her head. "Thanks, Katherine—and thank Mrs. Abbott for me, too—but I really need to lie down. I still feel woozy."

She watched her friend head back down the long corridor and disappear into the shadows. Iris half-turned back toward the chapel, wondering if Jerry was still in there. Then she shook her head and flitted like a ghost to her room.

CHAPTER FIVE

"Mail call!" Iris sang out, waving a letter close to Archie's face. Some of the patients whose eyesight had been damaged would've minded: one man who had no sight left in his right eye actually tensed up like a wild animal if he sensed her coming up that side. But Archie never minded. He was pitifully grateful that anyone would come near him, would talk and clown with him as if he still had his face. "It's a Theona-gram!" She sat down on the chair by his bedside.

"Never misses a week," he said proudly. Theona was his sweetheart back home. "I don't always get 'em right on time, 'course, but she's regular about writing them."

He loved talking to Iris about Theona and their homespun courtship, which had begun at a Grange picnic; she knew that taking out and sharing those memory-pictures with her helped him pretend that he was whole again. He took the letter eagerly and peered at it for a while. "Always writes in a nice clear hand, Theona does." He caressed the envelope, then passed it back to Iris. "My head's hurting some this morning, Sister Iris—you reckon you could read this one?"

"Of course, Archie." It was one of their little fictions—that Archie could read without difficulty, that it was just "this danged headache" or "a little eyestrain" that kept him from reading the letters on his own. But it was becoming clearer that his eyes had been more damaged by the shrapnel than they'd realized at first: Iris herself had heard tall, caustic Dr. Pratt mutter something about "gradually deteriorating eyesight" to Sister Katherine after examining Archie yesterday. Not where Archie could overhear him, of course, but on some level, Archie knew, Iris was sure, and she grieved that one more thing would eventually be taken from him.

Theona's letter was cheery and affectionate. She wrote about her parents' farm and the various church and Grange doings. She was knitting socks for the Red Cross, she told him, but "saving the nicest to send you, along with some hot water bags and chocolate, you say it gets pretty cold there, and I know you don't get chocolate or sugar much. Thank goodness you don't smoke, but if you did, I'd send cigarettes, too, much as I dislike them, smelly things. As it is, I'm trying to find a way to send myself. I feel so badly, you lying there in that French hospital, all wounded and me not there to look after you. . . ."

Iris put the letter down. "Does she know?"

Archie made a weary motion with his bandaged left hand. "Didn't have the heart—or the guts—to tell her." He hesitated. "D'ye think she'll look at me like I'm some kind of monster? I couldn't bear that."

"Not the way she writes, Archie," she told him. "It'll take some getting used to, yes"—Iris pressed his hand – "but I think she'll be up for it because she knows that your face isn't all there is to you. And that's not what she fell in love with, anyhow."

"Prob'ly not." Archie grimaced, but his hazel eyes lightened a little. "Can't truthfully say that I was ever a pretty boy. This new look might actually be an improvement."

Iris smiled and finished reading Theona's letter. "I've got some news I've been saving for you, Archie," she said, folding it up and handing it back to him. "Sister Katherine had it from Dr. Brisbane first thing this morning. Francis Derwent Wood *is* coming out to France, and he'll be including this hospital as part of his tour. It sounds like he'll be here a while, and maybe he'll be able to make one of his masks for you." She swallowed hard, twisting her hands together as she cast about for the right words. "I know it's not the same as having your own face, but it would be—well, something, wouldn't it?"

"Yeah, it would be something, all right." He lay there quietly for a moment, then cleared his throat. "So, how's your Canadian fellow, Sister Iris?"

"He's not really Canadian, and he's not really my fellow," she protested, feeling her cheeks burn. "He's still here, though, acting as a sort of orderly—neither Dr. Brisbane nor Dr. Pratt can seem to figure out what to do with him."

"Shell shock's a mighty tricky thing," Archie commented. "I've seen fellers sent up to hospital before a battle because they were so scared, they were nothing but a liability out there on the field. Can't say as I blame 'em. Everybody's scared out in the trenches, and anyone who says he's not is a fool, a liar, or both. But shooting your trigger-finger off or putting a bullet in your foot, like this one feller in my battalion did, why, that's just the other side of crazy."

"Were you scared a lot, Archie?"

"Hell, yes," he replied, nodding. His voice, always difficult to make out, had started to slur, the way it always did when he was getting tired. "But, y'know, once you hear that whistle blowing and you start heading over the top, it all kinda flies out of you, and it's almost, well, kinda peaceful and purifying. Sounds funny, I expect, but that's how it is."

Iris nodded. She'd felt that way after she'd made up her mind to sign up with the Red Cross. And again, when she'd gone to face Alexander Maxwell and ask his forgiveness for running from him.

"Get some rest now," she told Archie, tucking the blankets in around him. She hoped—oh, God, how she hoped—that Theona would indeed be able to live up to her words when she saw that terrible ruin of a face.

She practically walked into Jerry's arms walking out of the ward. There was a fumbling of hands, a muttering of apologies, and a delicious warmth emanating from the lanky young Southerner. "How's he doing?" He jerked his head toward the door. She'd told him about Archie shortly after their meeting in the chapel, in one of those long, meandering conversations that happen when a friendship is taking root, and Jerry never forgot to ask after him after that.

Yet the one time Iris had asked if he'd like to come with her and talk to Archie—"It would do him a world of good, you know," she'd said, borrowing one of Katherine's favorite phrases—he'd balked. "No," Jerry had rejoined coolly, reaching for a cigarette with a trembling hand and stalking off. After that, she'd taken care to only mention Archie when he'd asked.

"He's in good spirits," Iris replied now. "He's had a letter from Theona—sounds like she's determined to find a way over here to see him."

They looked at each other. "Is that wise, Iris?" Jerry asked.

"I don't know, Jerry—I honestly don't know," she admitted with a sigh. "She sounds like she's got spunk, though."

"Spunk's mighty good," Jerry retorted, "but it'll only get you so far. And it ain't gonna hide that there horror in her eyes when she sees what the war done left her in place of a man. I heard of men not half as bad as your Archie doing themselves in after a visit from their wives or sweethearts. Sometimes before." He began fumbling for a cigarette.

Iris shuddered. "I don't think Archie would do that," she said slowly. "Not now that Derwent Wood's coming."

Jerry's hand halted right above his breast pocket. "Derwent who?"

So she told him everything that Katherine had told her about the middle-aged British sculptor-turned-Captain of the Royal Army Medical Corps. "Apparently when he was an orderly, he came up with this notion of molding and casting splints to fit the patient's arm, leg, or back. That way, he told the commanding officer, the splint not only fit better but also held the bone in place so that the doctors could more easily get at whatever wounds needed treating. So they put him in charge of the splint room, and that's where he came up with his idea for the masks. And now—"

"And now he's coming here, and maybe he can pull a miracle out of his ass for Archie," Jerry said, finishing the thought. He pulled out a cigarette and lit it. "Well, I'm glad—damn glad. He deserves something, Archie does. And maybe I'll pick up a few pointers for my own drawings. You never know." He took a long, thoughtful drag on his cigarette. "So that's two visitors we're getting."

Iris looked up. "Why, who's the other?"

"Black Jack Pershing himself," Jerry said. "Or 'Nigger Jack,' as some of the boys back at West Point used to call him."

"Why?" Iris frowned. She'd heard nothing but praise for the cool, reserved commander of the American Expeditionary Force.

He shrugged. "Pears back around 1895, he was part of the 10th Cavalry way out in Montana."

"So?"

"The 10th was a unit of coloreds, or 'buffalo soldiers,' as they used to call 'em. Anyway, Black Jack got on real well with the coloreds— fought alongside 'em, praised 'em to the skies, and looked after 'em, same as he would his own kind. I guess some of the West Pointers figured he got on with 'em a little *too* well and seeing as he was such a lover of coloreds, he might as well have the name, too."

Iris studied him. She herself had had very little contact with blacks, other than the few Negro soldiers who had come through the hospital. But there was no getting around the story's ugly bigotry, and she hated thinking that this man she was attracted to was smeared with it, too. *Might as well find out sooner than later*, she told herself. "And how about you? Do you feel like the West Pointers do?"

Jerry raised one eyebrow. "Now that's an interesting question, Flower-girl." He'd taken to calling her that lately. He played with the cigarette in his right hand, not seeming to notice how close his fingers were to the lit end. "Maybe once upon a time, I might've thought that way," he finally conceded, "but that was another lifetime ago. No, ma'am, war sure as hell don't care if it's a black man or a white man who gets himself blown in half"—his voice shook—"so I don't see why I should."

Well, at least, he's honest, Iris reasoned. "Well, I'm glad you're not like them—not anymore, that is."

There went that crooked grin of his again. "Well, then, maybe you'll go on a drive with me if they decide I'm right enough in the head to trust with the two-horse rig. Hell, I'll even be the horse." He let his hand rest on her forearm. "What d'ya say, Flower-girl?"

She could almost hear the Matron's stiff, starched voice: *No loitering or canoodling on the grounds. It's far too easy to put yourself in a situation.* And the Matron was right, of course.

"Why, I'd say—" She looked up into his dark eyes and felt something as summer-sweet and wild as honeysuckle wrap itself around her senses. She should, of course, immediately pull up the feeling by its roots, but . . . "I'd—I'd say, 'Yes.'"

After all, she argued with herself, *the worst the Matron can do is shake her double chins at me and say, 'Be it on your own head, girl' like she did to May when she caught her with that French soldier out in the old monastery garden . . .* "I'd better go now."

"Yeah, I guess." His hand stayed where it was, anchoring her to the spot. "I'll see about getting a rig and let you know if the good doctors'll let me have a horse."

He was always dancing around the subject of his shell shock, suddenly throwing out a cryptic comment about it in the midst of casual conversation. She never knew what to do with those comments, lying there curled up like snakes ready to bite. "Of course." Iris avoided his eyes. "I'll wait to hear from you."

He let his hand slide off her arm, so slowly that his letting go was almost as much of a seduction as his holding on had been. "Mind you do that," he told her. "And don't let ol' Black Jack or that sculptor fellow talk you into going off with them instead, hear?"

As it turned out, the little hospital needed supplies from the larger one in Compiègne, so the doctors were only too glad to let Jerry use the two-horse rig. The Matron agreed that Iris should go with him—she would, after all, be better able to make sure they received the right quantities of the medicines, bandages, splints, etc. that they needed—provided that another nurse accompanied her "for appearances' sake. Not that I'm casting aspersions, Miss Amory—you're a very serious, upright young lady, and I appreciate that, believe me, I do—but people *will* talk, and I want my nurses' reputations to remain unbesmirched."

So Iris promptly volunteered May, a move that caused the Matron's jaw to drop down to the floor. She still seemed to be looking for it when the younger woman left the room five minutes later.

"I swear, she made me think of one of those mechanical banks when you pull the handle!" Iris laughed to her roommate that night. Laughter came to her very easily when she was with May. With her, Iris could clown around and be the girl she'd never really had a chance to be. "I felt like popping a cent in her mouth!"

"Well, it's no secret that I'm hardly in the Matron's good graces since she caught me spooning out in the garden with René," laughed May from her cot. "But even *she* realizes I'm better than no chaperone at all. Believe you me, though, I'll disappear—*poof!*"—she snapped her fingers—"if the two of you want to get the least bit romantic." She gazed up at Iris, her morning-glory blue eyes friendly and thoughtful. "D'ya *want* to get romantic with him, Iris? You're a hard one to read sometimes—and that's coming from another woman."

Iris paced around the room, undoing her hair from its bun. The thick braid swished back and forth against her back like an angry cat's tail. "Yes—no—I don't know. It all makes my head ache," she muttered, flicking her hair pins into a cheap little china tray she'd picked up in Paris. She unhooked her uniform and hung it on one of the tarnished hooks hanging in the tiny alcove. She stood there in her chemise and sighed, shaking her head. "I just don't know, May," she said, finally throwing her hands up. "I like him, May, I truly do—but there's this whole business about his shell shock. I never know if I'm dealing with the real man or if this is just some kind of mask he's holding up to fool me. I keep thinking about what Katherine said—"

"Listen to your heart," May interjected crisply. "Not to Katherine and not even to me. Hearts are a lot wiser than people give them credit for being." She paused. "There was a man back home I could've married, you know—he was well-off and incredibly romantic. But there was something *empty* about him: he was like a paper doll with all his flowers and pretty speeches. So I told him no.

"A lot of folks thought I was foolish to turn him down and come over here. But Mama didn't. She said, 'If your heart's not with him a hundred percent, May Elizabeth, don't do it. Marriage is a hard enough row to hoe even when you've found a man you think the world of, and don't let anybody tell you different. Besides, he's a little *too* nice, and that ain't natural in a man. Always kinda makes me wonder what he's hiding.'" May yawned, stretching her arms above her head. "Mama's a good scout." She glanced at Iris, her eyes flickering with amusement. "So, what are you going to wear?"

And they both laughed. Of course, they'd have to wear their Red Cross uniforms, complete with capes and veils, since they'd be on hospital business. "Although maybe we could ditch the veils once we're on the road," May suggested. "I always feel like Queen Victoria in mine."

"Well, at least, you don't *look* like Queen Victoria," Iris soothed her.

"Oh, don't I?" cried May, tucking her face down so that it looked like she was sporting an extra chin or two. Rather like a mutinous bulldog. "We are not amused by your antics, Miss Amory. In fact, we are most grievously dismayed and would have you—" Then her lips began twitching, and soon both of them were howling with laughter.

A few days later, they were maneuvering their long skirts and billowing capes into the two-horse rig, as excited as little girls going on a picnic. "Watch your step," Jerry murmured, his hand on Iris's elbow as he helped her up. He had a bright, buoyant energy about him that she had never seen before. All his dark broodiness had fallen away from him like dead skin, and his eyes glowed amber. "It's the horses!" he exclaimed boyishly in response to Iris's questioning look. "Make me feel like I'm right back on the farm." He ran his hand affectionately along the side of the roan. "You're a good ol' girl, aren't you, honey?" The horse nickered and nuzzled his neck, and Jerry chuckled.

It was early, so the trees were still beaded with dew. As they pulled out of the rusty monastery gates and onto the wide, rutted country road, the sun came out, turning each bead into a rainbow-flashing crystal before it faded away. The day was unusually warm for late January, and in the pastures along the road, there were scatterings of bandit-eyed cows eying them so quizzically, Iris and May couldn't help laughing. "That one there," May gasped, holding her side, "she looks just like Mrs. Weston from our Grange! All she needs is an old-fashioned reticule and a hat with stringy feathers!"

The doctors at the hospital in Compiègne were too busy with the incoming wounded to do more than give Iris and May a few hasty messages for Doctors Brisbane and Pratt. Jerry loaded up the medical supplies, then suggested they explore the abandoned battlefields nearby.

Iris found Compiègne small but enchanting, with its woods and its royal chateau built by Louis XV. The Germans had held the town for thirteen days, then deserted it after the Battle of the Marne, Jerry explained. Talk had been at the time that the Kaiser had meant the Crown Prince to rule from there once he became Governor of France. The town had been bombarded several times, and once, a Zeppelin had actually been shot down over it. "Though that was some time back," Jerry remarked. "Probably all the pieces have been made off with by now."

May, who was a souvenir scavenger, looked disappointed. But Iris was so intently focusing on Jerry himself, she scarcely took in his words. Since their meeting in the chapel on Christmas Eve, he'd been a puzzlement to her. Physically, he was very fit; yet the doctors clearly weren't falling over themselves to send him back to the front lines. He worked around the wards with a fierce energy—"He *eats* work, that one does," marveled Mrs. Abbott once when she'd stopped in mid-conversation with Iris to watch him tote in load after load of wood—and was, for the most part, friendly and easygoing, always ready with a story or joke. But there were long stretches when he was aloof and monosyllabic, almost as if he'd withdrawn into a hole and pulled it in after himself.

Those were the days when he'd walk away from Iris without a word, when his eyes held a haunted, hunted look. Then it seemed as though a completely different personality had taken him over—so much so, she was beginning to find it easier to believe those old tales of demonic possession her grandmother used to spin by the stove on fall nights when the wind was gypsying through the fields, rattling the dead cornstalks.

Yet Iris was drawn to him and he to her: she could tell by the way he gazed at her, or stood so close to her she could feel his breath warm and teasing on her cheek.

They drove through more fields, sometimes seeing bits of German uniforms stuck on tall, twisted poles. The poles reminded Iris of the pictures she'd seen of Sir Harry Lauder's trademark walking-stick; then, of course, her mind wandered inevitably over to Joe, who'd spoken so proudly of his fellow Scotsman. *Where is Joe now?* she wondered—a little guiltily, for, as she'd grown more entranced with Jerry, there'd been less room in her world for Joe. *It's been more than a month since his last letter.*

"Now, that's a right proper scarecrow," Jerry chuckled as they passed one pole wearing a round Boche cape. He gave it a mock salute. "And the only German you'll ever catch yours truly here saluting."

The road grew bumpier as it took them into a thick, shadowy wood with funny little thatched huts sprouting up like so many mushrooms on either side. Or baskets, she thought, noting their walls made up of branches and heavy ferns woven over and under poles. "Are we still in the twentieth century?" she asked May, her voice low.

"It sure doesn't look like it," her friend answered. "I almost feel like I've died, and this is purgatory."

Jerry said nothing, but his lean face darkened. Iris and May glanced first his way, then at each other, and swallowed any further comments.

The woods took over for a while, only to give way to what had once been a village. Most of the houses still had all four walls, and some of them had even kept parts of their roofs. But the glass was gone from most of the windows and the doors from their hinges. Through the open doorways, they caught glimpses of broken chairs, twisted iron beds, and smashed crockery scattered all about.

"I hear tell that the Germans once set up camp here," Jerry said. "Guess they done made off with anything they could find a use for. Mighty thorough, those bastards."

Iris shivered. "Let's get out of here."

Jerry clucked his tongue at the horses, and they left the empty, echoing town behind, making their way through still more fields. Then they came to the trenches.

Somehow Iris had always imagined the trenches as being neat, orderly affairs with the Allies on one side and the Germans on the other. Rather like a chessboard. But, no, the trenches were running off every which way, constantly changing direction till she felt like she was looking at one huge dizzying maze. And the barbed wire was even worse, crisscrossing the rough wooden posts and iron supports over and over until the beginning of it all was lost.

They stared silently at it, and Iris knew that May and Jerry must be picturing it just as she was, not as it was now, picked clean like bones, but with bodies hanging from its brutal mesh, dying the slow, agonizing death of crucifixion. She and May had seen the pictures, and Jerry—well, he'd seen the reality.

He urged the horses on till they came to another cluster of huts, somewhat larger than the first ones they'd seen. "I think that these here horses could do with a spell of rest," he remarked. He jumped down and hitched the team to a rusted iron bar that had been stuck in the ground as a sort of makeshift hitching post.

He helped the girls down next—first May, then Iris, his hands lingering on the latter's waist. Their gazes met and meshed, then their lips: it was like touching a match to dry wood. When she finally did break away from him, Iris put her hand up to her mouth as though she'd been burned.

She glanced shyly about, wondering if May had witnessed the kiss. Her friend was standing a little ways off, staring at the huts. Standing a little *too* straight, Iris thought, and staring a little *too* fixedly. May turned at the sound of their footsteps, her oval face perfectly composed, with just a hint of laughter in her eyes.

The three of them wandered on among the trenches. Planks had been placed here and there as a sort of walkway, but most of them were sodden and crumbling from age. Jerry walked close by her side, not touching her or needing to. They stopped short at one good-sized trench, which had a door set into one end of it. The many-paneled door, its white paint clinging to it in flecks, must've been lifted from some fancy French chateau, Iris imagined.

Jerry slowly turned the weather-pitted doorknob. Iris grabbed May's hand and waited dry-mouthed for the explosion, a terrible tightness in her chest. But nothing happened. Jerry eased the door open and scanned the area around and behind it. "Looks clean," he finally pronounced. "There's some kinda fancy stairs going further down. Don't know how much good it would do anybody, though— probably just end up getting buried alive down there when the shells hit instead of being blown to bits."

Iris let go of May's hand and hurried over. *Well, he's sure not coloring the truth any*, she thought, staring down into the open doorway. The stairway was a long one and put together as nicely and evenly as any carpenter could wish. At the bottom, Iris caught sight of a battered table and chair. "Why, there are rooms at the bottom," she marveled. Something wild and adventurous called into being by Jerry's kiss took hold of her then, and she forgot her initial fear, recklessly putting one sensibly heeled shoe down on the moldering step. "It looks just like Mole's house in *The Wind in the Willows*!"

Jerry hooked his arm around her waist and yanked her back up. "God almighty, Iris, you're worse'n a kid!" he exploded. "You can't go rushing down there like you're on your way to some picnic! I said the doorway here was clean, I didn't say nothing about the rest of the damn burrow! And I'm not particularly hankering to be picking you up and sending you back to the States piecemeal." He set her down hard on the ground, almost pushing her away from him. Then he strode off, lighting a cigarette.

Iris frowned. She could understand his being annoyed at her carelessness, but there'd been a harshness, a coldness in his tone and movements, as if he'd wanted to put as much physical and emotional distance between them as possible.

They toured the rest of the deserted battleground in silence, then headed back toward Compiègne and from there, back to their own little hospital. Once they'd driven through the monastery gates, Jerry reined the horses in—a little more tightly than usual, Iris noticed—and said roughly, "You two might as well get off here—I'll drive the supplies around back."

Iris started to speak when she saw May shake her head ever so slightly. *Forget it*, she told herself, swallowing hard. *Don't let him see that he's hurt you.* She jumped down from the rig, then helped her friend down. Together, they watched Jerry drive off.

May squeezed her hand. "It's going to be all right, Iris, don't worry."

"But why—" Iris broke off, shaking her head. His coldness had felt like a slap after that kiss.

May shrugged. "Men are funny that way." She shook the dust from her skirt. "Besides, you don't know what he's seen. Those trenches probably stirred a lot of memories, and his kind of wounds don't heal all at once. If you remember anything Sister Katherine has said, remember that."

May's words helped ease the sting, and Iris held on to them through dinner and her evening rounds. *I can do this,* Iris kept repeating to herself. *I can live without him if I have to.* She had almost convinced herself of it by the time she got back to her room that night. May had already slipped out for one of her unauthorized walks with René, and the little room with its cots pressed up against each other suddenly seemed much too big and empty for her.

There was a knock at the door. Wearily, she opened it, wondering if it was Sister Katherine wanting her to go back on duty. But it was Jerry who stood there, his body taut and his eyes fixed hungrily on her.

"What—," Iris began, but he slipped into the room, closing the door firmly behind him, holding her and kissing her till she was drowning in his closeness. And reveling in it.

CHAPTER SIX

"So it looks like ol' Black Jack's comin' at last." Jerry whistled. He leaned against the whitewashed wall, resting a hand right above Iris's head.

She glanced up from the soiled bed linens that she was carting back to Mrs. Abbott's domain. "Really? When?"

"Thursday. Or so I happened to overhear Pratt tell Brisbane." Amazingly enough, they were alone in the hall. Jerry playfully tweaked a curl bent on escaping from her already tousled upsweep, and a delicious quivering went through her. "I'm right curious to meet him. Ever hear the story about him and them pigs down in the Philippines?"

"No." Iris wrenched her mind away from the memory of the last time they'd been together. That had been over a week ago. It wasn't easy finding the time or the privacy for lovemaking, though May had been good about slipping out of the room after the lights had been turned down. Sometimes Iris felt guilty about that; René had just gone back to the front, and her trysts with Jerry must make May miss her lover more than ever.

"Well, y'know, he was Military Governor of the Moro Province down in the Philippines before this war, and there was a right smart number of attacks by the Muslims there. So Black Jack, he captured fifty of 'em and ordered 'em shot.

"Then, after the Muslims are all tied up to the posts, he orders his men to bring in two hogs and kill 'em right in front of the prisoners. And he goes and tells his soldiers to soak every last damn bullet in pig's blood before they commence shooting. They kill forty-nine of the bastards and dump what's left of 'em in this big ol' hole, then—this was Black Jack's finishing touch, y'see—they dump all those pig guts and blood right a-top those Muslims. Then Black Jack, he just ups and lets the last feller go." Jerry chuckled. "Didn't have any more trouble with Muslims after that, I tell you."

Iris frowned. "I don't understand—"

"Muslims think pigs are filthy, same as Jews think. They won't even touch one, never mind eating one. Black Jack sure knew how to send 'em a message they wouldn't forget in a hurry." Jerry rested his hand on her shoulder, his fingers straying down her arm. "Well, Flower-girl, I'd best be going—Doc Brisbane's waiting on me."

"Do you think he'll say you're fit to go back?" she asked, her voice an aching whisper. She honestly didn't know what the right answer was. Of course she wanted him rid of his demons, whatever they were—he hadn't been able to talk to her about them yet, not even in bed—but even *thinking* of his leaving for the front, right in the midst of this precious new intimacy of theirs, hurt her.

"How the hell should I know?" He shrugged, his hand falling away from her arm. "I'll tell you when there's something to tell."

He was back again—that cold stranger who sometimes looked at her out of her lover's eyes and spoke with his voice. He would appear without warning, just as Iris was feeling closer than she'd ever imagined it possible to be with another person, and she'd draw back like a scalded cat, wondering what in creation she'd done to bring that darkness in him on.

But it always faded quickly, leaving room for those heart-stopping prismatic moments when their souls and bodies seemed to blur and blend, making it impossible to tell where she ended and he began. Which was the true Jerry? she wondered now. The dark cold-eyed stranger or the man who held her so tenderly during their rare lovemaking?

Avoiding his gaze, Iris tucked the renegade curl he'd been playing with earlier back into her nurse's cap. "Well, I hope all goes well," she said with starched politeness, moving away from him.

Then, suddenly, Jerry was holding on to her shoulders and kissing her in that way that made her want to go all warm and limp inside. "You make me crazy, Miss Iris Amory, that you do," he breathed into her ear. "Is May gonna be out tonight?"

"I—I don't know." His breath, warm on her cheek as he leaned closer, was a drug. "I can find out and let you know."

"You do that." He kissed her and let her go. "'Pears to me we got some unfinished business to tend to."

She watched him amble down the corridor, her head spinning and the rest of her trembling like a tree in the wind. Her eyes fell on the doll-sized painted figure of a saint standing at the base of one of the windows. Iris walked over to study her better. She did not, of course, know which saint she was, only that her eyes were gentle and blue and that she carried a single rose in her hands like a gift. Her painted gaze was serene and comforting, and Iris almost immediately began to feel the tension ease from her body.

"So you've found her." May was by her side, warm and whimsical as usual.

"Who is she?"

"St. Dorothea, the gardening saint. Not that I'm the authority on saints, mind you"—May had, Iris knew, been raised Congregationalist—"but René has pointed her and some of the other survivors out to me."

"Survivors?" Iris stretched her hand out to touch the chipped rose, to get a feel for the battered yet still sweet face. "I don't understand. Whatever did he tell you about her?"

"Only that when the monks left here, many of the little statues and other religious relics were stolen. René's from a village not far from here, so he knows the history." May shrugged. "I imagine the same happened at monasteries all over the country. And he really didn't tell me a lot about ol' Dorothea here—only that she was the patroness of gardens and gardeners and that they killed her for her beliefs."

"So it's about faith," Iris mused, more to herself than to her friend.

May turned her about so that they were facing each other. "Suppose *you* tell me what happened to put you in such a broody mood? I passed Jerry on my way over here. It wouldn't happen to have anything to do with him, would it?"

Her voice low, Iris repeated their unsettling exchange. May listened, her eyes a living version of the little wooden saint's. "Oh, Iris," she said softly. She put her arm around Iris's shoulders. "I guess it is about faith after all," she continued as they began walking down the hall. "Faith that it's all going to work out somehow."

He was quiet, almost self-effacing. Certainly not at all what Iris had imagined the Commander of the American Expeditionary Force would be like. Yet for all his old-fashioned reserve, there was a forcefulness about General Pershing's set mouth and eyes, a refreshing directness in his manner when he talked with the doctors or walked through the wards. He talked with everyone, too, she noticed: not a single wounded man escaped his notice. He made no glib speeches about a glorious cause or a war worth fighting, just thanked them for having given so much.

Iris was there by Archie's bedside, just about to change his dressings, when Pershing came in. The General's eyes, always a little sad, grew even sadder as they rested on each mutilated face, but he did not let it hamper his speech: he talked to each man simply and naturally. When he came to Archie's bed, his eyes traveled from the heavily bandaged man to the surgical scissors in Iris's hand, and he said, "If it's all right with this man, Sister, you may continue as you were. I don't want to interfere with your duties."

Iris touched her friend's shoulder, and he nodded, saying, "I reckon the General has seen worse."

So she went through their usual morning ritual—a little stiffly at first, conscious as she was of the great man standing by her side, then quickly losing herself in her work. But even so, part of her was still aware of how Pershing's eyes never left the ruin of Archie's face. When she finished applying salve and fresh bandages, Pershing shook Archie's hand. "Bless you, son," he said gruffly. "I don't know if I could have endured as much as you have."

"Comin' from you, sir, that means a lot," Archie rasped back. "I'll remember that."

"As I shall you." Pershing nodded and followed Iris out of the room. He cleared his throat. "That was some fine work you did in there, Sister."

She blushed. "Thank you, General. Archie's my friend, you see, and there's so little any of us can do for him, it hurts."

"Yes, he has paid a higher price than most." He passed his hand over his forehead and suddenly looked terribly, terribly old. "Does he have family back in the States?"

"Yes, General—his parents and a sweetheart. She hopes to be able to come here soon so she can be with him, but, she doesn't know the full extent of his injuries, you see. Derwent Wood is due for a visit here soon, and we're—we're hoping he might be able to do something for Archie before she arrives." She swallowed hard and forced herself to meet the older man's eyes. "I—I don't know if he could bear it, sir, if *she* couldn't bear it."

"Let's hope she's made of the same stuff that you are, Sister." Pershing sighed. "How old are you?"

"Nineteen, sir."

He suddenly smiled down at her, and it was like watching a sunburst break out over a somber winter landscape. "You're older than any of my girls would be now. If they'd had a chance"—his firm voice quavered, a ripple on a seemingly still pond—"I like to think they'd have shown half as much spirit as you have." He took off his general's cap and bowed. "Bless you for the work you're doing—"

"Amory, sir—Iris Amory," she blurted. "I'm not really a full-fledged Sister." She stared down at her tray of instruments and soiled bandages. "And I—I really don't do that much compared to some here."

"You do what you can," he told her. "That's more than enough." He placed his cap back on his head and nodded, then walked away, his face stern and sad again. Iris had an eerie prickling feeling that he was not walking alone; that at least one invisible companion walked with the great man wherever he went.

"That was quite the conversation," said a familiar voice behind her. Iris whirled around, almost dropping her tray. Katherine smiled tiredly. "I didn't mean to eavesdrop, dear, but I was so close, I couldn't help overhearing. The general seemed quite taken with you."

"He was very kind and complimented me on my work," Iris said slowly, "but there was a terrible sadness about him, Katherine, especially when he was talking about his 'girls.' And when he walked away just now, it was almost as if he was . . . well, *looking* for something or someone."

"Several someones," Katherine murmured. Iris shot her a puzzled look. "You didn't know about his wife and daughters?" Katherine asked. Iris shook her head.

"A few years ago, the general was in charge of the 8th Infantry in Mexico. His unit was transferred to Fort Bliss, Texas, and he was making arrangements for his family to join him there when a fire broke out in the house in Mexico. His wife and all three of his daughters died in the blaze. His five-year-old son was the only one who escaped, thanks to his black orderly." Katherine's voice was raw with pity. "That's when the general's hair went completely white, they say."

Iris glanced down the shadowy hallway. The general was gone by now, of course—Katherine wouldn't have spoken so freely of his personal tragedy otherwise—but something of the sorrow that he carried with such silent dignity lingered. She winced, feeling physically ill at the mental picture of those little girls twisting and shrieking as the fire ate away at them. "What a horrible way to die," she whispered.

Katherine put her hand on Iris's shoulder. "And what a horrible way for him to live," she said softly.

That night, Iris lay quietly in her bed, resting her tousled head against Jerry's shoulder. He would have to leave soon, of course—it would never do for the Matron to find him here—but she savored his closeness. In bed, he was all warmth and light and gentleness, whispering endearments; the boundaries between their souls and bodies seemed to break down, and they flowed into one another. Iris had never known a giving and a taking like this, and they filled her with wonder. "It's like magic," she had marveled once to Jerry.

"Feels like the most natural thing in the world to me," he'd breathed back.

Iris put a gently exploring hand up to his face now, and he turned to her. "I almost thought you'd fallen asleep," she laughed softly.

"Not with you so close," Jerry murmured. He eased the chemise off over her head and drew her close, their bodies quickly merging together in silent symphony. Afterward, he lay there, stroking her unbound hair. "It's like a blanket on your shoulders," he whispered, twisting a thick chestnut lock around his long fingers. She laughed and ran her hand against his cheek, smooth as tanned leather, and eased her head back down against his shoulder.

"Iris," Jerry said suddenly, "they're shipping me back to the front. End of the week."

She sat up, her hair falling around her. She couldn't speak at first: there was this terrible pain shooting through her, as if some wild thing was clawing around her entrails, eating her alive from the inside out. She had known that this was coming, of course. It had walked alongside them in the corridors and in the old garden with its curving paths that seemingly went nowhere; it had punctuated every conversation and hovered in the shadowy corners of the room every time they'd made love. But weeks had gone by without Jerry receiving orders. And as the weeks had turned into months, she'd let her hope grow . . . not a lot, just a little, as tentative as a green shoot in that overgrown garden that the monks had designed centuries ago. "But you're not well!" she blurted.

Jerry laughed harshly. "I'm well enough on the *outside*," he corrected, "and today, the good doctor finally upped and decided that my shell shock wasn't as severe as some of the cases that have come through here. In other words, he done run out of excuses and has no choice but to send me back if he's not gonna catch particular hell from someone higher up."

He made a quick, pained gesture with his hands, his anger and fear spilling out of him. "See, word is, they're expecting Brother

Boche to attack the French and British sectors northwest of the line, and they need every damn man they can get their hands on." He groaned. "And here I am, just startin' to feel like I got some kind of chance, don't you know."

Don't I, she thought and put her hand to her throat, hoping to keep the nausea she was suddenly feeling at bay. Was this how May had felt when she knew René must go back to the fighting? "I—I don't know what to say," she faltered.

"I don't rightly know as there's anything to say," he rejoined, his voice so quiet, so detached, he might as well already have left her. But then he turned toward her, and she saw that it wasn't that cold, dark, angry stranger who lay beside her—that his eyes were full of life and light as they rested on her. "Oh, Jesus," he whispered, "am I gonna miss you, Flower-girl. But I'll be back for you. One way or another, I'll find you, I swear. You know that, don't you?"

"Yes." When he was like this, Iris never doubted him because it was his best self who was speaking, the same man who had eased her horror and shame in the chapel on Christmas Eve. His look and tone now soothed the sore places in her soul, the wounds that his dark twin had sometimes left. And in the midst of her despair over his going, there was a little flicker of warmth stirring inside her, and she grasped it gratefully, not caring if she burned herself doing so. "But—but I'll worry about you. I can't help that."

Jerry caressed her shoulder. "I know that, honey. None of us can help it. But from what I hear tell, the Germans ain't doing as well as they'd like us to believe. That armistice of theirs with the Bolsheviks was a bad business, there's no getting around that. And look at how many positions the Canadians and Brits have won back—Ribecourt, Flesquières, Havrincourt, Marcoing, Passchendaele"—his voice shook—"and a whole slew of others. German Southwest Africa, too. Then there's all those countries breaking with Germany and Austria-Hungary. You think they ain't sweatin' over that?"

His hand fell away from her shoulder, and he sighed. "It's happening, all right—the signs are all there. What I keep asking myself, though, is how many of us are gonna be left standing once the shooting and the gassing's all done?" He shook his head. "The French high command ain't exactly been handling things brilliantly. René there once told me that even before he was wounded, some of the soldiers used to bleat like sheep whenever officers passed 'em on the road. Can't say as I blame 'em."

The wind withered outside, seeking entry through the monastery's walls. It screamed like a banshee in a glory of grieving, sorrowful and insatiable. Iris shivered and drew closer to her lover. He smiled at her, but the light in his dark eyes was flickering, fading fast.

"I never did tell you how come they sent me here, did I?" he asked. She could see that he was making a tremendous effort to fight the darkness inside him. "That wind out there, it kinda brings it all back to me in a rush like. There was one just like it the night after Gil died."

"Gil?"

"Gilbert Thompson." Jerry sat up. "He was the lieutenant of my battalion and a real gentleman and scholar. And he died at Passchendaele."

Passchendaele, Iris had heard the stories, of course. Sir Douglas Haig, the Commander-in-Chief of the British forces, had intended the whole campaign to be a ringing victory against the Germans. Instead, it had turned into more than three months of shelling, heavy rains, and mud so thick and deep, it clogged rifles and swallowed men and horses whole. Eventually, the Allies had won back the little village, but the price had been high: 325,000 men.

"I'd seen fighting, naturally, but nothing like that." Jerry continued in a low, hurried voice. "And that damn dank mud smell was everywhere, so strong sometimes, it was hard to tell what was worse—that or the stench of dead men and horses rotting away in it. Never had a real clear picture of Hell, Iris, till I saw all that.

"Gil, he made it through almost to the end. Then, in November, right before Haig called off the offensive, he was killed. That was one of the things that made it so damn hard. Just a little longer, and he'd have made it."

Iris laid her hand on his arm. "You thought a lot of him, didn't you?" she asked quietly, sensing that there was more to this particular story.

"Hell, yes. He was good to us, never pulled rank or sent us anywhere he wouldn't go himself. Looked after us like a brother, he did." He stared down at his hands; Iris, following his glance, saw that they were clenched so tightly, it looked as though his knuckle-bones would burst through the skin. "My rifle had gotten clogged with the mud, and Gil had stopped to help me with it. He saw the shell coming before I did and pushed me out of the way of it. Don't know as he thought about it—just kinda a reflex action, I guess. When I came to, I had this shell splinter in my arm."

He touched the inside of his upper left arm. Iris had run her hands over that long ragged scar hundreds of times since they'd become lovers but, mindful of his condition, had never asked him how it had happened.

"So, soon as I could, I crawled back over where we'd been, back through the muck and the dead. Some of 'em was just blown-up bits of men—arms, legs, and the like. Others, like Frankie Plante, one of my buddies, were still in one piece, still holding onto their rifles, their eyes wide-open and watching me. Then I found Gil."

The silence hung thick and cobwebby between them. Iris swallowed hard.

"He'd been cut in two," Jerry said, dragging each word out, "but he was still alive. And he—he *smiled* at me." His voice broke. "He *smiled* at me, Iris. Jesus, can you believe it? The poor bastard's cut in two, and he's *smiling* at me." He covered his face with his hands; when he took them away, there were tears in his eyes. "He couldn't move, of course, just kept on smiling and looking at me with these big begging eyes like an animal caught in a trap. And I—I knew what he was asking me. So I managed to wrest poor Frankie's rifle from him. It wasn't clogged, like mine was, and I—I shot Gil in the heart. I was holding him when they found me, his blood flowing all over me."

He was sobbing now. Iris pressed his shoulder. She had never seen a man come so undone. It was almost as though his entrails were spilling out of him onto her bed, and she didn't know how to stanch the bleeding. "It was the only thing you could do," she told him. "There was no saving him. You did the merciful thing."

Jerry smiled—a faint, ghastly smile. So, she thought, Lieutenant Gilbert Thompson must've smiled up at him, his eyes begging for release.

"I've been holding you at bay," he said suddenly. "I wanted you, all right, but I didn't want to want you. 'Cause then I'd have to feel again, and I didn't want to feel anything ever again after that day. I kept pushing you away, and you just stood there, taking it, like a good soldier." He rubbed his eyes. "Why are you still here, anyway? I ain't been that all-fire good to you, not outside of bed, at any rate."

She didn't know herself. Maybe it was because this intimacy of theirs was all so new to her, she just didn't know better. Or maybe it was, as Archie had told her, that for the most part, it really wasn't in her to run from a person or thing. Then it came to her, pulled from somewhere deep inside her, just as her decision to join up with the Red Cross had been. "This is where I'm supposed to be," she said simply. She smoothed his sweaty rumpled hair, and Jerry touched his fingers to her lips.

"Don't ever leave me, Flower-girl," he said.

She bit back the obvious answer—that he was the one doing the leaving. "I won't," she promised.

"We—we haven't got much longer," Jerry faltered. "And we barely been apart since we met that night in chapel." He ran his hands gently along her face, almost as if he were trying to learn the lines of it by heart. Much as—the thought came to her unbidden—as Archie had that first day in the ward. And a wellspring opened up in her, and she yearned over him, not as a lover, though that was there, too, naturally. It was simply that she could now truly see him, soul wounds and all. She saw, too, the light in him breaking out and fighting to push back the darkness.

It was his fight, of course: she couldn't help him with it, she knew that. Nor was there any guarantee that he would ever be whole again, let alone that they would ever have a future together once the war had burnt itself out. What was it Joe had said to her? *We can't be making promises.* Well, neither could she and this man who lay beside her. But she could give him something of her own light and warmth now to help him as he trudged back to the trenches, the shelling, the liquid fire, and the mustard gas. And maybe, if fate was kind and spared him another time, it would bring him back to her. For this man was her home and she his: she saw it all so clearly now.

"We'll make the most of it," Iris said, working hard to steady her voice. "And I think—I really do believe—that it'll be easier for you now that you've talked it out some. It's like"—she lay her hand on the ugly scar—"you've let the infection out, and you can heal now. You just have to remember, you did the last thing that anyone could possibly do for Gil then. You ended his pain."

The tightness in his face eased up, although the sadness in his eyes didn't. "Thanks, Iris," he said, giving her name back to her in the most loving, tender voice imaginable. "It's good to know that I can talk to you about things like this."

They nestled back down together for the time they had left, not saying a word, just watching the trees outside the narrow window thrash about in their battle with that eerie changeable wind.

CHAPTER SEVEN

She was still sitting on the bed, unmindful of the cold, when May crept back in at daybreak. Iris looked up at her friend and tried to smile; then her lips quivered, and she wrapped her bare arms around her midriff as the nausea and grief washed over her. "He's going back to the front," she whispered. "End of the week."

May threw her cape down; it missed her cot and slid onto the wooden floor in a swish of dark fabric. Kicking it aside, she hastened over to Iris and sat down on the rumpled bed. "Oh, honey, I am sorry," she said softly, putting her arms around her. "I wish there was some way to make it easier."

"There isn't." Iris rested her head against May's chest. "He's going, May, and I don't know what to do."

"You bear it," May said simply, "because there's nothing else you can do."

"It's too hard." She shivered. "It comes over me in waves, and each wave is bigger and harder to fend off than the last."

"Then don't."

Iris raised her head inquiringly.

"Let it wash over you," May continued. "It will stop after awhile, that I promise. But if you fight it, the pain'll go underground—oh,

I'm saying this so badly, I know—and get stronger. Like"—she floundered about for the right word—"like an infection or fever. You have to let it run its course." She stroked her friend's tangled chestnut hair. She might have been the mother whom Iris could barely remember. "Honey, I hate to ask this right now, but do you think—I mean, do you think there's any possibility you're pregnant?"

"I don't know." Her shoulders slumped even more. She didn't want to be pregnant, of course. How would she manage to fend for herself *and* a child? Would the Matron even let her stay on? And if she had to go back to the States . . . well, she knew there wasn't a board of school trustees anywhere that would hire an unwed woman with a child. Still, it would be a part of Jerry, a part of the magic they'd made between them.

She lifted her tired, aching head and saw May fiddling with her cheap celluloid vanity set, lifting first the brush, then the comb, and then the brush again. She finally set the imitation tortoiseshell brush back down on the bureau and turned to face Iris. "There is a way," she said hesitantly. "If you are pregnant, that is."

Iris stared. "I don't understand."

"René and I talked about it before he went back to the front," May continued, keeping her voice low. "There's a midwife in the village who knows how to make babies go away. I don't really know how she does it—whether she uses herbs or"—she shuddered—"some kind of instrument. It's dangerous, I do know that much. The girls don't . . . don't always live. And, of course, René, being Catholic, was set against it. But I thought—and I hated myself for thinking it, Iris, truly I did—what if he doesn't come back? So I found out the woman's name."

"But you have your mother. Surely she would—"

"Oh, Mama's a good scout, all right, just like I said. But if I *were* pregnant—and I'm not, thank goodness, just got my monthly—it would still be hard, folks back home snubbing me and the fellows either not wanting anything to do with me or wanting *too* much to do with me." May came and sat back down next to Iris. "So, what I'm saying is, if—if that happens to you, don't even begin to think you're alone. I'm here." May chafed her friend's hand in her own still cold ones. "For what it's worth."

"Stop," Iris whispered. "You'll make me cry. And I hurt too much already, May." Iris wrapped her arms around her waist. "I hurt everywhere."

"I know, I know," May soothed her. She helped Iris under the bedclothes and tucked them in around her. "Get some sleep if you can. We'll have to be up for our rounds before you know it."

"I can't sleep."

"Then just lie there still as you can and conserve your energy," the other girl advised. She slipped into her own cot without even bothering to remove her gown. "That's what I'm going to do."

An image of Antoinette Eno Wood at the Fourth of July ice-cream social flashed through Iris's mind just then, and a funny half-strangled laugh escaped her.

"Not that I'm not glad to hear you laugh," May remarked dubiously, "but I surely can't fathom the reason."

"I was just remembering someone who said those same words to me—'conserve your energy'—before I came over." Iris shook her head. "It seems like another lifetime ago, May, and . . . and right now, I'd give almost anything to go back and not know this pain."

"Well, whoever it was spoke true." May yawned. "Now let's see if we can get a bit of rest in *this* lifetime."

Iris turned her face to the wall. She lay there, watching the last streaks of dawn fan out into a glow against the wall's thick patchy whitewash, then fade away.

That day, Iris went through her rounds with all the sprightliness of a mechanical toy. May, knowing what she was going through, did what she could to ease her pain. Sister Katherine was wise enough to keep silent, though her gray eyes watched Iris constantly.

It was Archie who broke through her numbness, however. "You're not yourself, are you, Sister Iris?" he asked a couple of mornings after Jerry had broken the news to her. And haltingly—really, it was so minor after what Archie had gone through, end of the world though it was to her—she told him about Jerry's leaving for the front.

He listened, then gently touched her face with his scarred hands. "Aw, Sister Iris, I'm sorry," he rasped. "You're broken now like me, only it's all inside."

She held his hand, resting her cheek against it while a few tears slid furtively down her face. "Thanks, Archie," she finally said when she was ready to let go of it. "You're very good to me."

"Aw, I'm just giving back to you what you've always given to me, Sister Iris." He patted her arm. "Just don't tell Theona when she comes, or she'll be jealous."

Jerry came to her that night. They didn't make love, simply held each other in that narrow bed and talked. He was, she realized, conserving his energy, too, mentally preparing himself for going back to the barbed-wire madness of the front. She didn't mind. She didn't have it in her to make love, anyway: some vital spring in her had run dry and needed to replenish itself. Somehow just being here with him like this was enough.

It was as if they'd stepped out of time. Or maybe time had stopped altogether, the way it did in dreams. *Yes, that's it,* Iris thought the next morning, as she changed dressings, applied salves, and talked to the patients. *I'm dreaming all this. I'll wake up the next morning and find that nothing has changed, that Jerry's safe in my arms and not going back to the front . . .*

But that would still leave the war raging around them, swallowing men up whole or, as it had with Archie, spitting them out half-chewed. And there was no way that she could ever trick herself into believing that she'd dreamed up the horrors she'd seen here at the hospital, no way that Jerry or any of them would be safe until the war had finally burnt itself out. And the reports of Allied losses were hardly encouraging.

"I can't seem to see my way around it," she complained to May when they were out walking in the monastery garden that afternoon. Her shabby little shoe stuck in the mud. She tried to yank her foot free: the shoe flew one way, and she would've flown the other if May hadn't grabbed her arm. She stood there like a heron on one leg while her friend hunted up the shoe.

"Maybe you're not supposed to," May replied. "Here's your shoe." She grimaced. "I'm not sure if it's much better than no shoe at all, though."

Iris took it from her and shook it out, then winced as her stockinged foot made contact with the mud still sticking to the shoe's inside. "Yuck," she said, thinking that there was really no word in the English language to describe just how cold and clammy those vestiges of mud felt. She remembered Jerry's description of Passchendaele and shivered. Then her mind darted back to May's earlier comment. "What do you mean, I'm 'not supposed to'?"

"I just think there are times we're not supposed to see clearly, just stand our ground 'to the last man'—or woman—and ride out the storm, not knowing." May shrugged, but her eyes had a faraway look. "'Through a glass darkly,' as the Good Book says and all that."

Iris raised her eyebrows. "When did you get to be such a philosopher, Miss Prentiss?"

"I think this war makes you one—or makes you mad."

Iris winced, thinking of Jerry, and May squeezed her arm. "Sorry, Iris—I didn't mean that as a jab at Jerry." She paused, biting her lip.

"Honest, I didn't." She scanned the sodden landscape. "Looks like November, doesn't it? You'd never guess that spring was around the corner, would you?"

A cackling of voices—they really did sound like the wild turkeys Iris had often heard in the woods around the school back home—broke out over by the front of the monastery. May peered over the neglected hedge, and Iris, being a tad shorter, stood up on tiptoes.

A Sunbeam motorcar—such as the officers often requisitioned—was pulled up by the gates. The car was spattered with mud, and the driver looked as miserable as a half-drowned kitten. His seat had neither car- nor wind-screen: only the passengers had any kind of protection from the weather.

"Poor man, I hope they give him a brandy or something warm," Iris murmured.

"That shouldn't be a problem," May murmured back. They began walking toward the gate. "Brisbane keeps a flask of whiskey in his desk drawer. I saw him take a few belts once when I was coming in to ask him about George Harlow's complications. Poor Brisbane practically snorted the stuff up out of his nose and onto his lab coat. Not that I blamed him—he'd just done a double amputation. It's got to be a fearsome responsibility knowing that you've just taken away a man's legs, even if it was for the best."

They were almost around the hedge now, and the figures by the door were easier to make out. "Wonder who they are when they're at home, as Mrs. Abbott says?" May remarked. "That man with the mustache—the one talking to Platt and the Matron there—doesn't look like an officer. Do you think maybe he's another doctor?"

They were close enough for Iris to get a good read on the man in question. He was short and wiry with a quiet, somewhat detached manner and thoughtful, curious eyes. She shook her head. "I don't think so, May. There's something very different about him."

She thought she'd spoken quietly enough: Jerry had always teased her about being "a mourning-dove among the blue jays." But her voice must've carried in the clear, cold air, and the short man turned in their direction. He said something to the Matron, who nodded pleasantly enough—although Iris could see her smile begin to curdle at the sight of May—and beckoned them closer.

"Girls," she said briskly, "this is Captain Francis Derwent Wood, RAMC, from 3rd London General Hospital. He has been good enough to come here and see what he can do for one or two of the patients with more severe facial wounds."

Archie! Iris thought. The bleakness she'd been feeling receded slightly at the thought of the possible boon awaiting her friend. *Just when I was thinking life was too horrible . . .* Then she looked up to find Francis Derwent Wood watching her.

He strolled over to them without any ceremony. "How d'ya do?" he asked, shaking hands first with Iris, then with May. A surge of electricity went through Iris at his touch: the man's creative energy was so strong, it leaped out of him. "I'm very glad to meet you both," he continued, addressing May but still following Iris with his eyes. "I won't have much time here, unfortunately, but since you work so closely with the men, perhaps you can give me a better sense of—"

"Who needs you the most," Iris said, then writhed inwardly. Captain Wood must think her manners abysmal, her interrupting him like that.

But Derwent Wood's eyes met hers appreciatively. *Soul meeting soul*, a voice in her head said, although Iris wasn't entirely sure why. Yet somehow their souls *had* met and touched, although it wasn't, of course, anything like the merging of hers and Jerry's.

With that uncanny timing of his, Jerry himself happened to amble around the corner just then, carrying a small crate. Probably medical supplies, although she wondered why his eyes looked larger and darker and . . . well, *angrier* as they quickly traveled back and forth between her and Derwent Wood. It wasn't as though she and the artist were alone—there was May, not to mention the Matron and a whole slew of others—and, besides, Captain Wood wasn't even touching her. Then, just as suddenly as he'd appeared, Jerry turned away from them and disappeared through the shadowy doorway.

"Interesting," Derwent Wood murmured. He deftly turned Archie's marred face toward him and ran his fingers along the shattered jaw. "Most interesting." He straightened himself up and turned to Iris. "You have a photograph that I can work from?"

"Yes, sir. I wrote his fiancée as soon as we were sure you were coming, and she sent me the one that he had taken right before he shipped out." Guiltily, Iris jerked her thoughts away from Jerry, who seemed to be on the verge of making a religion out of avoiding her since the sculptor's arrival the day before; he hadn't even come to her room later that night, as he'd promised. She'd lain awake, her eyes stinging with the tears she couldn't quite bring herself to shed, and a terrible aching inside. "You'll be able to do something for him, Captain Wood?"

"Yes, I definitely think so. Hand me that clipboard, will you, Miss Amory? Thanks." Licking the tip of his pencil, he sketched out a few quick lines. Iris, mesmerized by the pencil's progress—really, it seemed to have taken on a life all its own—gasped.

With less effort than it took her to tuck in the corners of a patient's bed sheets, he had conjured up the face from Theona's photograph. "He has good bone structure, see"—Derwent Wood did some shading, defining the cheekbones more sharply—"and the damage to his jaw isn't as bad as it looks at first." He brought the clipboard up close to Archie; Iris had warned him beforehand about her friend's deteriorating eyesight. "What d'ye say, Archie? Shall we give it a go?"

Archie stared at the sketch. "It—it'd be like a miracle," he rasped. "I don't know how to thank you, doc."

"Don't thank me just yet," Derwent Wood cautioned him. He smiled wryly. "You should see what the critics wrote about some of the pieces I exhibited before I started working at London General."

"Aw," said Archie, "they was talking out of their asses—pardon my French, Sister Iris."

The sculptor gave a short laugh. "Very good, Archie—very good. I'll keep that in mind the next time I get a bad review. When this damnable war is over, that is."

"You think that'll be soon, doc?"

"Well, we can hope, Archie, can't we? We can always hope."

Out in the drafty corridor, Derwent Wood turned to go, saying he needed some time to look over the sketches and notes he'd made that morning before meeting with Drs. Pratt and Brisbane. Iris laid her hand on his arm. "Please, Captain Wood," she began, wondering at her own boldness, "I—I—" The words fell away from her like broken beads rattling onto the floor; but she managed to collect herself and string a few of them together haphazardly. "I just wanted to say 'Thank you' for Archie's sake—we're all so fond of him, you see."

"Is that all?" Derwent Wood asked with a tired, curious smile, and Iris noticed for the first time the shadows under his eyes.

She shook her head slowly. "No—no. I just wanted to know how—how do you do this? I mean, I know you're an artist, and you see things the rest of us don't, but how are you able to"—she lowered her voice—"look at him and see the man he was before? I can do it with most of the men in his ward, but I can't with him, his face is so far gone."

The sculptor regarded her with interest. "And how do you do it? With the other men, that is?"

So, haltingly, she described her first visit to Archie's ward. How she'd learned to focus on whatever intact features there were and reconstruct the rest of a patient's face in her head. "But I can't do it with Archie. I don't know why."

"Perhaps you're too close to him," Derwent Wood reflected. "And let's not forget, I had more than a fair amount of anatomical training at the art academy."

"So have I—here, I mean," Iris countered.

"True. But it's the kind that's born on the spot, of necessity. You know parts, Miss Amory, not the whole." He held up his sketch of Archie's face, pointing to each line with his pencil. "I've had time to study the human face and form thoroughly, and that kind of time is precisely what you don't have enough of here." He tapped the drawing with his pencil and tucked it back under his arm. "My training gives me an extra advantage—that and my 'artist's eye,' as my wife says."

He smiled, and once again, Iris had that sense of kindred spirit with him, of something that transcended romantic interest but that had just as powerful a pull.

There was a hand on her shoulder, and Iris jumped. Jerry was standing there in his old trench coat, holding his kit pack loosely. "Excuse me for interrupting"—he paused significantly—"but I need a word with you, Sister Iris."

She winced at the faint flick of sarcasm on the word "Sister" but felt the chill in her heart give way to warm relief. She had been so afraid that he would leave without a word. "Of course," she murmured, lowering her lashes against his scrutiny. "Please excuse us, Captain Wood."

Iris followed Jerry wordlessly down the hall into the chapel. He put his kit down on an empty pew, and, for a moment, she thought he was about to break out his usual cigarette. But he just put one foot up on the pew and leaned against the back of the one facing it. Iris, not sure what to do, remained standing. She stared at the dingy walls and the long-empty sconces and found herself thinking back to the night they'd met. How low in spirit she'd been and how he'd charmed her out of it with his odd mix of understanding and flirtatiousness.

The room itself hadn't changed any, of course. But they had because of this feeling that had sprung up and grown between them since that night. And, truth be told, she couldn't wish that undone, no matter how harsh or hurtful he'd been at times. Because of it, life would never be completely desolate or bereft of color for her again.

"What the hell was that all about?" Jerry's voice cracked through her reverie. "You looking' to replace me before I'm even gone?"

"I don't—don't know what you're talking about," Iris faltered.

"You and that artist fellow. He trying to talk you into posing for him in private?"

"No," she protested, staggered by what he was insinuating. "We were just discussing Archie's case. And—and, besides, Captain Wood's married."

"Don't make any difference." Jerry pulled out a cigarette but didn't light it, just kept flexing it between his fingers. "She ain't here." The cigarette snapped in two and fell on the floor. He poked it with the scuffed-up toe of his boot, then ground it into the chapel floor. "Turns out, the transport came through a few days earlier than expected. So I guess I'll be pushing up sooner rather than later."

Iris grabbed his wrist. "How much sooner?"

"Within the next couple of hours, I reckon." He stared down at her hand, then covered it with his. "This isn't the way I planned it, Flower-Girl."

A tenderness rushed through her, practically spilling out of her fingertips. He didn't respond at first; then, just as her fingers started to slip away from his, he bent over and kissed her long and deep, drawing the soul from her body.

He did not let her go once they had finished kissing: instead, he made a safe place for her in his arms, and she nestled against him, oddly blissful. How strange that happiness would come to her at this moment, when her lover was taking his leave of her, perhaps forever.

Without moving out of his embrace, she turned her gaze toward the chapel itself. The dingy whitewashed walls, the statuette of the Virgin Mary on the altar, its gilt paint chipped and peeling from its uplifted round face, its hands broken-fingered and outstretched; the tarnished brass censers and hanging lamps; the dusty, mute organ pipes—all these things were suddenly and heartbreakingly beautiful to her. If he was taking part of her away to the front with him, then he was leaving part of himself back here with her, she saw that clearly now. Some ties went deeper than flesh, and neither time nor the war could undo them.

"I don't know what I should do if anything happened to you," she mumbled against his chest.

"Let's not even think that way," he told her, his voice unsteady. He ran his hands along her shoulders and down her arms. "You're the only bit of heaven I've ever known, Iris Amory, and I want you to remember that." He gathered her hands up in his. "Look, I got something here for you."

Iris raised her eyebrows in question.

"Now, it isn't a giftie kind of thing, like jewelry or scent." He let go of her hands and, going over to the pew, began rifling through his pack. He pulled out a pale-green bottle and a smaller odd-shaped item that she couldn't quite make out from where she stood. Then he came back to her and put something cold and hard into her hand.

Iris looked down. It was a spur—one that had been used, yes, but one that had also been polished until it had the dull satiny gleam of old pewter. "I don't understand."

"It's my good-luck piece." He was grinning, but his eyes were serious. "Where I come from, if a fellow gives one of these to his girl, well, it means she *is* his girl, and no other fellow better trifle or flirt with her 'less he wants a good fight on his hands." He swallowed hard. "It ain't an engagement ring, mind you—I ain't got any business giving you one of those, not with this war going on and me with a houseful of haunts in my head. I just wanted you to know you matter more'n a bit to me."

Suddenly, the spur was more beautiful to her than any filigree brooch or cameo would've been. "Thank you," she whispered, her hand closing over it.

Jerry kissed her eyelids, then the tip of her nose. He kissed her lips—a short kiss this time, but sweet nonetheless. He turned to go, then glanced down at the bottle still dangling from his left hand. "Almost forgot." He offered it to her with a sheepish grin.

Tucking the spur into her dress pocket, Iris turned the bottle over. "*Vieille Grande Champagne,*'" she read in her shaky French. "*Ladies' Vintage.*' But you don't drink—at least, I've never seen you touch a drop."

"Oh, I'm no angel—you know that," Jerry remarked. "I just haven't touched any for a real long while now. It—it seemed to make the nightmares worse, and they was bad enough as it was." He reached out to push the hair away from her face. "But some day—when the war's over—we'll drink this here bottle together. Drink to the end of all nightmares, I guess." He pulled her close and kissed her hungrily. Lingeringly. "I'll be seeing you, Iris—don't you ever be doubting it."

"I won't," she promised, but her voice was as soft and uncertain as a summer breeze. He picked up his shabby pack and headed toward the chapel door, turning to give her a sad half-hearted wave before he walked slowly out of it. She stared after him, listening until the familiar sound of his footsteps disappeared down the hallway. She touched the spur in her pocket and wished hard. Then she remembered the cognac that she'd set down on the floor. She picked it up and stared at the label. "'To the end of all nightmares,'" she whispered, and, suddenly, the green bottle felt very heavy in her hands.

CHAPTER EIGHT

The mask took shape slowly. First, there were the fittings. Iris stole what time she could from her rounds and hovered nearby, watching Derwent Wood smear oil over Archie's cratered face, then place small pieces of tissue paper over his eyes. "Don't want any of the plaster getting in there," he murmured. He was very careful to explain each step to Archie.

Then came a thin plaster coating, followed by yet a heavier coating. The sculptor kept adding more plaster until Iris wondered how Archie's skin could possibly breathe under it. But then she remembered that what Archie had left, most folks wouldn't have considered skin.

Finally, when the plaster had hardened completely, Derwent Wood eased it off. Iris peeked inside the mask and stifled a gasp. Within was a negative or inverted casting of Archie's face. Used to that face as she was, she couldn't help blanching when she saw it—it looked so much more gargoyle-ish that way.

Derwent Wood shot her a look. Iris nodded guiltily, knowing that he would make her leave if she couldn't keep her feelings off her own face. And she wanted to be involved so badly—both for Archie's sake and her own. Watching the process unfold took her mind off Jerry back at the front.

Not all of the work was done with Archie present, of course. Much of it Derwent Wood did in a well-lit room off the chapel where he'd set up a makeshift studio. Iris slipped in periodically to see how he was progressing. She watched him scrape the lumps and bumps off the plaster mask and fill in the cracks before using it to craft a second mask out of plasticine. Putting his cigarette to the side—he was a worse smoker than Jerry, unable to go more than a few minutes, it seemed, without lighting one up—he cut eye holes in it, then shaped yet another negative from plaster of Paris. The plaster-of-paris mold became the basis for a positive cast.

"Now we can really get started," he announced, setting it down on the table in front of him and picking up his discarded cigarette.

"But it's so heavy!" Iris protested.

"Oh, the final mask won't be made of this stuff," Derwent Wood assured her.

"What will you use then? Cloth? Papier mâché?"

He shook his head. "Cloth doesn't hold up well—you can't get a good shape from it—and papier mâché's almost as heavy as this. No, we're going to use electroplate—a very, very thin electroplate, light and durable."

But the metallic creation that he showed her a few days later was, Iris thought, almost as bad as that first plaster casting. "This"—Derwent Wood touched a small piece of metal sticking out between the eye holes—"will form the bridge of his new nose. And this"—he ran his hand along the curving side of the mask—"will be his cheek. It's hard to see it now, I know"—he threw her a smile—"but it's really coming together, I can feel it. Of course, I'd never let Archie see it at this stage."

Which was, Iris thought, a blessing. But once it had been electroplated, she found herself seeing it with new eyes. "It's so delicate," she breathed, hardly daring to touch it. "It's like hand-blown glass."

She thought she saw the Englishman wince. "Yes. It's very fragile." He turned the mask over in his hands, then placed it back down on the table. "At least I won't have to put glass eyes in this one," he mused, starting to mix paints. "Amazing that his eyes did escape."

"Not entirely," Iris said sadly.

"Well, relatively." He was frowning at the color he'd come up with. "Hmm, almost but not quite. I don't want his skin tones coming out all pinky-white, but he does need some color. After all, he was a farmer, so he would've had something of a weathered wind-burned look." He stirred the paints a tad more. "There, that's more like."

"How did you start doing all this?" Iris asked suddenly. "The masks, I mean. I know about the splints—Sister Katherine told me the story behind them when I first arrived—but these masks . . ." Her voice trailed off as Derwent Wood put down his paintbrush and pushed his chair back.

He didn't say anything at first, just pushed open the casement window slightly and stared moodily outside. Spring was a little further along now than it had been the day that she and May had been tramping about the muddy monastery garden; it was calling to them, beckoning to them with its birdsong and slowly greening landscape. But the sculptor seemed oblivious to it—indeed, oblivious to everything around him at that moment, including herself.

"At No. 3 London General," he finally said, and his voice had a faraway quality to it, "there were a number of men who were almost as disfigured as Archie. No surprise that: with the ambulances and faster transport to the hospitals, many survived that would have died in other wars." He began pacing back and forth, every step, Iris noticed, taking him further away from his worktable with the unfinished mask lying on it. "These chaps were fine as long as they stayed bandaged. Once the bandages came away, that's when the horror show began, people gawking at them like they were sideshow freaks. Even the sweethearts and war brides who were so damnably proud of them for signing up in the first place."

He paused, striking his palm with his fist. "Within minutes, I swear, they'd be in the Matron's office, wailing like banshees about how they didn't know what they were going to do and not thinking about the poor sods lying disfigured in their beds." His tone softened. "They meant well, those pretty blubbering young things— they just didn't know what to do. How could they? There's been nothing in our experience to prepare us for this kind of horror."

Iris stood there, watching him, not knowing what to say.

"The worst of it is," Derwent Wood continued, "these masks won't last. Two years—maybe, *maybe* three. That's all the time I can buy the poor blighters." His shoulders slumped. "What then, Iris?"

Iris noted his use of her first name but brushed it aside. She was learning that there were as many different kinds of intimacies as there'd been herbs and flowers in her grandmother's garden. There'd been her friendship with Joe, unfolding as gently and sweetly as the flower she'd been named for; her romance with Jerry, heady and sensuous as honeysuckle; and her bond with Archie, bracing and healing as bergamot or comfrey. She wasn't exactly sure how to describe this friendship that seemed to be springing up with Derwent Wood, only that it had a power all its own. *But wasn't it intimacy really any time one soul opened up to another?* Iris mused, remembering that night in her bed, when Jerry had told her about Passchendaele.

"But you're doing *something*," she argued, pulling herself back to the present moment. "Surely that's better than sitting back and ignoring their plight, saying it's all in God's hands. You're giving them hope."

He leaned on the scarred refectory table and stared at her. "But what if it's false hope?" He lit up another cigarette.

There was no breaking away from that gaze. "I don't think it is," she began slowly, seeing Archie's ravaged face in her mind's eye, hearing again the raspy gratitude in his voice when he realized what Derwent Wood was offering him. "But even if it is"—her voice trembled—"isn't that better than nothing at all?"

His eyes never left her face, but she noticed his arms relaxing. "Yes," he said, straightening himself up. "Yes, it is." He came over to her and touched her hand. "You're an incredible young woman, Iris Amory."

Joe had once said the same to her, she remembered. "Thank you, sir," she said, not knowing what else to say. She brushed her skirts out and headed toward the door. "It's almost time for me to start my rounds. I'd best be going."

She was just reaching for the doorknob when she heard him say, "I would like to sketch you before I go back to England, Iris. If that's all right with you, that is."

Jerry would be furious, she knew. . . "Yes," Iris said, her voice not much more than a whisper, and she walked out of the room.

She had a letter from Jerry later that afternoon—her first one in the four weeks he'd been gone. Her fingers trembled as she slit open the envelope with the inexpensive silver letter opener that May had picked up for her in Paris. A photograph tumbled out. She picked it up, and, sitting down on her bed, studied the lean, familiar face. She smiled in spite of herself. Trust Jerry to lean against an artillery shell and playfully spar with a small black kitten as if there was no war going on! But she could understand why—it was such a clown-kitten with funny silvery streaks in its fur (which she first mistook for water spots on the photograph) and crescent-moon markings like half-glasses over its round, serious eyes. And then, too, Jerry was always at his best with animals. She remembered how he'd been with the horses the day they'd gone to Compiègne. Sighing, she set the picture down on her pillow and picked up his letter.

Dear Iris,

As you can see, I've found myself a comrade-in-arms—kinda small but feisty, with one of the best left hooks I ever saw. And, would you believe it, he retrieves, too—comes trotting back with anything he can fit those jaws of his around, even spent bullets. We call him "Hawkeye" because he doesn't miss a trick. He's got this real serious, thoughtful ex-pression that always puts me in mind of you somehow. And this is the damn spooky part about him: he can sense a landmine or sniper more'n a mile away.

A couple of weeks ago, I was out on patrol with Tom Ungar, one of the other fellows in the unit, and Hawk comes along with us, run-ning a little ways ahead and miaowing. Then, all of a sudden, he sets down on his furry haunches and just <u>stares</u> at us out of those big round yellow eyes of his. He commences mewing pitifully, then scoots past us, back toward camp.

Tom was all for keeping on, but I felt this chill all up and down my spine and told Tom no, let's just head back. I've been around animals enough to know they don't generally spook for no reason. That kit, he knows something, I says. Anyway, we were just turning when someone starts shouting at us. And there was this Hun bastard pointing his gun at us. Tom, whipped out his Enfield rifle, picking off that Hun with a single shot.

We shared our rations with Hawk that night.

Mostly, we move by night and hide out in the woods by day. We dig small holes and such with whatever we can lay our hands on. The kitchen follows when it can, and we generally have to eat whenever both it and the opportunity present themselves. Same goes for filling our canteens.

Water's so hard to come by, some fellows actually use gasoline to clean themselves with. I draw the line at that one, though. I'd rather have the stink of mud and sweat on me than make it any easier for the Germans to blow me to kingdom come.

When we do get water, sometimes there's just enough for shaving. We gotta shave as often as possible because beards make it difficult to get our gas masks on, and we only have maybe six seconds to do that and adjust our rifles. Some poor bastard always seems to be a day late and a dollar short, and next thing you know, his eyes and nose are running and burning, and he's slobbering like a damn rabid dog.

Sometimes when I'm out here, I ask myself if there'll ever be a time again that I'll hear the phoebes singing instead of shellfire and cannon. Other times, I try to pretend that all the cannonading around me is just another thunderstorm. That the planes flying overhead are just barn swallows. Then I come back to myself and lose my vision gazing into the darkness. It's always night here somehow, Iris—least, it feels that way.

I try not to think of you too much because it hurts too much. And then I get to wondering, has our coming together been a blessing—a curse—or both? Other times, just knowing you're out there is a little light to hold on to in all this darkness.

Thinking of you—whether I like it or not—
Jerry

Iris read the letter over again, remembering the smell and feel of his skin against hers, and she ached with the remembering.

She had heard, of course, that the Germans had already begun *Kaiserschlacht,* a series of major offensives. Not that Jerry could say much about that, not with the officers instructed to read all the soldiers' mail before sending it on to the censoring center in Paris. Still, he'd managed to paint a word-picture so vivid, she could just about smell the sweat and the gasoline "some fellows actually use"—see the flying-machines overhead like eerie birds, the soldier gagging from the gas . . . .

What if, Iris wondered, she and Jerry had met *before* all this, before the war had damaged him? Would there have been the sweetness without the bitterness? She smoothed the pages out and slid them back into their envelope. Then she picked up the photograph of Jerry play-fighting with the kitten. "Take care of him for me, Hawkeye," she whispered, touching her lips to it. She slipped it into the envelope along with the letter and placed it under some worn chemises in her top bureau drawer before hurrying out of the room.

"Turn your head to the right—*so,*" Derwent Wood told her. "Yes, that's right. And, remember, you're looking down at the soldier—no, no, not down*cast,* simply downward."

"But if he's a dead soldier, shouldn't I be looking at him sadly?"

"No, most definitely not." He ran his fingers through his thinning brown hair. "Remember, this is not a man but War itself. That's why you've got your hand stretched out like that—you've got him by the throat, and you're not letting go. Here." He came over and rearranged her right hand. Squaring her shoulders and narrowing her eyes, Iris tried to imagine herself grabbing the invisible warrior by the throat. "No, no, that's not it either, Iris. You look like you're taking his pulse. This is not Archie or one of the men in the wards."

Finally, they got the pose right between them. "Do I talk or sit completely still?"

Derwent Wood glanced up over his sketch pad, his eyebrows raised. "Do you wish to talk?"

Iris started to shrug, then stopped herself. "Not really, I guess. I just thought you expected me to."

"Well, it's easier for me if you don't." She flinched at the curtness in his voice. He must've caught her reaction because he quickly threw her a smile. "Don't mind me, Iris. I'm a crusty old sod when I'm working. My wife, Florence, always gives me wide berth at times like these. Of course, she's an artist of sorts, too—she sings—so we each understand what the other's about."

"Oh." Iris tried to imagine what it must feel like to be so close to another human being, you knew their moods as well as you knew your own. She and Joe had hovered on the edge of that territory before they'd parted. And, of course, she'd ventured more deeply into it with Jerry. She was still mulling it all over when she suddenly became aware of Derwent Wood, who was standing so close there wasn't even room for his shadow between them.

He placed one hand on the back of her head, cradling it as he would have an infant's. Then he gently angled it so that she was looking downward to the right. "There," he said with satisfaction. "Much better."

He stepped back and studied her as though she were a most interesting problem. "If you'll excuse me," the sculptor murmured, and there he was, in front of her, undoing her collar buttons. Iris's head swiveled around so fast, their faces almost collided, but he paid her no mind, just kept unbuttoning until her nursing uniform was open to the breastbone. She opened her mouth to squawk a protest, but no words came out, only short, hurried breaths.

Derwent Wood slid the gown down around her shoulders. Iris's pulse quickened, an animal coming back to life after hibernation. *Does he mean to make love to me?* she wondered. *Do I let him? He has a wife . . .* But even as the thought was shimmying into her brain, his long, fine fingers were moving away from her. "We can leave your chemise in place," he assured her. "God knows, I don't want to frighten a child like you."

"And what if the Matron should walk in?" she retorted in a pert, sassy voice that took her by surprise, it was so unlike her everyday voice.

Their eyes met, and low, easy laughter rippled from him to her, chasing away the tension. Emboldened by it, Iris slipped her chemise straps down and sat there, glowing with this newfound freedom—really, she felt like an actress or a Gibson Girl in a low-cut gown—while his pencil moved rapidly over the paper. The silence in the tiny makeshift studio was friendly yet purring with possibility. The memory of Derwent Wood's touch lingered pleasantly, and Iris, bereft of her lover, couldn't help wondering what it would be like to lie with him.

The sound of the artist closing his portfolio and pushing his chair back pulled her out of her reverie. "That should do it," he told her, as he stood up and stretched. He walked over to her and touched her face. "You're a beautiful young woman, Iris Amory, and some day, you'll be a beautiful old woman." He traced the curve of her cheek, his voice low and musing. "It's in your bones, yes—you'll age well—but you've got a kind of inner light that shines through you."

He lowered his face. He *must* mean to kiss her. But then, just as suddenly as he had come to her, his hand dropped away from her face, and he drew back into himself. "Now go get yourself respectable for the Matron and scurry off."

Iris stared at him, then nodded, relieved yet disappointed, too. The interlude had reawakened her body, lifting her up like the swan in flight that she and Joe had watched by the river so long ago. And now that she knew that Derwent Wood wasn't going to forget himself—or his wife—and make love to her, she felt flat and foolish as if that mesmerizing swan had just fallen flat on its bill. She put her chemise straps back into place and rebuttoned her bodice with fumbling fingers before sliding off the stool and making for the door. She turned and looked at Derwent Wood once last time.

"I'll see you in the morning," he told her, lighting up yet another cigarette. "Archie's mask should be dry and ready for him then." He smiled, but it was a tight, unconvincing smile and didn't seem to belong to him at all. "I can't wait to see it on him, can you?"

"No," Iris whispered. "I can't either."

The mask fit beautifully, and Archie's joy when he saw himself in the mirror wearing it was contagious. It pulled Iris out of herself and made her forget—at least for the moment—last night's unsettling encounter.

Derwent Wood was there, of course, as were the Matron, Sister Katherine, and Dr. Pratt. Dr. Brisbane was checking on a young New Zealander who'd been brought in severely gassed, but he sent word that he would be in to see Archie later. Iris sighed inwardly with relief. With all these other people in the room, it should be easy to be matter-of-fact in the sculptor's presence.

Anyway, she reminded herself severely, *this is about Archie, not about me. I'm certainly not going to go around acting like some little tragedienne, emoting all over the place.* She took the cheap hand mirror from Derwent Wood's hand as calmly as if nothing had ever happened. Technically, she supposed, nothing had.

She felt a hand against hers and started. It was Archie groping for her hand. He squeezed it hard. "I can't believe it," he rasped. "I—I never thought there was anything like hope for me."

His eyes were suspiciously bright, even through the mask. "Stop that, Archie," Dr. Pratt commanded, trying to keep the usual crispness in his voice and failing. "I won't have you crying and ruining your eyes."

Archie laughed weakly. "That would be a shame, wouldn't it? Especially now that I've got this good-lookin' face here."

"Especially now," Iris whispered back. The mask was indeed a thing of beauty: and in the light filtering in through the shades made from old linens, it looked almost natural. She nodded and excused herself from the room.

She was almost halfway down the corridor when she heard her name being called. She whirled around and saw Derwent Wood coming toward her.

He took her hands in his with the directness that had cut through all the stiff, starched regulations right from the beginning of their friendship. "I wanted to say good-bye," he told her. "I'll be leaving this afternoon, now that the mask's done."

Iris nodded in the direction of Archie's room. "Will everything be all right for now?"

Derwent Wood shrugged. "I've made it as 'all right' as I possibly can, Iris. As I told you, the mask won't last forever." He lowered his voice. "Look here, I don't want you to feel foolish about last night. These things happen during a war, you know that."

She frowned. "But nothing *did* happen."

He smiled, and all the warmth he had ever shown her was back in that smile. "There are all kinds of affairs, Iris, and not all of them are physical." He stared at her hands, which lay trembling in his. "Some day," he told her, his voice low and husky, "some day, you'll see the piece of work that will come from that drawing I did of you, and then you'll know."

"Know what?" she asked breathlessly.

"How tempted I was to come looking for you after you left." Derwent Wood brought her hands up to his lips and kissed them. "Good-bye, Iris Amory. You've been a bright spot in the darkness, and I'll always think of you that way."

He let go of her hands and, with one last smile, was gone. Iris stood there, staring after him, her lips slightly parted and her world a little grayer for his going.

CHAPTER NINE

Jerry's letters came more frequently. As with the first one, there was very little mention of what was actually happening on the front, but he'd always slip in just enough details that she could rough out a reasonably good picture. A smudged picture, yes, but it was better than nothing. What she didn't have to guess at anymore was the strength of his feelings for her: there was a warmth to his letters that hung over each sentence like the frost on those Paris streets, only more abiding. His darker, brooding twin was nowhere in sight; it was as if Jerry had turned a corner in his mind and left that other self and its "haunts" behind.

Consequently, Iris was able to be more herself when she wrote to him, to not worry so much about stepping on some loose creaking board in that interesting room he called his mind. It wasn't the same as having him right by her side, of course, but she felt closer to him than she would've once believed possible.

If only she had an equally strong sense that the war was close to ending and in the Allied forces' favor! The reports from the front made, as May said emphatically, for a very mixed bag. The Germans were launching offensive after offensive, reaching as far as Château-Thierry—which was, after all, only fifty-six miles from Paris. *That* was certainly news guaranteed to put your heart up your throat, Iris thought, and they all prepared themselves for the worst.

But, then, just as suddenly—or so it seemed to them back at the hospital, living on such scraps of news that came their way and rarely seeing a newspaper that wasn't at least three weeks old—the enemy was turned back at Arras. Then the Australians stopped them short at Villers-Bretonneux. Was the darkness finally lifting? Iris wondered. She and May tried to read between the lines of Jerry's and René's letters, but the censors had done their work too well.

Jerry did, however, pass along a song that was, he explained, set to the tune of "If You Were the Only Girl in the World." It was "making the rounds in Trenchland, and we all think it real poetic":

"If you were the only Boche in the trench
And I had the only bomb,
Nothing else would matter in the world that day,
I would blow you up into eternity.
Chamber of Horrors, just made for two,
With nothing to spoil our fun;
There would be such wonderful things to do,
I should get your rifle and bayonet too,
If you were the only Boche in the trench
And I had the only gun."

She and May laughed over it, shuddered, and then laughed again, shaking their heads. What else could you do? Iris argued with herself. A year ago, she would have stopped her ears against such a gruesome little ditty; now she found herself humming it as she went from ward to ward.

May, of course, had to take it a step further: she actually got some of the abler-bodied patients singing it one evening, when they were sitting in the darkening "common room," having talked themselves out. Iris, drawn by the laughing out-of-tune voices, poked her head in the doorway. The Regina was playing a sad, sweet protest in the corner, but nobody seemed to be paying it any mind.

"Come on, Iris," May urged. "The boys and I have even managed to come up with a new verse or two."

They had, too, and ones that were strong enough to take the fuzz off a peach, as Iris's grandfather used to say.

"C'mon, Miss Amory," urged Abraham Wagner, a young black man from South Africa who had served with the Auxiliary Horse Transport, in a raspy voice. He had been gassed while trying to get an injured horse off the battlefield and into the veterinary wagon, and the chafing of his lungs had made him an easy target for the bronchitis that was always lurking nearby, along with the influenza. Iris always enjoyed talking with him; he was wonderfully kind, and his love for horses reminded her of Jerry.

"I can't sing," Iris gasped.

"Neither can I!" laughed May. "But I'm certainly not letting that stop me!"

"That's for sure, Miss Prentiss," agreed Abraham, his face solemn. But the corners of his mouth were twitching.

May laughed again and beckoned to her friend. "Come on, Iris—let's show this fine gentleman from the colonies just how truly badly we Yanks can sing."

Buoyed by the laughter and camaraderie, Iris moved slowly toward the group congregating by the unlit stove in the center of the room. And she surprised herself by singing, really singing, for the first time in her life. She couldn't make the high notes, and May was a little flat; still, all that was lost in the wave of voices as the patients all joined in. And even though they were singing about the very thing that threatened them, doing so helped them push the war that much further away from them.

Abraham and the other men had, with some help from May, just come up with a verse that threatened to take way more than the bloom from the peach when the Matron stuck her graying head around the door jamb. Sister Katherine was standing right behind her. "What on God's green earth is going on here, Miss Prentiss?" the Matron barked, fixing her eyes on May.

"Looks like a grizzled mongoose, don't she, Miss Amory?" whispered Tim Skinner. A rifleman with one of the Australian regiments, he'd had his arms impaled on a fallen barn door by the Germans. Somehow Dr. Pratt had managed to save the young man's arms, and now Tim was gradually regaining the use of them. Sometimes Iris could see how the slowness of his recovery frustrated him, but he usually kept his feelings hidden under his humorous banter.

"What's a mongoose?" she whispered back.

"Big weasel." He made a wild animal face. "Goes after cobras in India." Still keeping his mongoose face, Tim pretended to be holding up a cobra like a string of sausages and gulping it down one snake bit at a time. Iris collapsed in hysterics, laughing so hard that her side ached.

The Matron's eyes slewed 'round toward her. "And what have you got to say for yourself, Miss Amory?"

"Nothing," Iris gasped, still clutching her side. "The men were just singing to kill time, you see—"

"Yes, I see." The older woman's voice was icy.

"I don't think any harm was done, Matron," Sister Katherine said quietly. "As Miss Amory says, they were just killing time, and the good Lord knows, the days here are hard enough to get through sometimes." She turned to the soldiers. "If you boys—and nurses"— she smiled at Iris and May—"could simply keep it down a little, that would be easier all around, especially on the soldiers who have just been brought in and need their rest. I think that that would be all right, don't you, Matron?"

The Matron relaxed her vigilant mongoose stance. "Well, yes, I suppose that would do," she allowed grudgingly. She nodded curtly and stalked out. Sister Katherine followed her, stopping only briefly to shake her head at the girls, her lips twitching in spite of herself.

"Close call, ladies," murmured Abraham, winking at Iris and May.

"I'll say," Tim remarked emphatically. "Ought to send the old lady after the enemy. Just tell her that the Kaiser is a big bloody cobra, and, crikey, Nurse Mongoose there'll make quick work of him." He reprised his snake-gulping mongoose role for the rest of the company, filling the room with waves of laughter.

May made her way over to Iris. "What a hoot!" she said with a low laugh. For the first time since René's departure, her blue eyes were light and dancing. "Did you ever think that we could have this much fun during a war?"

"No," said Iris ruefully. She remembered the girl sitting in Mrs. Banning's garden with her copy of *The Country of the Pointed Firs*. "No, I didn't."

Shortly afterward, real news from the front did come to them, through a young American doctor. Dr. Daniel Blaine had been taken prisoner by the Germans during their advance but had managed to escape after a couple of weeks. He had a few wounds, superficial in themselves, that had gone septic while he'd been hiding out in the Forêt de Compiègne; he was also malnourished, and his hands shook constantly.

"Ague?" Iris murmured to Dr. Pratt, as she handed him a lance.

"No," he muttered. "Probably a slight fever from all the infection brewing in him." And Pratt, with a gentleness that his habitual brusqueness belied, lanced the biggest pustule on Blaine's arm. The yellow fluid oozed out like cream gone bad into the tin basin that Iris was holding. She shuddered inwardly, then scolded herself: *After all the things I've seen—!* But somehow that yellow ooze turned her stomach in a way that Archie's face never had.

"So, how did the Germans treat you?" Pratt was asking the younger doctor.

Blaine glanced up. "Surprisingly well. I think it was because I was an American, and some of them had family over in the States or had even gone to school there. They were very courteous, especially once they found out I was a doctor—although they were kerflummexed by what I was doing with a British regiment." He chuckled wearily, then slumped back into his chair, closing his eyes. "They're losing, you know."

"Really?" Pratt kept lancing pustules. His voice was as cool and clipped as usual, but Iris heard a subtle upturn in it that might, she suppose, pass for excitement. "They seem to be pushing pretty steadily ahead for men who are losing."

He doesn't dare hope, Iris realized. *He's afraid, just like the rest of us. We've lived like rats scurrying about in the darkness so long, we can't imagine anything else.*

"Empty victories," Blaine replied. He was sitting up now, and his voice, despite his fatigue, had a sureness about it. "They're costing the Germans more than they're gaining. Their troops are underfed—I saw that with my own eyes—their people back home are out-and-out starving—and the Americans entering the war has got them scared beyond reckoning." He looked down at his arm and smiled. "Nice, neat work, Pratt. I'd recommend your work any time. Can I offer my services in return?"

"You can bloody well get off your feet," the older man told him roughly. "It's a miracle you're not losing this arm, considering what I drained out of it." He tapped him on the wrist. "When you're up and about again, we'll settle up." He gave one of his wintry smiles. "I won't say no to an extra pair of hands then."

Blaine slowly got to his feet. His whole body was shivering, as he headed, wobbly-legged, to the door. Iris was just about to offer him her arm when there was a clatter out in the hallway. She caught the Matron's voice, a very clipped British voice that she guessed was a military one, and one or two other muffled ones that sounded suspiciously foreign. Not French, though. Her French might not be all that good, but she could pick that much out. She glanced at Dr. Pratt.

"Go see to it, Miss Amory," he said. "I'll show Dr. Blaine to his quarters."

She nodded and hurried out of the room, moving soundlessly in her worn shoes toward the foyer where the voices were coming from. There the Matron stood, talking intently to a British officer. Standing very ill at ease were several young blond-haired blue-eyed boys in tired, tattered German uniforms.

"Little beggars don't look old enough to shave," muttered a familiar voice at her shoulder.

Iris turned and found herself looking into Tim Skinner's sharp blue-green eyes. "I had students about that age back home when I taught," she said, her voice almost as shaky as Dr. Blaine's hands.

"I'll bet you did," Tim replied. "I'll bet you did. The Yanks is doing the same thing, shipping off fourteen- and fifteen-year-olds over here to fight in the mud and get themselves strung up on barbed wire. It ain't bloody right, I tell you. I don't care if they're Brits, Huns, or Hottentots." He took a last drag of his cigarette, then ground it into the floor with the uneven heel of his boot. His left ankle had been broken, too, so he tended to bear down more heavily on his right foot. "Makes you bloody start wondering who the monsters really are."

Iris stared. Somehow she hadn't expected Tim to speak up on behalf of a handful of Germans, no matter how young they were. "That you can say that after all you went through—!" she marveled.

"I was bloody crucified by men, not by little boys like this," he shot back. "They should be playing cricket or making cow-eyes at some little *fräulein* in braids." He limped away angrily.

Iris sighed. She stood there, not sure what she should do next. Then she glimpsed Drs. Pratt and Blaine emerging from the tiny room where she'd left them. Blaine was still shaking slightly and leaning on his colleague's arm. But he straightened up suddenly when he saw the young German soldiers and, letting go of Pratt, went straight to them.

"Wissen Sie Englisch?" he asked the boys haltingly.

"Ja, ja, selbstverständlich," blurted the tallest one. He blushed. "I mean 'certainly.'"

"Good. My German is"—Blaine gestured weakly—"very *schlecht*, very bad, and the rest of me's not much better at the moment. But once I'm rested and feeling myself, I would like to talk with you more."

The boy nodded, his face lighting up at the unexpected kindness in the doctor's voice. Then the British captain barked an order, and the young Germans followed him meekly down the corridor. Blaine made his way back over to Pratt, and they walked off in the other direction, passing by Iris but paying her no more mind than if she had been wooden and painted like St. Dorothea's statuette.

"Why did you do it?" Pratt demanded in a low, savage voice. "Sick as you are and after all you've been through, why in God's name would you make any effort to befriend one of *them?*"

Blaine smiled, and there was a world of warmth in that smile. "Because I've been where they are, my friend, and there were nurses and soldiers who were kind to me."

Iris was still mulling the words over in her head later that afternoon when she brought Archie his letter from Theona. He was sitting up in bed, running his fingers over his mask while he studied it in the cheap hand mirror. He looked up at the sound of Iris's footsteps. "Excuse me, Sister Iris," he rasped, laying the mirror down on the blanket. "Don't think I'm gettin' vain or nothin'—it's just that this new face here is still like magic to me. I can't seem to get over it. You don't know what it's like, goin' from no face 't all to this."

"No, I don't," Iris agreed quietly, sitting down on the chair next to his bed. "I have a letter here for you." She handed the envelope to him, smiling.

He couldn't show expression or animation with the mask, of course, no more than he'd been able to with the ruination of his real face, but the hand that grasped the letter was quick and eager. "I knew there was a letter comin'!" he said. "I kinda felt it in my bones, like my ma says."

"I have a letter, too," she told him happily. Only to him and May would she speak of Jerry.

"That's good, that's good." Archie leaned back, still holding on to Theona's letter. "What's he say?"

"I don't know—I haven't had time to read it yet. But I'll let you know when I have." Iris touched the envelope in his hands gently. "Would you like me to read this to you now, Archie?"

"In a bit—in a bit," he answered. "I kinda want to savor it, Sister Iris, and not rush through it." He patted her hand. "So, what's new out there?"

She patted his hand in return, then smoothed out her skirts. "Well, we have visitors."

"That a fact? What kind?"

"Well, there's an American doctor who escaped from a German prison camp. Some of his wounds got infected, so Dr. Pratt had to lance them. They'll keep him here for a bit—just to make sure the infection's all out—then ship him home, I suppose." She stared out the window. The trees that had held just a promise of green during

111

Derwent Wood's visit were thick with leaves and May blossom, and the late-afternoon sun was casting its shimmer over it all like a spell.

"This Dr. Blaine says that the Germans are in worse shape than they're letting on—that their men are undernourished and that the longer the war goes on, the weaker they're getting. He made it sound like the beginning of the end, Archie." She paused. "And there's another thing."

"What's that?"

"The other 'visitors'—they're captured German soldiers." She shook her head. "And they're *young*, Archie, maybe sixteen at most. They shouldn't be here."

The eyes behind the mask closed briefly, and he let loose a long, ragged breath. "No, they shouldn't. None of us should be here, and that's a fact. But we're here, and that's a fact, too." He raised himself up a bit and, turning to her, handed her the envelope. "All right then, let's say we have a look at that there letter."

It was a typically Theona-ish letter—cheerful and crammed with farm and Grange doings. She had an eye for detail and could, Iris thought, turn a phrase as neatly as she probably could the hem of a dress. Iris had grown to enjoy the letters herself; they took her away to a world she had almost forgotten existed. And Theona's affection for Archie was in every word, warm and homey as the scent of sweet grass:

. . . *So, my dear boy, I've saved the best news for last. Finally, after much scrimping and help from the folks here at the Grange, I've put together enough to come see you. I know, I can hardly believe it myself. It has been so long since I've laid eyes on you, and I have worried so about you being stuck away at the front. I expect to be there by the end of June.* . . ." Theona then went into details about the ship she was booking passage on and concluded the letter with her "undying love."

Iris put the letter down by his hands. But Archie did not touch it. He just sat there, a carved idol in the dappled light. "That's good news, isn't it, Archie?"

"Yeah, it is." He stared at the wall. "Yeah, I reckon it is."

There was a break in his voice. It was almost inaudible, but, knowing him as she did, Iris caught it. "It'll be fine, Archie—you'll see. You've got this now." She reached over and touched the mask lightly. *Please God*, she prayed, *let me be right about this*.

He turned to her. "So I have—so I have. Tell that fellow of yours he's lucky there's a Theona, or I'd be wanting you for my girl."

"I will," she laughed, relieved at the lightening of his mood. "I certainly will."

They sat there together outside of time, the golden glow of the late afternoon washing over them.

CHAPTER TEN

The four young German soldiers blended into life at the hospital so easily, Iris barely noticed the transition. They worked as orderlies around the wards, much as Jerry had, scrubbing floors, polishing bedside lockers, and helping with all the heavy chores. They were scrupulously polite, saluting all the doctors and nurses. Even Mrs. Abbott spoke highly of them. They might be Huns, she said feelingly, but it was clear their mums had brought them up right, that's what.

Only May remained hostile to them. It was not a blatant hostility, but a quietly perking one that showed itself in little things like the way she almost physically drew into herself whenever she passed them. Or her stiff, taut voice whenever she was forced to talk to any of them. One morning, when the prisoners had been there about three weeks, the hostility bubbled over, and she lashed out at Fritz, the oldest, tallest boy, who had spoken with Dr. Blaine that day in the hallway. It wasn't so much *what* she said as *how* she said it, Iris thought as she saw the young boy's eyes darken with hurt.

"I'm sure she didn't mean it," she assured him carefully after her friend flounced off. "Her young man's at the front, you know, and her nerves are terribly strained."

She was really just putting a useless little bandage on the hurt, and they both knew it. But Fritz smiled at her anyhow. *"Danke, Amme*—I mean, Nurse Iris." And he gathered up what was left of his dignity and walked away like the good soldier he had so obviously been taught to be.

"That was a nice thing what you tried to do."

Iris turned and once again found Tim Skinner standing nearby. Now that his ankle was mending, he moved so quietly, you never heard him coming.

"I don't understand it!" she burst out. "That was so unlike May! She's usually the kindest soul alive."

Tim shrugged. "He just happened to be there when it all got too much for her to bear." He cocked his head to the side. "She heard from her Frenchie lately?"

Iris frowned. "No," she said slowly, "come to think of it, I haven't heard her mention him in a few weeks."

"About the time Fritz & Co. arrived here," Tim reflected. He gave a long, low whistle and pulled a cigarette out of his breast pocket. "Odds are, it's got everything to do with him and nothing to do with the boy or anyone else hereabouts." He tapped Iris on the shoulder with his cigarette. "'Ta, Sister. And remember, even the kindest soul alive can only take so much."

"'Bye," Iris said, giving him a little half-smile. He tipped an imaginary cap to her and, whistling, went on his way.

She stood there idly—a strange sensation in itself these days—replaying both the incident and Tim's words in her head. "He's right," she murmured, then caught sight of the Matron emerging from a doorway down the hall. Her head was turned, and she was clearly talking to somebody. Sister Katherine, maybe. They were supposed to be inspecting the wards today, Iris suddenly remembered. Guiltily, she tucked a stray curl back up under her cap and hurried down the hall.

She went about the rest of her rounds mechanically, unable to get her mind past what had happened. *It fits, it really does*, she thought as she doled out medicine—they were running low again—and soaked a new patient's ankle in a saline bath. *How could I have been so blind?* The saline stung her hand, and she bit back a yelp: she'd forgotten about that scratch on her left hand, and now she'd have to worry about it going septic. Not that she could've done much about it, seeing as they were out of rubber gloves, and, anyway, there were never enough to go around for the doctors *and* the nurses. She'd just have to remember to soak it in disinfectant later. So she scooted up to their room as soon as her rounds were over.

She was just sitting down on her cot, the basin of disinfectant balanced on her knees, when May came in. Iris shot her a worried glance over the basin. May—blonde, voluptuous May with the painted-china complexion—was gone, leaving this sharp-faced wraith in her place. Even the circles under her eyes had circles under them. It *must* have something to do with René. Iris remembered how kind May had been when Jerry was leaving for the front, and she ached to return the kindness. But how? She lowered her hand into the disinfectant more quickly than she'd meant to and this time couldn't quite swallow her yelp.

May raised her eyebrows. "Got bit by the saline again, did you?"

"Yes." The stinging sensation was fading now. "I forgot about this new scratch of mine."

"You are the most careless kid," May said, and Iris caught just a hint of the old warmth and playfulness in her friend's voice, like the whiff of a remembered perfume. *She's in there somewhere*, a voice in Iris's head said. *If only I can find her and pull her out.* She sighed. It was almost like dealing with Jerry on one of his bad days.

May came over to where Iris sat and pulled the scratched hand out of the disinfectant. She examined it critically, turning it this

116

way and that, running her finger along the welt. "It doesn't look like it's about to go septic," she finally said. "I think it'll be all right."

"And what about you?" Iris could've smacked herself. Talk about the words coming out all wrong. Still, she and May had always been so open with each other.

"What about me?"

"We haven't talked much lately," Iris faltered. "And you were so sharp with that boy, Fritz, this morning—"

May let go of Iris's hand. "I'm not feeling much like a Hun sympathizer these days," she replied stiffly, as she headed over to the bureau they shared. She yanked her drawer open and began rummaging through it, then stopped short. She closed her eyes tightly, and a funny strangled sound escaped her lips.

Iris got up and, forgetting her own fear, went straight to May. "What is it?"

May lowered her head. A tear splashed down, then another and another, and, suddenly, they were coming down all at once, like the rain outside their window. "He's gone missing, Iris," she choked. "He could be dead or in a German prison or dying s-slowly out in the woods or mud like—like some w-w-wild animal."

Iris stroked her friend's hair. "How do you know?" she asked quietly.

"I just *know*." May rested her head against Iris's shoulder. "I haven't heard anything from him for weeks, and that's just not like René."

"The mail can get held up by the censors for a long time."

"Yes," May replied. "But—it's—it's hard to explain—one night, after I finished my rounds—it was that day we'd had all those casualties from Amiens, and I was done in, my head aching so bad, I thought it would burst—I was passing the chapel, and I had this sudden urge to go in. Now that's just not like me."

That was true, Iris thought. May had always joked how her religion was like her best dress—something that she wore once in a while but kept carefully pressed and tucked away in her wardrobe most days.

"But my feet seemed to have a mind of their own, and next thing I know, I'm sitting at one of the pews up front," May continued wearily. "It's raining to beat the band, and the sound's kind of soothing—you know, the way it is when you're lying in your bed at night, all snug and secure.

"Then, all at once it seemed, this nausea came out of nowhere and took hold of me. My insides were all a-roil, just like Tim Skinner says. No, I didn't vomit, Iris, but, oh, God, I wanted to."

"That could've been the tail end of the headache," Iris argued. But even she could hear the unsteadiness in her own voice. Given her odd upbringing and all the things she had seen or heard in the past year, she knew that there were things that just couldn't be explained away. Jerry's Hawkeye instinctively knowing where the landmines and snipers were lying in wait, for instance. It was, as May had once said, a time of not knowing or seeing clearly, which only sharpened your sense of the *un*seen . . . of knowing things without knowing *how* you knew them.

Then her grandmother's face came to her. Iris had never been particularly good at picturing people in their entirety once they were gone: she tended to remember parts rather than the whole. Like her grandfather's oddly wasp-waisted thumbs as he mended fences or soothed a spooked animal; Joe's blue-gray eyes, light- and laughter-filled; and Jerry's tanned-leather skin, and the way he used to run his foot gently against hers in bed. But she saw her grandmother now in detail, every wrinkle etched into the old paper-thin skin, the eyes oddly lit as she told one of her weird tales. "May?" Iris asked abruptly.

Her friend looked up wearily, her eyes more washed-out than St. Dorothea's and red-rimmed.

"Did you feel a chill? That night, I mean?"

May's mouth fell open. "A chill?" she demanded flatly.

"My grandmother used to say"—Iris began fumbling around with her words like a child trying to arrange blocks in some kind of pattern—"that when somebody died, you could feel them around you. That there'd be this *chill*, only not like any you'd ever felt before, and it would cut through you, quick as a knife, and drop you to your knees. Those were her exact words, May. I know they sound"—she fell back on one of Tim Skinner's cleaner phrases—"barmy, but they kind of make sense. Well, as much as anything does out here." She placed her hand over May's. "I—I don't see how René could've passed without your somehow knowing it."

May smiled. It was a weak-tea kind of smile, but there was a light in her blue eyes that made Iris think of the summer sun breaking out over the water. "Do you really think that?"

"Yes, I do," Iris replied. She had learned to take her own happiness in half-measures and to be glad for whatever grace the day brought with it. But she had to believe that it would come out all right for May and René—that somehow there would be at least one happy ending in the midst of all the suffering threatening to swallow them whole. "I really do."

May stared down at her hands. "I was horrible to that boy, wasn't I?" she asked, flexing her fingers and glancing up.

Iris met her gaze but said nothing.

"It's not his fault." May sighed. "My nerves have just been worn ragged—it's the not knowing I can't take."

"Maybe it's one of those 'times we're not supposed to see clearly,'" Iris quoted softly.

"Says who?"

"Said you. And not so very long ago, either."

May rolled her eyes and groaned. "Did I really? Iris, as your friend, I'm officially telling you that I'm an idiot. Easy enough to be handing out platitudes when you're not the one who's hurting." She leaned back against the rough whitewashed wall. "Do me a favor, will you, Iris? The next time I get up on my soapbox like that, just shoot me."

Iris shook her head, smiling. "I've never handled a gun, May—I'd probably miss and hit the Matron."

"Oh, well, all for the greater good, my dear." May smiled back. She almost sounded like herself. "You know, I think I just might be able to sleep tonight. These last few weeks, I'd just lie awake, all sorts of imaginings playing themselves over and over in my head like a ghastly moving-picture show or newsreel that I couldn't shut off." She sighed. "It doesn't seem as awful now that we've talked about it. Not that I know any more than I did fifteen minutes ago. No offense, but your granny's spirit lore isn't much to hold on to."

"No, it isn't," Iris agreed. "But it's something."

The letter came a few days later. It was from Jean Brunelle, René's commanding officer, and, judging from the battered, mud-streaked envelope, it had been through something of a war itself trying to reach May. The postmark was badly smudged, but the letter was dated—both May and Iris drew their breaths in sharply and stared at each other—the day after the Amiens casualties had been brought into their little hospital.

It was a very straightforward letter, written in simple, precise French. Fortunately, Iris reflected, resting a hand on May's shoulder and glancing quickly at the elegant slanted writing, her friend's French was flawless, so they didn't have to call upon any of the French patients to interpret.

René was missing in action. "They presume that he has been taken prisoner," May said in a dull, dead little voice. The letter slid from her trembling hands. "Those *bastards!*"

Iris understood, of course; still, she hoped that Fritz and the other German prisoners gave May a very wide berth for a long time. She picked up the letter and scanned it quickly. "He says that he regrets having to write you these words but that as René's fiancée, you naturally have first right to know." She mustered up a smile. "Why, May, you never told me you were engaged."

May looked up. "I didn't know we were."

"Well, René must've told Captain Brunelle that you were, or he wouldn't have written to you first."

"Fat lot of good it does me now that the Huns have got him," May sniffed.

"At least you know," Iris reminded her gently, handing the letter back.

"Not much more than I did before." May put her hand in front of her face now. Iris was about to get up and slip away when May jerked up and said in a shaky voice, "Iris, what if—what if they're torturing him?"

"Dr. Blaine says they treated him well."

"Only because he was a doctor, and they thought he might be useful to them. Look what they did to poor Tim Skinner."

"I don't think that Tim would care much for your calling him 'poor,'" Iris replied, smiling in spite of herself. "Anyway, I wouldn't go borrowing trouble, as Mrs. Abbott says—we've got plenty of it here."

"Still, I couldn't bear it if—" May shut her eyes tightly and shivered.

"Don't even let yourself think it." Iris pressed her friend's shoulder and rose from the side of the bed where they'd been sitting.

"Rest, and I'll tell the Matron—well, what there is to be told. I'm sure she'll understand and give you leave to skip your rounds tonight."

May raised an eyebrow. "Live long enough, and you'll see everything," she murmured, a faint flicker of amusement lightening her thin face.

"There you go." Iris smiled as she left the room, glad to see May's sense of humor struggling to reassert itself. She hurried down the corridor, anxious to catch the Matron alone. She was a crusty old mongoose, all right, just as Tim had said, but there was much kindness in her, too. You just had to approach her properly.

"Nurse Iris?" She whipped her head around. There stood Fritz, smiling shyly.

"Yes, Fritz, what is it?" she asked, trying not to speak impatiently.

"I need to ask a *gunst*—how you say"—he gestured uncertainly with his hands—"a favor."

"Of course, Fritz." He was so nervous and young, he brought the teacher in her to the surface. Iris patted his arm. "What is it?"

The words came in a rush now. "I need—that is, we all need—to write our mothers. You see, they know not how we are faring or if we are even alive—and you were so kind the other day when the other nurse, she lose her temper with me—"

Iris shook her head. "I still don't see where I come into all this, Fritz."

"We are not allowed to write ourselves. They, the officers, think we will send valuable war information to *our* commanding officers." Fritz hung his head. "And all we wish to do is let the *mutters* know we are alive." He hesitated, then looked up at Iris, his blue eyes large and wistful. "*Please,* Nurse Iris, it would mean much to me—to all of us."

"Of course." The words came forth almost before she knew that she was saying them. He pressed her hand gratefully, clicked his heels, and left.

Iris stood there for a while after he'd gone, wondering just what kind of fool she was. *This*, she thought wryly, *is not going to make me popular hereabouts. Archie'll understand, of course, and so will Tim Skinner. But what will the Matron say?* She shook her head and continued walking. She was almost at the door of the Matron's office when another thought came to her like a malicious, unwelcome guest. How would May herself feel? She was in a fragile enough state as it was; anything connected with the Germans, remotely or otherwise, was bound to be anathema to her right now.

But he's only a boy! Iris silently argued. *Besides, I promised.*

Sighing, Iris shut her mind to her doubts and rapped on the Matron's door.

Word did get out about her writing the letters for the German prisoners, of course, and almost as soon as she had posted them. Iris had known, even as she was addressing the envelopes—they had to go through Switzerland—that it would. The Matron lambasted her for sticking her nose where she shouldn't. "It's military business, Miss Amory, and you're just an insignificant little nurse from the States, remember that."

"It wasn't military business," Iris replied, nettled. "Just a handful of boys wanting their mothers to know that they were kicking and breathing. Or breathing, at any rate." She stared down at her hands.

"*You* see it that way, but that doesn't mean the brass will, if they get wind of it," the older woman told her shortly. "They, if they're so minded, could accuse you of aiding and abetting the enemy." Her tone softened. "I know you meant well, Miss Amory, but you've got us here at the hospital in one very sticky wicket. The whole thing can be taken out of context so blessed easily, don't you see?"

Iris did see in the weeks that followed. Mrs. Abbott, who had been so kind and understanding after that awful encounter with

Alexander Maxwell, told her that "she had less morals than Mata Hari. Your parents must be turning in their graves, that's what." The other nurses gave her equally nasty little jabs, and Drs. Pratt and Brisbane only spoke to her when they absolutely had to and never by name anymore. It was always "Nurse" or "You there." Pratt in particular looked at her as though she was one large, loathsome human cootie.

Archie and Tim Skinner took her part, just as she had guessed they would. "You did what's right," Tim told her roughly, "and you did it knowing that it was probably going to blow up in your face like some bloody potato masher grenade. That takes guts, Sister."

Surprisingly, the rest of the wounded men took pretty much the same point of view. So did Dr. Blaine, who, seeing how swamped with casualties the hospital was, had stayed on to help once he was fully healed. "I'm glad you helped those boys out, Miss Amory," he told her one day as they were preparing a soldier for surgery. Generally a quiet-spoken man, he took care that his words should carry. "Their mothers'll rest all that much easier knowing that they're safe. I'd want somebody to do as much for my sons if I had any."

Iris looked up from the bloody pant leg that she was trying to carefully scissor off the unconscious man. "You mean that, sir?"

"I most certainly do," he said warmly. Then, as her eyes began tearing up, he shook his head. "None of that now. And watch what you're doing with those scissors there. We don't want to be cutting up any more of this boy than we have to." But his voice and eyes were kind.

After that, the cold front at the hospital began to thaw. Dr. Pratt grew civil again, and Mrs. Abbott apologized for the Mata Hari slur. "I shouldn't've been saying it, and that's a fact." She put her roughened red hand on Iris's forearm—looking, for all the world, like she was being sworn in in court. "It weren't good manners nor religion, and it weren't true besides. And I'm hoping you'll forgive me."

"Of course," Iris replied. And meant it. Mrs. Abbott's attack had been aboveboard, nothing like the other nurses' sniping had been. Anyway, nothing hurt like May's attitude. She didn't say nasty, cutting things, and she didn't go out of her way to avoid Iris: she just suddenly acted as though her friend had ceased to exist.

"It's like I'm a ghost, and she can't see me," Iris told Archie as she sponged him one morning, her voice unsteady. They had moved Archie into a little alcove of a room, apart from the others because the risk of infection was so much greater for him. "We've been through so much together, and she seemed to be coming round, even after we got the letter from René's commanding officer and—"

"After *she* got the letter," Archie corrected her gently. "Don't you see, Sister Iris, this is *her* tragedy, not yours, and she's hurting pretty bad. She's about as raw on the inside as I am on the outside, and your writing those letters for them German boys just set her back some, that's what. It ain't rational, I know, but she ain't exactly thinking rationally right now. Give her time." He reached over and patted Iris's hand. "For what it's worth, I'm behind what you done. Them little boys shouldn't ought to be fighting a grown man's war."

His voice was growing fainter, like field grasses rustling in the wind. Iris hurried him through the rest of his sponge bath and into a fresh nightshirt; then, not knowing why she did it, she bent over and kissed his forehead, right where the mask met his hairline. "You're a peach, Sister Iris—a reg-lar peach," he slurred as he settled back down among his pillows.

"You're sure you don't want me to take the mask off?" she asked.

He shook his head slowly. "No, I figure I might as well see what it feels like sleeping with it on."

Iris knew he was thinking about Theona, about how much he feared her seeing him without the mask on. She watched Archie drift off to sleep in the late-morning sunshine, then slipped out of the room, silent as a shadow.

After finishing her rounds, she stopped off in the mailroom and found a package from Jerry waiting for her. Clasping it to her chest, she stole away to her room, which was, thankfully, empty. Iris sat down on her hard, narrow bed and pored over Jerry's letter. It was loving, affectionate, and as newsy as the censors would allow. There had been very little delay in the mail lately, so Jerry knew all about the uproar over the letters.

Don't know what all the damn belly-aching's about, Flower-girl, he wrote. *Way I look at it, you just wrote a handful of German Fraus that their boys were all nice and tucked into bed. Hardly what I'd characterize as an international incident. Just rest that pretty head of yours and get a good look at the floor 'cause you aren't gonna be seeing it for a while once I get back.*

The letter fluttered down onto the bed. Blushing, she put her hand to her throat and felt laughter burbling up there. She should be properly shocked, she supposed, but . . . The corners of her mouth still twitching, she picked up Jerry's letter and began reading again.

You know I'm not much for gifties, the letter continued, *but this is something that came my way unexpected-like. There's this estaminet at a farmhouse here in Amiens where, for just a little bit of money, even a private like myself can get a pretty good feed. Nothing fancy—just eggs and chips and sometimes even chicken or seafood.*

Anyways, I met up with this flyer from the States, and he had this interesting box on him. Made it from an Avro airplane propeller himself, he says. He was trying to get the madame running the estaminet to take it as trade for food, but she wasn't interested. I took a good look at it and decided she wasn't using the eyes God had given her. There was something so out of the ordinary and elegant about it, Flower-girl, it reminded me of you. And, all at once, I wanted you to have it. So, seeing as I happened to have some extra cash on hand for once—I treated him to a hearty meal in exchange . . . .

Iris laid the letter aside and picked up the parcel. It took some doing to untie all the string—Jerry knew how to wrap a package every which way and then some—but the oval box was every bit as elegant and unusual as he'd said. She ran her hands over the ridged lid, loving its cool, hard smoothness and warm chestnut color. The lid lifted off easily, revealing a shadowy place for treasures. Letters. And a single spur with the dull, satiny patina of old pewter, lovingly polished. Smiling, Iris closed the box and placed it alongside her. She picked up the letter and began reading where she'd left off, swinging one shabby little boot to invisible music.

Anyway, Jerry concluded, *it's a right smart little box. It ain't got a lining, but I figure we can go to Paris once this here fighting's done and pick you out some blue velvet for that. I recollect your saying how much you enjoyed poking around those little shops there when you went with May. Till next time, Your Jerry.*

She glowed over that. *Her* Jerry. Suddenly, for no particular reason, she found herself remembering the time she and her grandfather had rescued a half-drowned kitten. Her grandfather had wrapped the kitten up in an old hucksack towel and handed it to her: she remembered holding it and feeling the warmth seep back into its sodden gray-striped body.

It's like that, just like that, she mused. And hope, that half-drowned kitten, took hold of her as she sat there, re-reading her lover's letter.

CHAPTER ELEVEN

Theona was almost as good as her word; she arrived in early July. She was round-faced and rosy-cheeked with strawberry-blonde hair and friendly eyes. Had Theona been a flower, Iris thought, she would've been a cheerful, hardy marigold protecting the fancier flowers from insect attack. "Thank you for being so good to Archie," she said, shaking the hand that Iris offered her and smiling.

"Archie's been a good friend to me," Iris replied, trying not to frown. Something suddenly felt a little off. Was it the handshake? It had been a weak-tea sort of thing, a little too lady-fied, and didn't have the warm capableness you'd expect from a farm girl. Of course, women didn't usually put the strength in their handshakes that men did, but still . . . . Iris put on a smile and led her into the Matron's office.

The Matron greeted Theona briskly. "Go and fetch the tea, will you, Miss Amory?"

Iris went and fetched. When she came back with the tray, the two women were talking animatedly. Or, rather, Theona was. The Matron was studying her visitor, wearing what Tim Skinner would've called her Mongoose Look.

Suddenly, Theona seemed to catch on that she was giving more to the conversation than she was getting back, and her voice came to an abrupt halt like a motorcar pulling up short at a railway crossing. She began fidgeting with her mug of tea, then glanced over at the Matron. "Please," she said, setting the mug down on the older woman's desk with a less-than-steady hand, "when can I see Archie?"

The Matron put her own mug down. "You're aware of the extent of Archie's injuries, Miss Fuller?"

"Yes, I know his face was badly scarred but—"

"Not 'scarred,' Miss Fuller," the Matron corrected sharply. "Obliterated."

The marigold drooped and shrank into herself. "Obliterated," she repeated dully. "So there is"—she swallowed hard—"nothing left?"

"Nothing but eyes and a voice, and both are badly damaged. Of course, he'll be wearing the mask that Captain Derwent Wood made for him a good deal of the time." The lines of Theona's face relaxed, and she sat up a tad straighter. But the mongoose wasn't done shaking her about. "Still, married life being what it is, it's inevitable that you'll see the damage that the war has wrought. And, woman to woman, I'm wondering if you can deal with it."

Theona opened her mouth, but the Matron motioned for her to stay quiet. "Because if you can't, m'dear"—never, Iris mused, had a term of endearment sounded less like one—"then you'd better march yourself out that door at once and get on the first ship back to the States. I won't have you giving that poor man false hope, not after all he's been through." She placed her hands on the table and made a little steeple with her forefingers. "So, have you got it in you, girl?"

"Yes, I believe so." Iris thought she heard a quiver in Theona's voice but wasn't sure.

"Very well then." The Matron rose from her chair. For a short, stocky woman, she had an incredible amount of presence at that moment. "Miss Amory will take you in to see Archie. I have a requisition for medical supplies that I have to get ready by four, but I'll be here ready to discuss his care in more detail with you afterward."

Theona hesitated, then picked up her purse and rose slowly to her feet. Iris tried to muster up what she hoped was an encouraging smile as she escorted her to the door. Theona smiled back, but her eyes had a haunted look, and her feet moved leadenly out into the hallway. She was—the comparison came unbidden into Iris's mind—doing a chilling imitation of someone being led to execution. *So, does that make me the chaplain reading the final prayers?* Iris wondered. She did her best to push the thought out of her mind, but it insisted on following them all the way to Archie's room.

Theona just stood there, staring at the door. Iris waited a few moments, then reached around her and turned the doorknob.

Archie jerked his head in their direction. "Sister Iris?" he queried. Then, more hesitantly, "Theona?"

"I'm here, Archie dear." Theona went to him and sat down on the chair alongside the bed.

"I—I can't believe it's you, Theona." Archie put his hand up to his sweetheart's face, much as he had to Iris's that first day. Theona caught at the hand before it could touch her face; holding it down firmly, she began chatting away about her voyage.

Iris's heart turned inside her, and her eyes filled with tears. "I'll leave you two alone now." She could feel the tears threatening to spill onto her cheeks like raindrops against a windowpane. "I'll be back in a half-hour or so," she mumbled, ducking out of the room.

She tried to steady her nerves by making a linseed poultice—there was always a soldier with chest congestion in need of one—but her hands trembled, and she made such a mess of it that Sister Katherine finally shooed her out of the room. "You're no good to us here," she told Iris matter-of-factly but kindly. "Your head's elsewhere."

"I know," Iris replied, her voice small and tight. "I feel like there's a train wreck happening back in that room, and there's nothing I can do to stop it."

"Well, there isn't now, is there?" Sister Katherine said. "But maybe she'll rise to the occasion, Iris. We can hope."

"Maybe." Iris slipped out the door and made her way slowly down the corridor back to Archie's room. It was her turn to stare at the door now; and she stared at it until she was sure she must know every grain of wood by heart. Then, shaking her head slightly, she turned the knob and went in.

They were sitting there, just as she'd left them, only Theona wasn't holding his hand anymore. Iris went straight to Archie and placed her hand on his shoulder. "Is everything"—her throat tightened up, and she had to work to get the words out—"all right, Archie?"

He groped for her hand, and she saw that the eyes behind the mask were bright with unshed tears. At the same time, she also noticed that the mask was ever-so-slightly askew, right by the jaw line. Almost as if . . .

No, he couldn't have, she thought, chafing his hand in hers. She darted a look at Theona, who was wearing her smile like a badly fitting hat. Archie cleared his throat. "'Bout as well as you could imagine," he said. He tightened his hold on her hand, and Iris winced.

Theona slowly stood up and began fiddling with her purse. She looked down at the man she'd traveled so far to see. Her smile trembled and faded away, leaving her face plain and pasty, the marigold with all its jaunty color drained from its petals. "I suppose I should go now, Archie."

"Yes, I expect you'd better, Theona," he replied, nodding. "You have a safe voyage back now, you hear? And"—the eyes behind the mask grew brighter—"tell—tell the folks back home I—I think of them all the time."

"I will," Theona told him. There were tears in her eyes, too. So she *had* loved him, Iris thought. Just not enough. "Good-bye, Archie."

"'Bye, Theona." He turned his face to the wall.

"I'll show you back to the Matron's office," Iris said, struggling to keep her voice even. "I'll be back later to check in on you, Archie."

He did not reply. Iris walked Theona out of the room and down the long corridor, her heels clicking angrily.

"You hate me, don't you?" Theona's voice cut through the starched, polite silence. "You think I'm unkind. Unwomanly."

Iris stopped short and turned to face her. "Not unwomanly," she said. "But unkind, yes."

"I thought I could handle it, I honestly did." Theona stared down at the floor. "I mean, I've seen injuries among the hired men on my parents' farm but nothing like this. It—it beggars the imagination. What I saw wasn't a face anymore, just a bombed-out crater of a thing with Archie's eyes peering out of it."

She looked up, sickened. "That's what made it worse. I couldn't tell myself it wasn't Archie, not with those eyes following me about." She swallowed hard, as she rooted about in her little purse. She pulled out a pretty linen handkerchief with coral tatting she had probably made herself and dabbed her eyes with it. "You know, they had that same gentle, pleading look they'd had when he was asking me to marry him. Strange that I should think of that, isn't it?"

Iris fought the urge to slap her. "Don't you see? It still *is* Archie—he's still the same good, kind man who offered you all those things. Of course, he needs a lot more care—"

"I can't do it," Theona said, her voice flat and unyielding. "I can't."

Iris stared. "Then I'm sorry for you," she replied quietly, "and sorrier for Archie. You may"—she made a dismissive motion—"find another man, but I'll wager you'll never find one who will give you half the love he has." She turned to go, but Theona caught her by the wrist.

"Doesn't his face bother you, Iris?"

Iris gently disengaged the other woman's fingers. "No," she retorted, picking up her pace. "You see, I love Archie. He's like a brother to me."

Theona hitched up her skirt slightly to keep with her. "But what if he was your beau? Would you feel the same then?"

Iris's mind darted back to Jerry's lean face and warm dark eyes. She tried to picture that same face—what was the word the Matron had used?—obliterated—and knew that some part of her would always yearn over him. "I would still want to be with him," she said simply. "No matter what."

"No matter what," Theona repeated dully. She shook her head. "I don't understand it."

"You're not supposed to," Iris told her. "It just *is*."

They had reached the office. Iris rapped on the door, anxious to be rid of her charge. "Come in," the Matron called in her usual crisp tone. But when they entered, the faithful old mongoose was just sitting there, a very faraway look in her eyes . . . and, Iris suspected, no further along on that requisition for supplies than she had been before.

The older woman glanced first at Theona's face, then at Iris's. "I'll take it from here, Miss Amory." Iris stared at her supervisor. "Just go back and check on him." Her voice was unusually gentle. "Just go."

Iris moved slowly back down the hall, trying out all sorts of different speeches in her mind. *It will be all right. You're better off. The hurt will go away after a while.* But each phrase was a bell out of tune, and she knew she couldn't say any of them. Not in good conscience. Because that pain wasn't going anywhere. It was going to sit there in Archie's heart and soul, gnawing away at him like a rat from the inside till the day he died.

Quietly, she pushed open the door to his room. Archie lay there, so still, she caught herself automatically checking for the rise and fall of his bedclothes. "Archie?" she whispered.

"Here, Sister Iris, right where she—where you left me."

Iris sat down on the rickety chair by the bed. The mask lay abandoned on the little table. She glanced at it and opened her mouth, only to shut it again. Finally, she shook her head. "I don't know what to say."

"There's nothin' to say." He sighed as he turned toward her. "It is what it is." He gestured wearily with his right hand, then let it fall limply back onto the blanket. "I—I didn't mean for her t'see me like this, not just yet, at any rate. But I'd had it on so long while I was waitin' for her, it was gettin' uncomfortable, and she said she could take seein' it. And I believed her." He stared at the whitewashed wall in front of him. "You know what the worst of it is, Sister Iris? She took part of me with her for keeps, like, and she don't even want it."

"I know, Archie." She was remembering herself in the chapel the day that Jerry had left for the front, that left-behind feeling, that sense of having your heart ripped out of your own keeping. "I know."

He sighed again. "You'll stay?"

"Of course." She stared down at her hands, rough and worn with their cross-hatching of septic scars, lying against the even more worn blanket: they didn't look like her hands at all anymore, she thought, and she had the strangest sense of disappearing. She pulled herself out of her reverie and looked at her friend. "I just wish I could do more for you, Archie," she murmured.

He looked at her, and her heart hurt all the more for him. "You stayed, Sister Iris," he said, touching her face. "You stayed. That's gift enough."

CHAPTER TWELVE

Late summer brought more Allied victories and a general lift of everyone's spirits. "It's a black day for Germany, all right!" Tim crowed, paraphrasing Ludendorff's words after the success of the Anglo-French counterattack at Amiens. He grabbed Iris by the waist and waltzed her along the hallway.

"It feels like Christmas morning, presents and all," Iris laughed, making him a quick curtsy as he released her.

"Not for the Boche it isn't," he said, bowing back. "Of course, we've still got a piece to go. But I think we're finally seeing that light at the bloody end of the bloody tunnel."

The Allied army kept pushing forward. Dr. Blaine had been right: the German army was a rag-and-bone force, a skeleton collapsing in on itself. Mihiel, Ypres, the Argonne offensive. . . . The names of the battles were a joyful litany to Iris. Only later would she learn the reality behind the litany—stories like that of the Lost Battalion, the American unit that was almost wiped out by both German and Allied fire. Only later would she learn that General Pershing, for all the compassion she'd witnessed in him, was just as capable of throwing men's lives away as his English and French counterparts, Haig and Joffre. But for now, all Iris saw was the rainbow after the storm, the promise that they were indeed nearing the end of a tunnel that had been bloody beyond imagining.

Then the influenza stole in upon them like a sneak thief in the night. It prowled the whitewashed halls of the monastery, snatching up lives where it pleased. Iris had, of course, seen the grippe before. But this was a far stronger, more malevolent version of what she'd heard Mrs. Banning call "the old person's friend." It fed indiscriminately upon the inhabitants of the hospital. One of the men it took was Abraham Wagner. Abraham had fought for all he was worth, but his already damaged lungs had made it a losing battle almost from the start. Tim, who'd befriended the gentle black man, wandered the corridors, totally bereft. Oh, he helped wherever possible, but gone were the jokes and the lightning flashes of humor that everyone (even the Matron, though she never would admit it) had enjoyed.

"He's the one who died, and it's me what's feeling like a ghost," he said wearily to Iris one afternoon. He passed his hand over his forehead. "He was twice the man that some of these bigotty whites from the States are."

"Oh, not all of us Yanks are so 'bigotty.'" Iris told him Jerry's story about General Pershing and how he'd earned his "Black Jack" moniker. It would, she figured, give him something else to think about.

"Really?" Tim's face took on something of its old keenness. "I'm glad to hear it. That's a bloody sight better than those congenital idiots grounding that black flyer chap when his squadron got itself transferred to Yank command. I wonder if Abe ever heard that story your beau told you?" He shook his head, wistfulness settling in on his face like fog. "It would've pleased him, that it would've. He didn't like to say much—he tried to hide it, Abe did—but a blind man could've seen it bothered him when some folk treated him less decently than they ought." He sighed. "Well, I'll be seeing you, Miss Iris."

She nodded and watched him go before she began retracing her steps down the hallway. She wasn't really watching where she was going, she was that tired, and practically collided into Sister Katherine.

"Why, Iris!" the older woman laughed, catching her by the arm. "Looks like you need bed rest more than some of our patients. When was the last time you slept?"

Sister Katherine's touch—that touch that had always been so sturdy and competent—felt thin and, well . . . *insubstantial*. It seemed to go right through her. Iris glanced up quickly. Sister Katherine's squarish face with its pink-and-white porcelain complexion was oddly gray and hollow-cheeked. When had that happened? Iris wondered. She had been so caught up with Archie, May, Fritz, and the other German boys, she hadn't noticed the change coming on. Then, too, Sister Katherine had been quietly disapproving of Iris's involvement with Jerry, and Iris had found it easier to keep her distance. "Are you all right yourself, Sister Katherine?" she asked uneasily.

The older woman smiled. Her eyes still had that shimmery stained-glass quality, but they looked far too big in her pinched face. "I'm fine, dear," she replied quickly. "Just a little done in, as we all are. Now, off with you—see if you can rest your eyes a bit." And she was gone before Iris could ask her anything more.

Slowly, Iris trudged up to her room. She shut the door behind her and leaned against it, closing her eyes against the harsh sunlight filling the room. Summoning up what energy she had left, she crept across the room and collapsed onto her cot.

Almost immediately, she fell into that light, restless sleep where dream and reality meet and blur. A little black cat with silver-gilt streaks scattered throughout his fur was sitting on her pillow, regarding her with serious yellow eyes. She touched him; her fingers grazed fur smooth as watered silk. With a funny, squawky miaow, he leaped off the bed, and she suddenly found herself following him through a shadowy wood.

The trees were crowding in on them, pushing and poking Iris with their gnarled branches. It was getting harder to see the cat in the gathering darkness. She reached out, wanting only to feel his comforting warmth again. At last, she thought she had him; but when she brought her hand close to her, she found that she held only his long black tail. *No,* she thought with a sickening twist of her gut, *no, not this, too.*

Out of the darkness came a squawk. Iris looked up, terrified of what she would see next. But the little cat sat calmly on a tree stump in the clearing, looking the same except for his missing tail. Slowly, he raised his left front paw, just as though he was checking for rain. Then the paw curved inward, beckoning her. She went to him like . . . *like it was the most natural thing in the world.* Jerry had said that to her once, she could almost hear his voice, low and musical in her ear . . . could almost touch him . . . Her feet slipped on the uneven ground, and the cold took hold of her, a fierce, demanding lover.

Finally, she made it to where the cat was waiting, his yellow eyes ever watchful. Opening her clenched hand, she looked past the little raggedy reddish half-moons in the skin where her nails had dug too deeply and saw the tail, still lithe and twitching as though it had a life all its own. She reached over and reattached it to the cat. He lowered his head, as though bowing to her, and leaped ahead. She gathered up her sodden skirts and made to follow him, but *"that damn dank mud smell"*—where had she heard those words before?—was clinging to her, suffocating her . . .

She woke up in a clammy sweat, her clothes sticking to her. Her mind still cobwebby from the dream, she stumbled to her feet and over to the window. She tussled with the latch—it always put up a fight—but a few minutes and a couple of broken fingernails later, she had gotten it unstuck and stood there, greedily gulping in the cool autumn breeze. Then she froze.

Outside, in the field just past the monastery gates, she saw a man walking. Still slightly sleep-dazed, she stared at him, not really taking him all in; then, as he drew closer, her heart leaped up inside her. Those lean, lanky lines were as familiar to her as this room or her grandmother's garden. But it couldn't be. She leaned out the window, trying to see his face . . . trying to make sure that her heart wasn't misleading her. But the October sun shone hot and hard down on him, obscuring his features. He might as well have had no face at all.

And then, just as suddenly, he vanished. She hadn't taken her eyes off him a second, but he was gone, melted away like her dream or the morning dew. Iris drew back into the room, shivering. She dropped to her knees and clung to the window ledge, brittle as a dead leaf.

"Why, Iris, are you all right?"

May dropped the letters she was carrying and rushed over to her. She caught Iris by the shoulders, then felt her forehead. "You're all clammy. You'd better get into bed." May helped her up and back over to the cot. "You rest a spell, and I'll let the Matron know you'll be out of commission for the rest of the day. You don't want to end up sick like the others."

It was the old May, all warmth and caring. The frost that had grown thick between them had evaporated, just like the man by the gates had. Something of the old glow had come back into her eyes, too. Iris leaned against her friend, pushing the strangeness of the last hour or so away from her. "What others?" she asked.

"Pretty much what you'd expect—a lot of the patients whose lungs have already been weakened from gassing and a few of the other nurses. Penny Gower and Jen Silcox, for instance." May drew her breath in, and her eyes dimmed like a kerosene lamp being turned down. "And—and your little German friend, Fritz. He has it real bad, and—oh, honey, I'm sorry."

Iris stared at her. In the midst of her worry over Fritz, she couldn't help being struck by something in May's voice and eyes that hadn't been there for a long, long time. "You don't hate him anymore," she said curiously.

May looked down, flinching ever so slightly. "No, I don't. I was wrong, Iris—wrong in the way I treated him—wrong in the way I acted when you tried to help him and those other boys. I was hurting so over René, I took it out on you both."

"And you're not hurting now." It was a statement, not a question. "You've had word."

May gasped. "How did you know?"

Iris shrugged. "I just did." *Maybe there's a little bit of my grandmother in me, after all,* she thought. "Tell me."

The blonde nodded. She touched her bodice, and there was the faint rustle of paper. "He doesn't write much, only that he has escaped and is being treated at a clearing station not far from here. And—and they won't be sending him back to the front again." She smiled with the radiance of the Madonna in the chapel's stained-glass window. "Oh, Iris, I'm so lucky. And so thankful."

Iris hugged her, then smoothed her crumpled skirt and apron. "Ready?"

"You're not going to rest?"

"No." Iris shook her head slowly as she rose to her feet. "You said that Fritz is ill. I *have* to go to him—he has no one."

"But—but you're ill yourself. Anyone can see that."

"Not ill," Iris replied. "Just heart- and soul-weary. And this is the only cure I know."

May stared. "But, Iris, you know as well as I do, there's not much we can do—this is such a ferocious strain, Brisbane says—"

"Not for him," Iris interrupted. "For *me*. The only cure I know for *me*."

Iris worked over Fritz like a sinner trying to expiate her sin. She didn't neglect her other duties or Archie—who, of course, had ceased to be a duty to her long ago. But every spare moment she had, she gave over to Fritz's care. She bolted down her rations and barely slept. There were days when her vision was so blurred, she could barely distinguish one person's face from another. Other times, usually at night, she saw with an eerie clarity the shadow behind the shadow, the soul within the most commonplace of things.

She was, Iris sometimes thought, between worlds, neither of the living nor of the dead. Early one morning, just before dawn, she felt a cold, gentle touch on her shoulder while she sat, half-dozing, at Fritz's bedside. She jerked her head up and found herself staring into Abraham Wagner's deep-set brown eyes. He smiled at her, then at the boy, who was lying still after having been thrashing about most of the night in a fevered sleep. Iris looked up at the dead man fearfully, but he only smiled and, taking her hand in his, placed it on Fritz's forehead. Iris gasped: he was still hot but no longer burning up.

Suddenly, Fritz sat up. His eyes looked beyond Iris. She turned and saw Abraham, still smiling, backing up toward the open doorway, where a woman stood waiting for him. The woman's features were blurred, but she felt familiar somehow, just as the man outside the gates had. And there were other presences, more shadowy still, out in the hallway behind her. Like Abraham and the woman, they were silent, but Iris felt their pain. Fear gave way to wonderment, and her heart broke open inside as she felt some of that wonderment wash over her. Fritz slumped back down onto the cot, but Iris knew from his breathing that he was going to be all right now. She sat there, exhausted but humbled and thankful for what she'd seen.

"Miss Amory." The hand on her arm this time was warm and living. Iris jerked her head up from the counterpane. Dr. Blaine was gazing down at her, his green eyes kinder and wearier than usual, his clothes a tad more rumpled. "So you've been here all night." He gestured toward Fritz. "How's this fellow doing?"

"Better—I think," said Iris, her brain still blurred and confused. Her eyes felt dry and gritty and her mouth even worse, as though she'd been licking out a dustbin. She started to get up, but there was a feeble tug on her hand. It was Fritz, his blue eyes fixed on her face, battered and washed out like cornflowers after a heavy rain. "*Danke schön,*" he whispered. "You saved me. The black man, he would've taken me with him, but you stayed, and he took the woman instead."

Iris remembered Abraham's face, and her throat tightened. "No, no, Fritz," she murmured, struggling to let the words out, "it wasn't like that, not exactly." But the boy had drifted back to sleep.

Iris eased her hand out from under his and stood up. Dr. Blaine was watching her, the most curious expression on his face. "Come with me, Miss Amory," he said abruptly. "You need the air."

He walked her down the still, dim hallway, past Mrs. Abbott, who was laden down with billowing white cloth. *A wedding gown,* Iris thought tiredly, then realized she was looking at an armful of shrouds. So Fritz had lived, but others had followed Abraham into the night. She shivered and let Dr. Blaine lead her out into the overgrown monastery garden. He eased her down onto the stone bench but did not sit down himself, just kept pacing by the stone wall and throwing her an occasional glance.

Iris looked about her. The grayness of the pre-dawn had given way to a deep, rich apricot sky smudged with purple and red, and the trees were taking on a mysterious glow with the coming of the light. The air was chilly—it was, after all, October—but she didn't mind. After the stuffiness and sickroom odors inside, the cold air was a tonic. She gulped it in eagerly, then laughed. "I'm like a horse at the watering trough."

Blaine stopped pacing and smiled. "Best medicine in the world for you right now." He sat down on the wall and leaned his head back. "It's been one helluva night, hasn't it?" He paused. "What was the boy talking about?"

Haltingly, she told him. He leaned forward, clasping his hands in front of him, listening hard. "You think I'm foolish," she said once she'd finished her story. "Or dreaming things."

"I've heard stranger," he said tersely. He got up and resumed pacing, then turned to her. "There's no good way to say this," Blaine said awkwardly. "Sister Katherine died last night."

The world fell away then, along with the joy she'd been feeling at Fritz's recovery. *It isn't possible*, Iris told herself numbly. *God wouldn't let it happen.* But God had let a young man like Alexander Maxwell lose his legs and Abraham, a man with a wife and young children waiting for him back in South Africa, die. And He had let first Archie's face and then his heart be torn up past repair. "Influenza?" she whispered.

"No, it was her heart," Blaine replied. "She had a very weak heart—it ran in her family, she told me—and it finally gave out. Actually, it amazes me that it held out as long as it did."

"She never told me," Iris said in that same soft paper-thin voice.

"Only the other doctors and I knew, and that was just because she had such a sharp attack not long ago, she couldn't hide it from us. Dr. Pratt and I tried to get her to go back to England then, but she wouldn't. The war was so close to ending, she said, and she wanted to see it out." He came over and knelt down in front of her, taking her scarred hands in his own equally scarred ones. "I know how hard this must be for you. Sister Katherine thought the world of you—in fact, she told me once that you resembled her younger sister Margaret."

"Margaret?"

"She died of consumption before the war. Their parents had died when she was a baby, so Sister Katherine had raised her. They hadn't any other family to speak of, so Margaret's death was even harder on her."

I never knew she had a sister, Iris thought. So much she hadn't known. She remembered walking through the wards with Sister Katherine that first day and how the Englishwoman had joked with all the patients and shown her the ropes. *And while we're at it, dear, I'm not much for formalities at the best of times, and these hardly qualify as that. So call me Katherine, and let's have done with all the bowing and scraping.* Iris cried then, great big gulping sobs that racked her body. She cried not just for Sister Katherine but for the distance that had grown between them. For all that time lost that she could never make good now.

Blaine put his arm around her, and Iris leaned against him, forgetful of proprieties. Only when she had cried herself out did they move apart. But not too far apart.

They were silent together for a while. The sky was paler now, and the sun was limning the weave of white and silver birches across from where they sat. *"There's something about this place that soothes the soul,"* Sister Katherine had said that first morning. Iris felt it now despite her sadness, a sort of grace and godliness that lingered. Somewhere, too, Sister Katherine and Abraham must be lingering, somewhere just out of sight. "It's fitting, isn't it?" she remarked suddenly.

"What is?"

"That Sister Katherine would've taken a child's place—well, not a child, exactly, but someone young, maybe even the same age her sister had been—"

Blaine smiled, and the light of that smile brightened his sallow, tired face. "Yes, it is fitting—very fitting. It's what she would've chosen." He touched her shoulder. "Come on—it's time you went in and got some sleep."

"But my rounds—"

He tried to pull a stern face and almost succeeded. "Doctor's orders, Miss Amory." He patted her arm. "Someone else can do your rounds this morning. You're no good to any of the patients when you're this done in."

Iris followed him back into the monastery, glad for once to let someone else take charge. She slipped into her room and tumbled onto the bed, falling into a deep, kind sleep, without nightmares or haunting dreams that were worse than nightmares, following you around for a long time afterward. Her grief over Sister Katherine hit her full in the face when she woke up, but she knew that she couldn't give in to it just now. She could almost hear Sister Katherine's voice: *You'll be better once you're working. Not right away, but gradually. That ache will go, you'll see.*

Besides, the grief couldn't entirely crowd out the gladness she felt over Fritz's recovery. Sunshine and shadow, just like the pattern on one of Mrs. Banning's quilts. Sister Katherine would've understood. And Dr. Blaine *did* understand—his words out in the garden had shown her that.

She got through the rest of the day and the day after that. She even got through the simple funeral service in the chapel and watched the cart carry Sister Katherine's body in its shroud and plain pine box off to the village cemetery. *I can bear this,* she said to herself, amazed, although she was glad she didn't have to watch that box go into the ground. There was a comfort in that—an odd-fitting hand-me-down kind of comfort, but a comfort nonetheless. And that night, as she and May listened to the Matron and Mrs. Abbott discuss the service and exchange teary reminiscences over their tea, she still felt it.

Mrs. Abbott finally pushed her teacup away from her. "Ah, well, she's sleeping now, may she rest easy."

The Matron fidgeted with her empty cup, her eyes broody. "I don't know about that."

"Why, what d'ya mean?" Mrs. Abbott exclaimed sharply.

"Sister Katherine left a handwritten will." The Matron paused. "She must've known how things was with her—she was too good a nurse not to, see what I'm saying?—and she'd written it just weeks ago. Anyway, in it, she said she wanted her body given to the nearest medical school." She shook her head, a rueful smile creeping onto her face. "She even tried to make a joke about it. 'If they can use Mata Hari's body,' she says, 'they can use mine. And at least mine isn't sexually diseased and full of bullet holes.'"

May stifled a cry. Iris felt sick. "But Dr. Pratt said they were taking her to the village for burial!"

"That's where the folks from the medical college were going to meet them and—well, collect her, I guess you could say."

Mrs. Abbott got up and began gathering up their tea things. "I would've waked her proper, that I would've," she muttered, sniffling. "Like I did my Samuel when he died. And there should've been hymns and flowers thrown on the casket as they lowered her down. I mean, she used to sing in her church choir as a girl—she told me so often enough, Delphina. This cutting her up is just barbaric, it is."

The Matron went to her and placed her hand on the other woman's shoulder. "It was what she wanted, Agatha."

"But not what she should've had!" The cup slid from her hand, smashing against the floor, and she crumpled against the taller, stouter Matron's shoulder. "Hasn't there been butchery enough?" she sobbed. "And now there isn't even a grave to go to!"

"Now, Agatha," soothed the Matron, "it's just the shell—you and I have seen enough to know that. That wasn't Sister Katherine they took away, any more than it's your husband in that old London cemetery. Just shells, that's all."

"It's true," Iris chimed in. She told them what she had seen that night, sitting by Fritz's bedside. She hadn't meant to speak of it to anyone other than Dr. Blaine, but she wanted more than anything to drive away the misery from Mrs. Abbott's face.

"Glory be," said the Matron, gently letting go of her friend and crossing herself. "Could you ask for proof better than that, Agatha?"

Mrs. Abbott fished a handkerchief out of her apron pocket. It was one of her best ones, edged with yards and yards of black tatted lace. She'd last carried it at her husband's funeral, she'd told them earlier.

"No, I couldn't," she said, wiping her eyes. Tucking the precious handkerchief back in her pocket, she went over and hugged both Iris and May. "Blessed are they who mourn, dears, for they shall be comforted," she told them, her voice shaky.

Iris stared. She must've heard those words a thousand times before, but she'd always thought them one of those awful platitudes that people gave out at funerals, like unwanted dishes or clothing—something that made the speaker feel better but did nothing for the bereaved. But now, looking into Mrs. Abbott's sad but steadfast brown eyes, she thought she caught just a glimmering sense of what they really meant . . .

But the next afternoon, when a letter came telling her that Jerry had been killed by a sniper's bullet, she knew that she really didn't understand it at all. Pain beyond her imagining tore through her like a wildfire as the company commander's words branded themselves upon her brain. She crumpled the letter and thrust it from her. She knew now whose figure she had seen beyond the monastery gates. There was no comfort anywhere, only a dream now burnt cinder-black.

For a moment, she could've sworn that Sister Katherine was standing before her. *You were afraid he would hurt me*, Iris cried silently, *and he did—but not the way you thought he would.* Then the figure had faded as quickly as it had come, and Iris sat huddled on the landing, watching the shadows grow longer, unable to cry. May found her there at teatime, took one look into her eyes, and silently helped her back up to their room.

CHAPTER THIRTEEN

The package arrived a few weeks later, a tad battered and torn but somehow still intact. Tom Ungar's name was scrawled in the upper left-hand corner in big, messy letters. Finding it just as she was coming off her rounds, Iris clutched it to her breast like a child holding a beloved toy and stole off to the common room.

It was just starting to rain, making the room feel even colder and emptier. She drew Mrs. Abbott's makeshift curtains and lit the kerosene lamp; then she went over to the music box and rummaged through the small pile of zinc discs alongside it on the table till she found what she was looking for. Her fingers trembled a little as she slid the disc over the machine's musical comb. It would hurt her to listen to that love song about the "long, long trail a-winding in the land of my dreams"—she knew that—but she couldn't live with this horrible numbness any longer. What had Tim Skinner said to her after Abraham's death? *He's the one who died, and it's me what's feeling like a ghost.* Iris sighed. Well, that was about the size of it.

She sank down onto the shabby settee and cut the strings on the package with an old butter knife she had filched from the kitchen. There wasn't much inside. The letters she had written Jerry. A nearly empty billfold. And, at the very bottom, a handful of drawings with

Jerry's name scribbled underneath. Some were just rough sketches of the various men in his division; one more detailed picture, which made Iris smile in spite of herself, was of Hawkeye, that "right sociable kit" who had kept Jerry safe for as long as he could.

But the drawing that made her cry out softly was the most detailed of all. It was of herself, her hair loosened and rippling down her back. He had captured everything from her cleft chin to the quizzical expression in her eyes more faithfully than a mirror could have. Iris stared at the drawing, shaking her head. She remembered that first meeting in the chapel and the little caricature he'd given her. *A souvenir of our meeting....* Iris shivered. Best read the note now, which had fallen out from among the drawings.

For an exquisite heart-stopping moment, she thought it might be a last letter from Jerry. But it was Tom's handwriting splattered across the page:

Dear Miss Amory,

Hope you won't think I'm terrible forward, writing you like this, but I kind of felt obliged to, for Jerry's sake and all. By now, you've gotten the commander's letter, so you know the worst of it. But you don't know the best of it. See, Jerry wouldn't say so himself, of course, but he thought the world of you. He drew this picture of you 'cause he didn't have a snap of you to show me. I recollect his face as he was bent over drawing you and how it was all lit up like. It was the same when he talked about you. "She's no Lillie Langtry," he said to me a few nights before the end come, "but she's my rock, Tom, my North Star, the one thing I can hold on to in this here darkness."

We none of us can tell the future, naturally, but that speech alone made me feel sure he was meaning to make his way back to you. Don't know as that helps much now, but I felt beholden to tell you.
Yours respectfully,
Thomas Ungar

P. S. Still no sign of Hawk.

Iris leaned back, letting the paper fall onto her lap. The rain was coming down more heavily now, grieving with her and shedding the tears she still couldn't, not even after reading Tom's letter. There was just that fearful emptiness. For all his faults, Jerry had given her something heart-piercingly beautiful—something as sweet and wild as the red rambler roses tumbling onto the grass in Mrs. Banning's yard. And now an unseen hand had torn the roses apart and scattered the bruised petals in the mud of the trenches.

"I don't deserve this," she hissed at the shadows in the room. Anger took hold of her, making her ache to strike out. At the Serbs for starting it all and at the Germans for taking it up several hideous notches. At the government officials who kept this Grand Guignol going, sparing no one. At women like Theona who threw love away with both hands just because it had—literally—changed its face. The tears came then, only they were hard as bullets, hurting more to shed than to keep locked inside. She rested her face against the settee's cool worn chintz and felt the gray fog seep further into her soul.

"Need a little more light on the subject?"

It was Tim Skinner, shining a small kerosene lamp into her face. The lamp was smoking a tad, and the brass fittings were rusty and pitted, but the glass base was a deep teal, glowing jewel-like in the dusk, and Iris found just looking at it oddly comforting.

"May sent me looking for you," he explained, sitting down next to her and setting his lamp on the table. "Anything I can do?"

She showed him first the letter, then the sketch. "Why couldn't he tell me these things when he was alive?" she cried. "Why do I have to find them out now, second-hand, when they can't possibly do me any good?"

"Are you sure about that?" Tim asked, raising an eyebrow.

"They're just words and lines!" Iris pushed the papers away from her. "I can't live with a ghost."

"No, you can't," Tim agreed. "Not in one sense. But it seems to me—and I could be looking at this wrong, mind you—that in another sense, we're all of us living with ghosts. They follow us whether we ask 'em to or not. Abraham, Sister Katherine, and now your Jerry here . . . You wouldn't want to be forgetting any of them now, would you?"

"No," she whispered, staring down at her hands.

"The pain goes away after a while, you know, and it leaves a kind of blessing behind." He took hold of her hands. "Keep the letter and the drawings. Put 'em away somewhere—you don't have to be looking at 'em all the time. But you'll be glad of 'em some day."

She leaned back, letting her hands rest safely in his a little longer. "How did you get to be so wise, Tim?"

He smiled, and there was a wistfulness in his blue-green eyes that she'd never glimpsed before. "I lost my first love a few years back. Typhoid. Her da owned a sheep-shearing station not far from our farm." He sighed, pushing his glasses back up onto his nose. "I'm not going to lie to you, Iris. You don't get over it. Part of you's like one of those bloody tombstones with 'Sacred to the memory of' stamped on it." Tim paused. "But it will stop hurting so hard, that I can promise you."

They sat there, lulled into a tired, friendly silence for the moment. The rain was tapering off now. Jerry had once told her that he'd loved the sound of rain at night. That same rain must be falling on his grave. "Tim, where do they bury them?"

"Somewhere in Normandy, right along the coast. He'd be in the British section, I expect, since he joined up with the Canadians."

"He didn't exactly join up. Not on his own, that is." And she told him the story that Jerry had told her that first day in the chapel.

"I heard stories of Canadian recruiting officers going across the border to reel in more men," Tim remarked. "The Canadians was in the war so much longer than the Yanks, they'd used up a helluva lot of manpower." He let go of her hands—reluctantly, she thought—and shook his head, looking off into the shadows. "So, despite everything he did to make it come out different, he ended up right where he was bloody well supposed to."

Iris shivered, both at his fatalism and his choice of words. "That's not very comforting."

"I don't see why not." Tim turned toward her. "See, he found *you*. You two was supposed to meet and do what you could for one another. It didn't last, but that was just sheer bad luck and some bloody Hun's damn good aim."

He caught her by the shoulder and shook her gently. "Listen to me here, Iris. This Jerry chap gets sent up here all in a funk, sickened in his heart and soul by what he'd done at Passchendaele. He ain't had no choice in the matter, no more than any of us, but he don't see it that way. He meets you, and you give him—how'd he put it?—'some light to hold on to.' That's no small thing, Iris—good God almighty, if that doesn't win you some stars in your crown in the hereafter, I don't know what will."

"I'm no saint, Tim," Iris demurred, flustered by his praise.

"Just as well." Tim grinned at her, and she found herself grinning back. She had thought she'd forgotten how.

Gradually, life came and found her. That was the funny thing, Iris thought: no matter how trampled upon your heart felt, life had this trick of sneaking up and tugging upon it like an excited child pointing out small newfound treasures. *Look at this!* life cried, and the sight of the trees' bare branches against a changeful blue sky set her spirit soaring, just as the swan on the river had so long ago. *Smell this!* it gasped, and the subtle scent of a yellow rose, blissfully unaware that it was late October, brought the light back to her blue-gray eyes.

"It's strange, how the little things bring you back to yourself," she mused aloud one afternoon, when she and Mrs. Abbott were rolling bandages.

Mrs. Abbott smiled over the bunches of rolled-up fabric. "It's mostly the little things what make up a life, dear." She looked up, her brown eyes sad and bemused. "I remember how it was when I lost my Samuel. Life won't let you sit with your grief too long— draws you back in the dance kicking and screaming, so to speak." With a deft flourish, she finished a roll and tossed it on top of the pile. "There, that's the last of them. For today, at any rate. Why don't you pop them over to the Matron now?"

Iris added hers to the pile and stretched. "Good idea, Mrs. Abbott. My fingers are starting to cramp." She flexed them and smiled. "It'll give me a chance to look in on Archie—he seems a little low lately."

Bemusement left the older woman's face, leaving only sadness. "I think he's more than a little low, Iris."

Iris felt fear weaseling its way through her, gnawing at the serenity she'd just been starting to reknit. "It's probably just a chill," Iris said quickly, gathering up all the bandages onto a metal tray. "You know how easily he catches them and how it takes him forever to throw them off." She nodded to Mrs. Abbott and walked out of the room faster than she had to.

154

She pushed the dispensary door open. The Matron was nowhere to be seen, but Dr. Pratt was standing by the window, tapping his fingers listlessly against the glass. Iris stared. She had never seen the tall arrogant physician like this, all his fierce, quick energy gone from him like air from a pricked balloon. "Yes, Miss Amory?" he asked, not moving.

"I've brought the bandages for the Matron, sir."

"Good. Just leave them on the table, please." His tone was preoccupied but not unkind.

Iris set the bandages down on the table. But she didn't go. She had never particularly liked Dr. Pratt, especially after the letter incident, and she had no reason to think that he liked her. Still, he would be honest with her, that much she was sure of. "Dr. Pratt?"

He turned around, looking surprised at finding her still there. "Yes?" he asked, raising an eyebrow.

"It's about Archie," she blurted. "Mrs. Abbott was saying—well, you know, he's been so low—and he's a friend of mine, not just a patient, and"—she lifted her head, preparing herself to meet his usual cool, critical gaze—"and I had to know how it really is with him."

"He's dying." Pratt looked away. But not before Iris saw that his eyes were neither cool nor critical now.

She gripped the edge of the table hard—so hard, she thought either it or her fingers must break. That her heart would break again was a foregone conclusion. "You're sure?"

Pratt nodded. He walked over to a longer table with drawers that served as a desk of sorts and sat down. "I could give you a whole slew of medical reasons why he's dying, Miss Amory—weakened constitution, infection, lungs and other organs too damaged to be functioning fully—but none of them is the real one." He began opening and closing drawers randomly, and the noise was more maddening than the tapping of his fingers on the glass had been.

"What is the real one?" she whispered.

"He's lost heart, Miss Amory—he doesn't care enough to live, not since that silly bitch of his ran out of here fit to puke at the sight of him." He slammed a drawer shut and snarled out an oath: he had mashed his fingers in the drawer.

"Anything I can do?" Iris jumped forward, forgetting her dislike of the man.

Pratt bit down hard on his lip and shook his head. He sat there studying his hand as though it belonged to someone else. "Looks like I might lose a nail or two—no matter," he observed calmly. Then he looked up at her. "I envy you, Miss Amory."

"Me?" She must've misheard him.

Pratt smiled a thin, wintry smile. "I've watched you with the patients, especially with Archie. You give yourself over to them heart and soul."

She hadn't the proverbial clue where he was going with this. "Oh, I know it's not very professional of me, sir—"

"'Professional' be damned," he told her roughly. "*You* worry that you feel too much—*I* worry that I can't feel anything, not even for Archie, whom I admire tremendously. That's why I slammed my hand in the drawer—just to feel *something*." Pratt slumped back into his chair, then began murmuring wearily,

"We are the Dead. Short days ago
We lived, felt dawn, saw sunset glow,
Loved and were loved, and now we lie
In Flanders fields." He sighed. "Sometimes it seems like I'm lying there with them."

"I've felt that way myself, doctor," Iris surprised herself by saying.

"Oh, yes—your young Canadian. Or was he a Yank? No matter. I was sorry when the Matron told me about it. The war breaks us one way or another." Pratt stretched his legs and rose to his feet, slowly, like an old man, his fine posture deserting him for the moment. He turned to Iris, regarding her steadily. "Still, he left you an incredible gift."

She stared. "Sir?"

"Compassion—the flower that only grows when your heart has been broken open." He smiled again, and some of the winter melted away from his face, revealing a kindness and understanding she'd never dreamed was there. "The healing herb."

Iris smiled back—a shy smile, faint and flickering as the sunlight filtering through a tangle of trees. "Yes, sir, I suppose it is."

Surprisingly, Death did not take Archie quickly. No, like a well-mannered caller, it simply bided by the threshold of the little alcove room, waiting for the right moment to announce itself. Or so it seemed to Iris as she went back and forth, doing what she could for her friend.

Archie said very little other than an occasional weak "Hello, Sister Iris." Mostly, he just lay there, staring across the room at something—or someone—that neither Iris nor the doctors could see. He would not eat, no matter how much she coaxed him. Sometimes she could get him to take a little water, but more often than not, it simply spilled over what was left of his chin, settling in the folds of his neck.

He wants to die, she realized as she sponged the water away. Her glance traveled over to Derwent Wood's mask lying mockingly on the table. She touched it, and her fingers came up dusty. She couldn't remember the last time she had seen him wear it. Not since Theona's visit, surely.

"How're you holding up, Iris?"

It was Dr. Blaine. They hadn't really talked since the morning after Sister Katherine's death. Yet she hadn't stopped thinking about him. Not in a romantic way; it was just that in the midst of all horrors and heartbreak happening around them, the memory of their talk in the garden had been something good to hold on to.

He motioned to her now, and she silently got up and joined him by the doorway. "This is hard for you, I know," he said.

Iris shrugged. "I know it's better for him to go," she whispered, looking down, "but I can't *feel* that it is."

"It *is* better for him," Blaine told her firmly. "And not just because of his face. He can't move from that bed, bathe himself, or even feed himself. He's losing his eyesight—you know that—and there's been damage beyond the telling to his heart and lungs. It's a limited life he'd be leading at best."

"Oh, I know it's selfish to want to keep him." She swiped at the tears that were pushing past her guard. "But I can't imagine life without him—he has been such a friend to me."

"Listen to me, Iris." Blaine took her cold hands in his, just as he had in that dawn-struck garden. "What sort of life would it be for him once the war's over? He wouldn't have you—he wouldn't have me. He wouldn't be getting the care he's been getting here. He'd be back in that one-horse town of his—oh, I know the type, all right, and I grew up in one—with only his elderly parents to tend to him and a kindly neighbor to sit with him now and then."

"There are doctors in those small towns," Iris argued weakly. "Good ones, too."

"Certainly. I worked with such a man once I finished medical school, and I never saw anyone who had the gift of healing in his hands that that man had." He was so caught up in what he was saying, he seemed unaware that he was still holding *her* hands. "But those doctors haven't had experience with wounds like Archie's." He shook his head. "No, Iris—nature is being kind to Archie, kinder than we're allowed to be."

She gasped. "You wouldn't—"

"Didn't you hear me, Iris?" Blaine let go of her hands, and they fell to her sides, rag-doll limp. "I'm not *allowed* to. Frankly, I'm not sure I could, even if I were. But if ever I saw a case that cried out for it . . ." He shook his head and slipped out the doorway.

Sighing, Iris went and sat back down by Archie's side. She studied his wreck of a face and remembered her conversation with Theona: *Doesn't his face bother you, Iris?*

No. You see, I love Archie. He's like a brother to me.

And then, from a little further back in the past came Derwent Wood's voice: *There are all kinds of affairs, Iris Amory, and not all of them are physical.*

So many different kinds of love, Iris mused, like so many— Daniel Blaine's words echoed in her mind—wounds. Some wounds healed easily, barely leaving a scar; some, like her love for Jerry, broke your heart wide open so that you never saw anything the same way again.

And then there was Archie here, who had come quiet as a shadow into her life—who had felt, at times, almost like her second self. She sat there, her hand resting alongside his on the coverlet, and wondered what might've been had they stumbled upon each other at another time. Not a passionate connection like the one that she and Jerry had shared. No, it would've been more of a warm, comfortable growing together, she was sure of that. Steadfast and true . . .

"Sister Iris?"

"I'm here, Archie." She leaned toward him, and he put his hands up to her face, just as he had the day they'd met.

"You're crying," he whispered.

"Oh, it's been such a long day, Archie." His fingers touched her mouth, and she smiled.

"That's better," Archie told her. "Don't want you crying over me. Just glad you're here—nobody wants to go out alone like some kinda animal."

She pushed the chair up closer to the bed and, leaning in more, put her arm around him. It was an awkward position, and her back ached from it, but it was the least she could do. "I'm here as long as you want me, Archie."

"That a fact?" he wheezed. "Flying colors, Sister Iris—flying colors." He turned toward her. Even though she knew he barely had any sight left, she could've sworn that he was looking straight at her, seeing her clearly. "Your Canadian feller says hello."

He put his head down on her breast, and Iris tightened her hold on him, trying not to hear the death rattle. She sat there, the tears running freely down her face now. She had seen Archie through to the end of his journey: in her own way, she had been able to do for him what she hadn't been able to do for Jerry, and there *was* comfort in that. Maybe she did understand those words about mourning and being blessed, after all.

Dr. Blaine stuck his head around the door jamb.

Their gazes locked, and she nodded. He came to her quickly and put his hand on her shoulder. "I'm sorry, Iris," he said. "Sorry for you—and for me because we'll miss him like hell—but glad for him. You understand that now, don't you?"

"I do," Iris told him softly. "And, Daniel"—the name slipped out almost without her realizing it—"I'm glad, too."

He eased Archie's body out of her arms. Together, they laid him out on the bed, Iris turning away only as Blaine began pulling the sheet over his face. "I'll see Mrs. Abbott about a shroud," she said, putting her hand to her mouth to stop the sob coming on. "What about his mask?"

Daniel ran his fingers through his already rumpled dark hair. "Good question." He picked the mask up from the table, studying both sides of it. "It's a work of art, all right, though I don't suppose anybody wants it except maybe a war museum in the distant future. What do you think, Iris?"

She took the mask from his hands and, staring at it, found herself remembering the morning that Derwent Wood had given Archie the finished mask. And she could just hear Archie's voice, all raspy and enraptured: *I can't believe it. I never thought there was anything like hope for me.* "I think it needs to be buried with him," she said firmly. "You see, it gave him hope."

He touched her cheek, and once again, there was that blurring of the borders between them. "It wasn't the only thing that gave him hope," he murmured, and there was a yearning, a quickening inside her that she hadn't felt since Jerry's leaving.

So she wasn't surprised when Daniel came to her in the old garden that evening. Or when he suddenly reached out and pulled her close, kissing her. Iris returned the kiss, then slowly broke away. She stared at him, not sure exactly what she was looking for but finding something in his steadfast gaze that felt right. She gave him her hand and walked quietly through the darkness with him to his room.

He was gentler than Jerry had been, his hands moving along her body like a musician's over a well-loved instrument. He kissed one breast, then the other: for a flickering flame of a moment, she saw Jerry's lean intense face with its half-crooked smile. Then she closed her mind to memory and lost herself in his warmth, in the urgent, excited murmuring of his voice in her ear. She ran her fingers through his chest hair and, wrapping her legs around him, cradled his body in hers.

They lay like that for a spell; he even dozed a little in her arms, and she was glad to have him there, a talisman against the things that hid in the shadows, whispering. She didn't know what the result of their lovemaking would be, only that she felt safe in his wiry, muscular arms.

Later, toward morning, she slipped back to her room, careful not to wake May. There were shadows here, too, but they were friendlier somehow, less likely to swallow her whole. Or maybe they were gradually losing their hold on her. Too tired to sleep—she'd have to start her rounds soon, anyway—she walked over to the window. The light was pearl-gray now, streaked with apricot and smoky purple smudges. She rested her forehead against the cold glass, and that vanishing figure she'd seen in the field beyond the gate came back to her with a sharpness that made her heart cry out. *Jerry, Jerry, you tried to come back to me, just like you said you would . . .*

Your Canadian feller says hello. Her head shot up, her exhaustion fallen away. Archie had been so ill, she had never told him about Jerry's death. She hadn't had to. In that passage between worlds, his spirit had met Jerry's and passed on the simple message he'd received before going over the top.

"Iris?" May's voice was sleep-muffled. "Where've you been?"

Listening to Dr. Pratt speak his fear aloud. By Archie's side as he lay dying. In Daniel's bed, feeling what it was like to be alive and with a man again. Sitting by this window and realizing that she'd just received one last message from Jerry.

She turned to May with a tired, wistful smile. "I'll tell you some time, May—really, I will. But not now. The story'll keep."

That drizzly day in November, the day that the war ended, was not all that different from any other day, as far as the hospital staff was concerned. Since the Armistice was not signed till eleven in the morning, the casualties kept coming in throughout the day—some slightly wounded, others whose luck had run out completely. *Just a few measly hours*, Iris thought angrily. *What a hideous waste.* She glanced at Daniel across the makeshift operating table, and he nodded wearily.

They had been together several times since that first night, and his lovemaking had touched a chord in her that she'd not known existed—one so sweet and heartbreakingly beautiful, she always felt like they were out of the body rather than in it. Yet there was a subtle chemistry between them that, strangely enough, had nothing to do with sex. Sometimes he would surprise her by coming out with the very words she was thinking. She felt at home with him. For the first time since Jerry's death, fear wasn't walking alongside her, its hand tight and clammy on her throat, and for that reason alone, Daniel Blaine would always matter to her.

Surgery over—for the moment, at least—Iris wandered out into the hushed hallway, wiping her hands off on her already bloodstained apron. She paused. Someone had left the front door ajar. Well, it was a heavy one, all ornate medieval carving and swollen with dampness: you had to use a little extra muscle to shut it properly in this cold, wet weather. She'd see to it now before the rain got any heavier and started coming in. Iris quickened her pace toward the door; then, following an impulse she scarcely understood, she pushed it further open and stepped out into the drizzle.

She stood on the sunken lichen-covered steps, the soft rain falling on her and turning the splotches on her apron an orangey-pink. So much blood, all of it spilling to the ground. She remembered her old nightmare of the death train spewing blood and torn limbs. And she remembered, too, the shy, young, inexperienced woman she had been. Just a little over a year since she'd come here, and yet it all seemed another lifetime ago.

A rustling sound caught her attention. After some peering about, Iris located the source. A wood dove sat under a half-dead shrub, unmindful of the weather. Not wanting to frighten her, Iris eased herself into a squatting position on the step.

She looked at the dove, and the dove looked back at her, the black eyes shy but determined. She must have a nest nearby, Iris thought. "Hello, bird," she said softly. She sat down on the step, barely noticing its dampness. "I won't hurt your nest. In fact, I won't even try to find it."

The dove cocked her head to one side, clearly intrigued by the sound of the human voice.

"You're brave," Iris told the bird. "I wish I could be half so brave. Or that I had something that mattered as much to me as those eggs do to you."

And that's the problem, Iris mused. With Jerry and Archie gone, she had lost the two people who had mattered most to her. And her romance with Daniel, while sweet beyond the telling, could not fill the emptiness they had left. It was too new.

The dove regarded her steadily. Curiously. Then, with feathery aplomb, it moved out from under the bush and came toward her. Not right up next to her. But closer, making Iris suddenly feel less alone. They sat there companionably; then, as the drizzle became heavier, Iris slowly rose to her feet. "Good-bye, bird," she said, hating to let go of the moment.

The dove stared at her—she could almost see it nod—and amiably wobble-footed back to the shelter of the bush. It preened its shimmery gray feathers and gave Iris one last look before settling back down on its watch.

Iris pushed the dripping chestnut tendrils off her forehead. It was, as she had once mused, about faith; but it was about purpose, too. This little Quaker-like bird had both. *And I have to find mine again*, Iris reflected, her hand on the door latch. She stepped in and found herself face-to-face with the Matron.

"I was just coming to look for you. I'm calling a meeting of the nursing staff in my office," the older woman said. She glanced at Iris. "Feeling at loose ends?"

Iris shrugged. "It's silly, I know. I'm glad the war's over, of course, but I just don't know where I belong anymore."

"None of us does, Miss Amory." The Matron gave one of her rare smiles. "We've all been living, eating, and breathing war for so long, we've forgotten there's anything else." She patted Iris's shoulder. "I know you've suffered plenty, losing your young man like that. It was a hard blow, there's no denying it, but you borne it like a trouper. He'd be proud of you, he would be."

Iris thought of Daniel and squirmed inwardly. But she clutched the praise to her gratefully. "But what do I do now, Matron? That's the part I can't figure out."

"That's the part that'll come to you," the Matron replied kindly. "You can't force it. But it'll come to you. Life's not done with you yet, Miss Amory, not by a long shot. Now, close the door, will you? This place is drafty enough as it is. And come down to my office as soon as you've had a bit of a wash-up." She nodded and ambled down the corridor, looking more like Tim Skinner's belligerent mongoose than ever.

Iris turned and glanced out the doorway at the shrub. The dove was still there, still bright-eyed and defiant despite the rain.

CHAPTER FOURTEEN

The war was over, but disbanding the hospital staff took a while longer. Patients had to be well enough to ship home or transfer to more permanent nursing facilities; once they were gone, the wards had to be scrubbed and disinfected. And throughout the whole dreary muscle-numbing process, there was paperwork. Always more paperwork.

It was, of course, easier to see some folks go than others. She was glad to see Fritz and the rest of his comrades depart for Germany—happy to know that these boys had escaped maiming or worse and curious as to what kind of men they'd become. Especially Fritz.

At least, she didn't have to think of doing without May yet. May had promised to travel with her to the British cemetery at Etaples so that she could visit Jerry's grave. They would sail home from there. René would be joining May as soon as his affairs were in order; later, they were to be married quietly at her mother's house in Dayton, Ohio. "I'd love for you to stand up with me as my maid-of-honor," May told her frankly, "but only if you think your nerves can handle it. If they can't, I'll understand." She looked up from the trunk that she was cramming clothes and battlefield souvenirs into. "But promise me you'll think about it, OK?"

"I will, May." Iris, busy clearing out her own bureau drawers, came across Jerry's box. She ran her fingers wistfully along the glossy wood. Part of her wanted to say yes to May's request very much; the other part of her was afraid that she'd start howling in front of everybody and spoil May's day. Perhaps after their pilgrimage to Jerry's grave, it would be easier.

When the day of their actual leave-taking came, it was pretty much a mixed bag, Iris decided. Dr. Brisbane mumbled something friendly at her. At least, it *sounded* friendly, she thought, trying not to wrinkle her nose at his whiskey breath. Dr. Pratt said very little but wrung her hand hard. Mrs. Abbott hugged both her and May and cried. "You'll always be my girls, that you will," she said emphatically. "I don't know how likely you are to be crossing the ocean again, but if you ever find yourselves in London, here's where you'll find me." She pressed a scrap of paper into each young woman's hand. "There'll always be a light in my doorway and plenty of scones on my table for you." And she hugged them again.

Saying good-bye to Daniel was even harder. "I'm not going to lie to you, Iris," he said. They were walking in the garden that had seen so much pass between them. "There was a girl back home, and we had a sort of understanding. But nothing as definite as an engagement, or I wouldn't have made love to you." He looked at Iris as though he wanted to kiss her but didn't. "You do believe me, don't you?"

She gazed at him, her blue-gray eyes unfaltering. "Yes, I do."

He moved closer—still not touching her, but close enough that she could savor his body's heat, and she moved toward it instinctively. "So, what do we do now, Iris?"

"We go back," she said simply, "although I'm not altogether sure where that is for me now. But you need to find out how things stand with you and—"

"Meg," he answered quietly.

"And Meg." Iris smiled. Strangely, she felt no jealousy of this unknown girl. "If the bond between you hasn't held, let me know. If it has—well, let me know that, too. We've always been honest with each other." She hesitated, casting about for the right words. "And, Daniel?"

"Yes?" His voice was low and strained.

"However it turns out, I'm not sorry for any of it. It has been something gentle, sweet, and sane to hold on to during this nightmare we've been living." She glanced down at the arm under her hand and thought about how tightly it had held her the night of Archie's death and all the nights after that. "More than ever now, I believe that people come into our lives for a reason, and you came into mine to show me that."

He kissed her then, and she returned the kiss with interest, melding into him. Slowly, reluctantly, they drew apart. "Iris?" he murmured.

"Yes?"

"Your kisses still excite the hell out of me." He smiled down at her, his eyes large and shining. "I just thought I'd like you to know that."

Parting with Tim Skinner hurt almost as much. Even though his injuries had healed a while back, he had stayed on—to help them all with the heavier muck work, he said, glancing sideways at Iris. And he *had* helped. With his mimicry and antics, his quirky blend of humor and understanding, he had gotten Iris through the roughest patches of her sojourn here. In some ways, he had taken Archie's place. But only in some. He was too colorful and complicated a character in his own right.

"I'll be heading back to my da's place in Australia," he remarked as they strolled about the grounds. "At least till I get my bearings back. Or until I remember how bleeding hellish the heat there can be. Right unmitigated shit the summers are." He grinned at her, and she grinned back. Somehow she never minded his swearing: it was just part of who he was. "And then—"

"And then what?" Iris prompted, smiling.

"I was just coming to that." Tim sat down on the low stone wall and Iris joined him. "Leg's playing me up a bit," he said, rubbing it ruefully. He looked about him, whistling, then turned to her. "I'm thinking about pulling up stakes, so to speak, and seeing for myself what your neck of the woods is like."

"Simsbury?" she exclaimed, her voice coming out like a cross between a squawk and a very squeaky hinge.

Tim pulled one of his faces. "Miss Amory, really. And here I was thinking you had such a *loverly* voice." He shrugged. "Honestly, Iris, I don't know where I'll end up. I'm just thinking that the old homestead won't suit me much after what we've been through. Never did care much for sheep. Too bloody stupid by half. But you and me, we'll keep in touch, and if I ever find myself anywhere near that patchwork quilt of a farm town of yours, I'll come by, and we'll have a bit of a catch-up. That I promise you—you're too good of a mate to lose."

He paused. "So, you really think you'll go back to teaching again?" He slid his glasses down the bridge of his nose and tried to look professorial.

She laughed a little and shrugged. "I guess I have to find out what I'm fit for now, same as you, Tim. Somehow I don't feel much like teaching anymore—although I'll do it, of course, till I figure things out."

"You could always write about it," Tim suggested, pushing his glasses back into place.

"'It'?" Iris stared, frowning.

"The war. The dying and the saving. Everything we've been through. C'mon, Iris, you could do it—I know you could."

"I'm not so sure about that."

"Crikey, why the bloody hell not? There are women writers a-plenty—women newspaper writers even. What was the name of that American one—y'know, that gutsy one who went into an asylum, pretending to be a patient, so's she could write up what was really going on there? Nellie . . . Nellie Bly, yes, that's it.

"The point is, Iris, you could write about all this"—he gestured toward the hospital—"the way she did about the asylum—firsthand, like. It'd be one helluva story, and you'd write it up bloody perfect. You've got a way with words, you have, having been a teacher and all that. But what really matters is that *you* see what matters. That's what makes a story stick with folks in the end."

"I don't know, Tim," Iris murmured, touched beyond the telling by his belief in a talent she didn't even know she possessed. She lifted her head and looked around her. The landscape had finally begun to resurrect itself. The field where Jerry's restless spirit had walked was slowly greening over, and the deep woods beyond it were lit up by the playful, flickering sunlight. She took a deep breath. "I just don't know."

They sat quietly together on the wall. "I ever tell you about the time I had to hide out in a shell hole, Iris?" Tim asked abruptly. "Before the Huns asked me to play Lord Jesus Christ on that bleeding barn door, that is?"

She shook her head.

"It were a regular scene from hell, Iris, it were. Bodies and bits o' bodies scattered far as my eyes could see, and each and every one of them somebody I'd shared smokes or dirty stories with. I was too scared to piss myself, I tell you." He ran his hand through his light-brown hair so that his cowlick stood at attention even more than usual. "And then—it was the most curious thing, Iris—a hand grips me by the shoulder. This voice says, 'Don't you worry a bit, Tim, you're gonna be all right,' and I whip around like a snake. Ain't no one there. But suddenly, I'm all calm and considering-like, making my way out of the fighting, bold as Daniel in the lions' den."

He picked absent-mindedly at a scab on his hand. "Makes you wonder, don't it? At what's hidden in the shadows, I mean? See, not all of it's bad, and what's good kind of emerges when we need it—or them. I never got the wind up me after that, even when they were nailing me up on that barn door."

St. Dorothea's painted face appeared in Iris's mind, her eyes borage-blue and soft. "So it's about faith," she murmured, remembering that long-ago conversation with May.

"Partly—partly," Tim acknowledged. "Of course, it doesn't hurt to be in the middle of the line."

"'Middle of the line'?" Iris echoed, puzzled.

"Well, back at the front, see, the German machine gunners used to start off firing to the right and the left of our lines." He leaned toward her, his voice rising in excitement with the telling. "You learned pretty damn quick to get front and center if you wanted a chance in hell of surviving. It helped being a scrawny scrapper, I tell you. I could slip in, quiet as a thought, without the officers noticing—they being officers and not overly acquainted with thoughts. You might say"—the corners of his mouth began twitching ever-so-slightly, just like a rabbit's whiskers—"I learned the value of a middle-of-the-*row* approach to life."

Iris laughed and groaned and laughed again. "Tim, that's the most awful pun imaginable!"

"Made you laugh, though, didn't I?" The sun skittered behind the clouds, taking all the luster and warmth of the day with it. It seemed almost autumn again. He jumped to his feet and held out his hand. "C'mon, I'll walk you back."

171

She took the offered hand and was, as always, energized by his touch. "I don't know what I shall do without you, Tim—really, I don't."

"Won't have to," he replied. They began strolling back to the monastery. "I'll always be there if you need me. Might take me awhile to get there, but get there I will, make no mistake about it."

But the very last person she saw as she and May were leaving the hospital was the Matron. "Well, God bless you, Miss Amory." Her tone started off matter-of-fact, then softened. "I'll be thinking of you—thinking and praying you find safe harbor and the happiness you deserve."

"Thank you," Iris said shyly. She hung back, wanting to ask the question that had been hovering in the back of her mind since the funeral tea for Sister Katherine. "Why 'Delphina'?"

The Matron laughed unexpectedly. Her laugh was a rich, generous one that invited you right in. "My father was a sea captain, and Delphina was the name of a *señorita* he romanced down in Argentina. Nothing came of it, mind you—at least, I'm not aware of any Spanish-speaking half-siblings—but the name stuck with him, and he gave it to me. Poor Mother didn't half hate it, she did, but he wouldn't hear otherwise. Right unbudgeable about it he was." She laughed again. "We've all got our stories, we do."

"We do indeed," Iris murmured.

The dawn light spilled rose and gold through the inn's bedroom window and onto Iris, sitting by it, her hands folded stiffly in her lap. She found herself thinking about that October afternoon and the phantom lover in the field who'd tried to do in death what he hadn't been able to in life. She brushed away a tear and, leaning her forehead against the cool windowpane, wondered if she would ever be able to go somewhere and *not* look for him.

"Iris?" May was sitting up in bed, yawning. "Why, you're dressed already!"

"Couldn't sleep." Iris shrugged. "Figured I might as well dress—at least, it felt like I was doing something then." She slumped back—well, slumped back as much as was possible—in the hard little ladder-back chair. "I wish it were over with, May."

"I know." Her friend's voice was all compassion. She threw back the woven navy-blue coverlet and scooted out of bed. "I'll hurry up and get myself presentable, and then we can find someone to guide us to the cemeteries. We can eat later—if you're feeling up to it, that is."

Iris nodded. She got up and pushed the chair back, then narrowed her eyes. Not quite right. She positioned and re-positioned that damn chair until she got it to her liking. Funny how you found yourself fidgeting with silly humdrum things like chairs and clothes when you felt yourself about ready to break into so many pieces that nobody—not all the king's horses, not all the king's men, not even God—could possibly put you back together again.

It was midmorning by the time they reached the British cemetery. The land rose up before them, a hilly knoll that just dropped down into the ocean. "Which row do you think it is?" May asked breathlessly.

Iris looked around at the sea of white headstones. "I don't know," she said blankly.

May rubbed her hand against her waist. "Believe I've taken a stitch in my side. Damn!" She glanced at Iris. "Listen, Iris, you take this end, and I'll take the far one. Whoever finds him, hollers. The Matron and Mrs. Abbott would be horrified, but I don't think these boys'll mind."

Iris nodded. She watched May move down the row and further afield, then shook herself and painstakingly began her own search.

Each stone called out to her—each one had its story, as the Matron would've said—but none of them was Jerry's. Her feet moved leadenly down one row and up another. She was just wondering whether this pilgrimage of theirs had all been a mistake—whether his company had ever recovered his body after all—when May called out, "Iris! Jerry's here! I've found him!"

Iris moistened her lips. "Where?"

"About three rows down on your left! Just follow my voice, and I'll bellow you on home!"

The feet that had been such dead weights suddenly came to life, and Iris tore down the rows, almost as though her lover were alive and could take her in his arms again. Then she reached the spot where May stood.

Slowly, Iris knelt alongside the grave. She placed her right hand down on it. "It's dry!" she cried. "The ground, it's bone-dry!" And the dreary little phrase suddenly seemed beautiful, like something right out of an illuminated manuscript. What had been committed to the earth would already have begun to become part of it; but the dryness of that earth now allowed her the blessing of holding on to the image of Jerry as he had been in life.

May smiled, her blue eyes awash with understanding tears. "That's good, Iris," she said softly.

Iris barely heard her. She brought her left hand down alongside the other and pressed both down hard against the soil. An almost electrical current ran through them; then, all in a flickering, her heart burst open, and the grief tamped up inside her spilled out. Oddly enough, though, it was Tim Skinner's voice she heard in her head: *The pain goes away after a while. . . . You two was supposed to meet and do what you could for one another. . . .*

Then Iris finally did understand it. What mattered was the sweetness of their beginning, not the sadness of an ending come too soon. The might-have-beens didn't count; all that mattered was the comfort that they'd found in each other at a time when comfort was in short supply and caring a downright luxury. Despite the war—despite Jerry's "haunts"—there *had* been magic between them, and nobody could take that away. She smiled, brushing the hair out of her eyes. Whatever had brought their two souls together hadn't died just because Jerry had; it had simply changed its shape.

The tears came then, spattering down her cheeks, easy as the first drops of rain against a windowpane. She ran her hands along his grave, full of gladness for the love they'd made, and wished she had thought to bring flowers. Nothing fancy, just a simple, colorful posy. Jerry would've liked that.

"Are there any wildflowers along the edge of the cemetery?" she asked abruptly.

"I'll check," May replied, and was off. She hadn't gone more than a few feet, however, when Iris heard her exclaim, "Well, hello, kitten-cat! What're *you* doing here?"

A chill passed through Iris, and she rose to her feet, turning her head in the direction of her friend's voice. There, on a little slope, just above where May stood, sat a small black cat. His plushy fur was flecked with silver, and there were silver "specs" around his far-seeing yellow eyes. He turned those eyes now on Iris. Then, just as he had in her dream, he bowed his head and vanished.

Back in Simsbury, Iris felt more at loose ends than ever. And lonely. May was married to René and living at her mother's house in Dayton for the time being; Iris had no hopes of being able to see her again any time soon. The school trustees offered Iris a new teaching position—one in the little high school, where she could make use of her newly acquired French. Trouble was, she couldn't quite see herself teaching anymore.

Then Joe MacCurdy reappeared in her life.

They ran into each other just as she was coming out of the post office one weekday morning; they smiled friendly, awkward smiles at each other and stopped to chat, the awkwardness evaporating as chatting soon turned to banter. Before she knew which end was up, Joe was walking her back to Mrs. Banning's.

A few days later, they took a walk along the river, just like old times. But there were no swans lifting their wings like the hands of a soul in prayer this time, and Iris wasn't the easily flustered innocent she'd been when they'd first met. Jerry, Daniel, and the war had changed her till it was a wonder she even recognized herself. Still, Iris admitted as she stood there, listening to Joe's conversation, glancing up at his shining eyes, she felt comfortable with him, almost as though they'd never been apart. He, too, had seen his share of horrors and could speak her language. And when he suddenly leaned forward and kissed her, she returned the kiss.

Without the war to slow him down this time around, Joe began haunting Mrs. Banning's antimacassared parlor, making himself as much of a fixture there as the rose-colored hurricane lamp with its gaudy beaded shade or the slate-blue horsehair "courting sofa."

"Not that much courting could ever be done on that damnable thing," Joe laughed, rubbing a smarting elbow after they slid off the stiff, uncompromising cushion. "They'd have done better calling it the 'touch-me-not' sofa."

"There's a poem with a line like that in it," Iris murmured, pulling herself off the floor and casting an eye about for a safer seat. "Only it was written by Sir Thomas Wyatt for Anne Boleyn. No horsehair sofa at all."

He caught her by the arm. "And how about you? Are you ready to lose your head over me, Miss Schoolmarm?"

She looked up into his eager face. "No," she laughed, trying to twirl away before he could kiss her again. But he was quicker, and she melted against him, letting him run his hands against her breasts and backside. It went no further than that, of course; it was too soon, and the frowning daguerreotypes and ferrotypes on Mrs. Banning's fussy wallpaper would've killed the most passionate interlude. But that night after he'd gone, she sat on the window seat in her bedroom for a long while, reliving the sweetness of it all.

Then she heard about him and Glenna Fraser.

It was, she supposed, a commonplace-enough story: man gets girl pregnant and tries to extricate himself by any means possible. Joe, preferring to take his chances with mustard gas and shrapnel, had enlisted—hoping, no doubt, that Glenna Fraser would've disappeared into another dimension or, at the very least, another town, by the time he came back. Unfortunately for him, she had already returned home with a dark-haired baby girl with enormous blue-gray eyes.

Joe didn't try to deny it when Iris confronted him with the story one night in Mrs. Banning's parlor. "She's a winsome little bairn," he said of his daughter. "And I'll do what I can by her. But I never made her mother any promises, and she's lying if she says I did."

"But"—Iris frowned, not sure where she stood in this mess—"shouldn't you do the right thing now? For the child's sake, I mean?"

"I was renting, not buying!" Joe shot back. He jumped to his feet and grabbed his cap off the table. "And you, my fine madam, might try getting off that high horse of yours. For, unless I'm mighty mistaken, you learned a trick or two in France yourself!" He stalked out of the room, leaving Iris staring after him, even more confused and lonelier than ever. She hadn't realized how much she had come to count on his being there.

She spent the next few days brooding in Mrs. Banning's garden, hiding from the whispers around town, big and nasty as black flies. But the garden brought neither comfort nor inspiration to her, and she was all too acutely aware of her landlady's fussy, sympathetic looks. So Iris hied herself over to the Center Cemetery in Simsbury, thinking that it would be really pleasurable to spend some time with folks who could keep their mouths shut.

She sat down on the grass not far from the site of Antoinette Eno Wood's proposed crypt and shook her head. Another cemetery! Only there was no May to stand by and help her through this one. And no solemn-eyed black cat watching her either. Least ways, Iris didn't think so. But, then, jumping from one continent to the next was probably nothing to a little spirit cat.

Iris picked a rosy-tipped clover blossom from the clump in front of her and twirled it about. In a way, Joe was right, she told herself. Who was she to pass judgment? After all, she'd had two lovers in a year's time: she just hadn't gotten pregnant. No, what bothered her (she plucked a second clover blossom and then a third and a fourth) was that she'd fallen under the spell of Joe's talk of "wanting to make a difference" when the only difference he'd been wanting to make was his geographic proximity to Glenna. And he'd been playing the perfect gentleman caller with her when he'd been sleeping with another woman all the while. She bit her lip as she began tying her blossoms together. "I can't trust him—I can't!" she muttered, tugging hard on one of the green knots and decapitating a pathetic little blossom.

"Having a good chat?" a slightly rough-around-the-edges but pleasant male voice asked.

Iris dropped her clover chain and put her hand up to her mouth. Where was a hole in the ground, she wondered, when you really needed one to swallow you up? George Whittaker was a farmer toward the north of town; his grandson, Jeffrey, had been one of Iris's favorite pupils back at the little elementary school. She jumped to her feet. "I didn't realize anyone else was near," she blurted, brushing imaginary dirt off her skirt.

"Came up to visit with the missus." The old man bent down to scratch his big, burly dog, who stood there regarding Iris with thoughtful, philosophical eyes. "I don't like her to think I've forgot all about her." He looked away for a moment, then swallowed hard and turned to Iris. "I wouldn't worry none about your talking to yourself. I do it all the time." He smiled a weather-beaten smile. "I like to think of it as a highly educational conversation with a right interesting party."

Iris laughed, already a little more at ease. "I'll have to remember that."

They began strolling among the headstones, with George and his dog, Max, taking the lead. Sometimes he would point one out to her and tell her the dear departed's history. "*She* was an infamous type of woman, she was. Wouldn't've guessed it to see her sitting all proper and holier than thou in church on a Sunday, though." Or "That one! He'd buy your soul dirt-cheap and sell it back to you at interest." Mostly, they just meandered about in friendly, comfortable silence.

"You seem kinda low somehow, Miss Amory, if you don't mind my saying so," George suddenly remarked as they turned down another row. He paused. "I guess what I'm trying to say is, if you need a set of ears, you can borrow mine. And I'm no gossiping old hen—it won't go no further than me and Max here." He reached down and stroked the dog's massive head, and Max promptly returned the favor by taking his owner's hand in his mouth and gumming it playfully.

Iris studied him, and something in his eyes told her that she could trust him, just as she'd been able to trust Archie. So she told

179

him—skimming over her own affairs, of course. George nodded once or twice, not speaking until she'd finished.

"I'd heard rumors," he admitted. "Can't keep much to yourself in a small town like this." He cracked his knuckles thoughtfully. "It's a mess, all right. But the way I look at it, there's only one question you need to get answered."

"What's that?" Iris asked, bending down to pat Max, who thumped his tail approvingly.

"Do you care about him? 'Cause if you do, then the rest of it's kinda secondary, seems to me."

"I don't know," Iris replied. Max was licking her hand now—great warm sloppy kisses that drew her out of herself, out of the trance she'd been in the last few days. She ruffled the fur along Max's ears and neck; satisfied, he settled against her feet and resumed tail-thumping. "I don't know. I hadn't thought—"

"To care for someone else again so soon after losing your young man over in France?" George gazed down at her, the blue eyes behind the specs compassionate. "No, I suppose not. But life has a knack for pulling the unexpected out of a hat, and that's what you've got here now, and that's what you gotta make a decision about."

"Someone else said something like that to me once," Iris mused, remembering Mrs. Abbott's words to her after Jerry's death. "So you think I should forgive him? Accept the situation—and him—for what they are?"

"If he matters to you, yes. You're the only one who can answer that. C'mon, Max buddy—time to rise and shine." The dog reluctantly got up, and the three of them started moving again, slowly, as though in a dream. Suddenly, George touched Iris on the shoulder. "Look at that, will you?"

Iris looked. Past the hodgepodge of stones—the simple Colonial markers with their blurred and lichen-spotted inscriptions, and the bigger, more imposing Victorian monuments that tried to defy mortality—she could see the Methodist church, its crenellated red tower with its bands of brighter red vivid against the summer sky, keeping watch with the shops on Main Street. The town was a youngster compared to the ones she had seen in France, of course, but there was something both timeless and comforting in the view.

"I never get tired of that there sight," George remarked. "'World without end, amen.'"

Iris nodded. "I don't know why, but it makes me feel like I could live forever."

"Do you now?" he queried, smiling. He glanced around him and nodded. "I know what you mean, though I can't put it into words either. The missus never seems very far away from me here, though."

They stood there for a while, neither one of them wanting to break the spell the place had laid upon them. Time did not exist, or if it did, they had somehow managed to step outside it. Finally, Max started whining and pushed hard against George, his black-and-white bulk nearly knocking the old man over. "C'mon, buddy," George said, coming out of his reverie. "Let's get you out of the sun."

They began moving, walking more quickly than they had before. "Do you really think it's 'world without end, amen'?" Iris asked. "That there's more than this?"

George never slackened his pace. "You mean, do we just fall asleep, and that's that?" He shook his head. "No, I don't believe that one iota. I've seen some mighty strange things. There's something beyond us, all right—and sometimes, if we're lucky, we get to see a small piece of it in the here and now."

They continued on in friendly silence down the hill. When they came to the cemetery gates, George turned to her. "Sometimes you kinda have to go half ways," he remarked. "I'm thinking this is probably one of those times for you."

"So you're saying I should take it slowly," Iris asked. "This business with Joe, I mean?"

"Take it *all* slowly is what I'm saying." He patted her shoulder paternally. "And I'd see if I could figure out some sort of answer to that question we was discussing earlier. It would be highly educational, I expect." He touched his hand to his cap and whistled—a thin, reedy whistle, plaintive as a phoebe's song. "C'mon, Max—time to go."

EPILOGUE

The room was darkening now. Iris reached over and flicked on the table lamp alongside her, creating a soft amber oasis of light, pushing the shadows back. Slowly, reluctant to step out of the world of her story, I got up and switched on the standing lamp over by the stairway. I sighed. The shadows hadn't been half-bad, I thought.

I strolled over to our cozy fireplace nook and slid back into my chair. "So you married him, anyway," I mused. "After all that."

Iris smiled up at me impishly. "After all that."

"And you were happy?"

She nodded. "In our fashion." She paused. "Of course, there were no children."

"But—" I glanced up at the photo of her and Lucy.

Iris followed my gaze calmly. "Oh, I love Lucy like she were my own. But she's not." She looked down at her hands—thin and scarred but the lines of them still beautiful. "She's Glenna's."

I opened my mouth and shut it almost immediately. Iris reached over and placed one of those lovely old hands with their crepe-paper-thin skin and bird-like bones on mine. "Glenna died when Lucy was seven. A botched abortion, though that, of course, was hushed up. By then I'd had several miscarriages, and I wanted a child"—she swallowed hard, her throat quivering—"very much. Lucy was such a little scrap of a thing. Nobody else wanted her, and I—I told Joe we'd take her." She stared into the empty fireplace—seeing the scene replay itself, I didn't doubt. "It was easier adopting then, and, besides, Joe *was* her father, there was no question of that."

"After everything that had happened," I marveled, practically repeating myself. I shook my head. "That was pretty saint-like of you."

"I'm no saint, Dawn—you know that by now. But Lucy was such a pretty, affectionate child with Joe's eyes and coloring, she was in my heart before I knew it." Iris reached for a faded navy-blue book lying on the table and handed it to me. "Ever read this?"

"No," I replied, frowning at her non sequitur. I peered at the title. *My Lady of Cleves*, by Margaret Campbell Barnes. Iris had shared her books generously with me; I hadn't read this particular one, but I'd seen it on the lower shelf, where she kept her very best favorites, the ones that she liked to flip through on what she called her "gray days." I handed it back to her. "I know you like historical novels, Iris, but I can't say I get the connection."

"Then I'll show you." She flipped through the book till she found what she was looking for and then, the schoolteacher in her taking over, read, "*The only way to triumph over frustration was to make a free gift of the thing denied.*" Iris sighed, the way a true reader does when satisfied by the turn of a line or the vividness of an image, and closed the volume softly. "That's how it was with me, Dawn. Barnes didn't write this book till many years later, but she knew—she knew. Like Anne in the story, I had to find a child who needed what I had to give. In the end, it didn't matter whose daughter she was."

"And Lucy"—I hesitated, afraid of blundering in with the wrong words—"she regards you as her mother?"

Iris nodded. "Glenna had pretty much neglected her, I'm afraid—she wasn't all that old herself when Lucy was born—and

I never saw a child who wanted to be loved so badly." She leaned back in her chair and gazed at the photo. Seeing her face unguarded like that, I knew where she had finally found the ease her heart had been looking for since losing Jerry.

"You must miss her," I said.

Iris withdrew her eyes reluctantly from the picture. "Yes, I do," she admitted. "But it was too good an opportunity for her to let slip by. Anyway, it's a short-term appointment, and she'll be back soon. Wants to get back to doing her own painting, she says, instead of teaching about other people's. So that's something to look forward to."

The lamplight touched the cut-glass vases and bowls on the long radiator shelf, coaxing out some of their pale-purple-and-gold shimmer. "What about the others at the hospital?" I asked. "Did you ever hear from any of them again? Other than May, I mean?"

The glass bric-a-brac wasn't the only thing that the light worked its magic on. Iris's eyes glowed, and I knew that for her, the friendly room with its "interesting clutter" had receded, that she was back in a past infinitely more real to her than the here and now we shared. "Derwent Wood, no," she said, "although I read of his passing, of course—let me see, that was in 1926, just after his statue for the British Machine Gun Corps Memorial was erected. Lung cancer." She shook her head, her eyes wistful. "All those cigarettes." A shiver ran through her, and she pulled the turquoise afghan down off the back of the chair and wrapped it around her.

"Did you ever see the piece that you modeled for?" I asked quickly. The ghosts—especially the one of a man who had passed through her life so briefly—should really ease up on her some. Talk about taking up space without paying rent.

She perked up and gently—graciously, as was her wont—sent the sculptor's ghost back into the shadows. "Lucy found a sketch of it in one of her art books. It had a very allegorical sort of name—something like 'Humanity Overcoming War.' He had a strong classical style. Can't say it resembled me much, except"—she grinned wickedly—"the shoulders and the *et ceteras.*"

I laughed. "Oh, Iris, you wanton hussy."

"I've had my moments," she agreed. "Now, let me see, where were we? Oh, yes. The others. Not a word from Fritz, although I always hoped he made it out of Germany before Hitler came to power. He was such a sensitive, beautiful soul. The Matron and Mrs. Abbott I heard from regularly till their deaths in the Blitz. They died together, you know—Delphina happened to be visiting Agatha at the time." Iris shuddered. "At least, they weren't alone. It helps knowing that."

"They probably never even knew what—" My voice trailed off awkwardly.

"What hit them?" Iris finished. "Probably not. There's a comfort in that, too."

"And Daniel Blaine?"

Iris smiled, and her smile held all the vibrant magic and honeysuckle sweetness of a June morning. "Oh, he came back to me, all right." She smoothed the folds of her afghan, running her fingers along the crocheted medallions. "But it was a long time afterward. His Meg had just died, and Joe had been dead a good eight years. Anyway, he looked me up, and we began seeing each other again." She paused. "We talked of getting married."

I looked up. Here was a plot twist I hadn't foreseen. Like Iris's grin, it was totally unexpected. And yet, when I turned it over in my mind, it fit. "What happened?"

"He died," she replied softly. "In his sleep. His heart just stopped. In one sense, that is. In another . . . well, he was the most compassionate man I ever met, and I don't think that changed just because he left his body."

"So, you don't feel cheated?" *I would've,* I thought. *I would've been howling to the universe like a freakin' banshee about the unfairness of it all.*

She turned to me, and the look she gave me was one part Psyche, one part *Pietà,* and wholly transcendent, lighting up the worn cameo elegance of her face. "No," Iris said slowly, "I don't. After all, I had him—twice. And the second time was sweeter. There was no war, no other lovers dead or waiting in the wings." Her hands came to rest against her afghaned lap. "Don't get me wrong, Dawn—when he died, I grieved for him and grieved for him hard. That's my nature. But I also knew what we'd been to each other, and it seemed—well, *selfish* to ask for more.

"Folks talk a lot about soul mates these days, Dawn. Well, I don't buy it. Never did. That is far too much weight to place on another's soul. There are simply people we're more 'right' with than others." She began rummaging through the table's drawer. "In some ways, Daniel Blaine was more right for me than either Jerry Enright or Joe MacCurdy—in some ways, not." She pulled a small snapshot out of the drawer. "Here he is," Iris said, and I never heard a more satisfied purr. She handed the picture to me.

I studied it thoughtfully. Yes, he looked the part. "He has the sort of face I would like to sculpt if I were an artist," I reflected, handing the photo back to her. "But I thought his hair would be darker."

"It was, when I knew him during the war. But this was taken the second time around, when he was considerably older." She touched the photo gently, then propped it up against the table lamp. "There you go, Daniel."

"What about Tim Skinner?" He'd been one of my favorite characters. If *I'd* been writing this story, I'd have had Iris choose *him.* Speaking for myself, I could never have resisted a man who could do a mongoose impersonation.

"Oh, Tim's still alive and kicking—emphasis on 'kicking.' He lives up in Springfield, Massachusetts, with his son and daughter-in-law and has an in-law apartment attached to the garage. So he has somebody to check in on him and his independence both, which is nice for him. He has missed his wife dreadfully." Seeing my disappointed look, Iris chuckled. "Why, Dawn, you wanted me to end up with Tim."

No use denying it. "Yep."

"Yep," she repeated, still chuckling. "Oh, Dawnie"—her voice softened as it did in her more motherly moments, when she called me that—"what makes you think we *didn't* have our happy ending?"

"But—"

"Remember, all kinds of affairs—all kinds of love. Nothing is clear-cut once the emotions step in. If you're to become a truly superior writer, that's the first thing you've got to get a handle on."

"But I'm just—"

She pulled a face, but her eyes were kind. "Too many 'buts.'" She looked at me—and through me—and spoke in a rapt faraway voice: the priestess at Delphi or the Sibyl of Cumae. "I believe you have it in you to be a great writer—you just haven't found the right story to tell yet."

Her words caught me off guard, bringing some of those less-than-clear-cut emotions burbling up to the surface in me. "So, what about you and Tim?"

"Oh"—Iris was back to her everyday self now—"he used to come down here periodically for visits, or I'd head up there. Of course, neither of us drives anymore, but we keep in touch by letter and phone, same as May and I do."

How much of her life I still didn't know, I marveled. I squeezed her hand. "Thanks for a superior story."

"You're very welcome." She inclined her head graciously, but I could tell how much the telling had tired her. I got up and kissed her on the cheek. "You rest now—I'll be back before you know it."

"I'll be here." Iris closed her eyes and was so quiet, I thought she might've drifted off, the way she did sometimes. But, as I went to let myself out, she surprised me by saying, "You can have it, you know. The story, that is. I'll never write it now."

I nodded. "Thanks," I whispered. I locked the back door from the inside and slid out as noiselessly as one of her shadow-folk.

What was left of the fall played itself out quietly. I had always stuck to journalism, fearful of the creative leaps of faith that fiction-writing demanded. But I was trying my hand at some short stories now and liking it: the results were rough, yet I saw something real and heartfelt emerging on the page. Some of the better ones I shared with Iris. Somehow she always saw what I'd been trying to accomplish, even when the story itself seemed like a badly put-together crazy quilt to me.

More and more frequently, Mary, her physical therapist, was there, doing whatever she could to relieve the pain in Iris's degenerating spine. Afterwards, we'd sit there, chatting over our soup and sandwiches; then, as I grew more comfortable with Mary, I began sharing my stories with her as well. She, too, was enthusiastic, and I—well, I was more in my glory in that living room with the two of them listening to my yarns than any Pulitzer Prize–winning author could imagine.

With all of this going on, the holidays just sorta snuck up on us. For Iris, the real presents, of course, were a transatlantic phone call from Lucy and a watercolor she'd done while visiting Wales. Still, Iris fussed over our gifts. Mary had made her a pillow for her back, and I had put together a little stocking of soaps, hand creams, and the like since Iris had been emphatic about not wanting any *more* "interesting clutter" at her age. I must've overdone it with the soaps, though: after pulling out the third one, Iris turned to me and asked,

"Are you trying to tell me something?"

She tried to look pained but the corners of her mouth twitched. And then she found the crystal leaf prism—the one frivolous gift I'd dared sneak into her stocking—and her eyes turned entirely blue, shimmering like sunlight on the water. Suddenly, I wanted to freeze-frame the moment, etching every line of her fine-boned face into my brain.

Shortly after the New Year, Iris began slipping away from us— slowly, genteelly, like a guest who knows it's time to leave but who doesn't want to be rude or make a fuss about it. She tired more easily and was content to sit and listen; her mind was still laser-sharp, but it seemed as if spoken words, too, had become just more interesting clutter to let go of. Still, I kept getting the sense that she *was* in silent conversation with someone, some thoughtful presence whom I couldn't see myself but who was nonetheless real. Jerry? Daniel Blaine? Archie maybe? Somehow I didn't think it was Joe, despite their having been married all those years and raising a child together. No, it was another soul communing with her, one that had touched hers to the quick and never really let go.

Mary and I watched her with our hearts in our throats, never saying a word, just looking into each other's eyes and turning away, sighing. But one February afternoon, when Iris was especially list-less, Mary stopped me in the kitchen on my way out. "I've called Lucy," she said, keeping her voice low as possible. "She'll be in early tomorrow morning."

I closed my eyes. It was happening. "Does she need a ride from the airport?"

Mary shook her head. "She said she'd rent a car." She pressed a small book into my hands. Glancing down, I saw that it was Iris's address book. "If you could call some of the folks in this book, that—that would be a help. I know Lucy from her visits but not the others." She swallowed hard, twisting her hands. "It's not like there are all that many to call. Most of her friends are gone, and she didn't have any family other than Lucy."

"And us," I choked. "Don't worry, I'll take care of it."

As Mary had pointed out, there weren't many calls to make. Most of the entries were followed by scribbled-in dates of death. Iris had spoken true: of her old comrades, only May and Tim remained.

I called May first. The phone kept ringing, and I was just about to hang up when somebody finally picked up. "Hello?" a quavery voice said. An old woman's voice. May's.

It really threw me. I guess part of me had stupidly been expecting the vibrant young woman of Iris's story to answer. That's what stories did to you, the really good ones, that is—they caught you up in their spell and, like Iris's unseen caller, never quite let go of you. Quietly, as kindly as I could, I broke the news to her.

A long drawn-out animal moan came over the line, making me forget my own grief. Then silence. I stood there, cradling the receiver, wondering what to do when May spoke again.

"Tell her"—that quavery old voice got even more quavery—"I'll be seeing her soon." There was the sound of the phone dropping, followed by a quiet buzz of voices very close by. Then another younger—well, middle-aged—voice spoke. "Hello, this is Tara Shaughnessy, Mrs. LaJoie's nurse. I just want to thank you for calling to let us know about Mrs. MacCurdy—Mrs. LaJoie speaks of her so often."

"I'm sorry there wasn't a better way of letting her know."

"There never is," Tara said matter-of-factly. "Hold on just a few while I make sure she's settled."

I held on, twisting the phone cord. She was back in a few minutes. "Sorry to keep you hanging." Tara sounded a tad breathless. "I just wanted to get Mrs. LaJoie settled in the next room. The truth is,

I'm with hospice. You see, Mrs. LaJoie is in the end stages of uterine cancer, and today was a bad day."

And I just made it worse, I thought. *Way to go, Dawn—tell the dying woman that her oldest friend's about to beat her across the finish line to the mortuary.* "I'm so sorry to hear that," I said. "I—I hope whatever time she has left is as painless as possible." I hung up and wished myself somewhere else . . . London . . . through the looking-glass . . . it didn't matter where. Your favorite story characters aren't supposed to die; they're supposed to stay safely tucked in their books, waiting for you to come visit.

Finally, I flexed my foot, which had fallen asleep while I was sitting there at my desk, and dialed Tim Skinner's number. A young man I figured was probably his grandson answered. "I'll get him," he said, and in moments, Tim's voice was coming at me—strong and penetrating and still retaining a good measure of his Australian accent.

He was slightly deaf, so I had to repeat a few things, but his mind was wonderfully clear, and he rapped out question after question about Iris's condition as though *he* were the doctor handling her case. Then he said, "Tell Iris I'll be down as soon as I can. My fool family won't let me drive anymore, or I'd be down there faster than—"

"A mongoose on a cobra?" The words popped out of my mouth before I knew it.

He laughed, and I joined in, glad, as I felt he must be, to have a little comic relief. "So Iris told you that one, did she? Full marks—full marks." Tim chuckled, then sighed. "Those were harsh times—what did you say your name was, miss?"

"Dawn. Dawn Kailey."

"Well, Dawn Kailey, those were harsh times, like I was saying. And yet . . . and yet I don't think I've ever felt more alive. The war wouldn't let us take anything for granted, see what I'm saying? Besides, I never would've met Iris, Abraham, or May. Come to think of it, you called May yet?"

"Ye-es," I replied reluctantly, "but—"

"Spit it out, girl! I've lived through a world war and my very own private crucifixion. I expect I can take it."

So, feeling more than a little like the Grim Reaper's personal secretary by this point, I told him what Tara Shaughnessy had said. He was silent for a moment. "So, that's two of them," he said heavily. "I'm sorry to hear that, I am. May was always a good scout. Well, that settles it. I can't let my Flower-girl go out alone."

"That's what Jerry called her," I murmured, my mind drifting back to the love story that I suspected Iris might've regarded as *her* "very own private crucifixion."

"I stole it from him," Tim admitted. "Suited her, it did. I don't know as he would've made her happy if he'd come back, mind you, but he did love her. I saw the letters he sent her and the sketch he done of her, and I never doubted *that*. Listen, my daughter-in-law is yammering at me about taking my damned medication, and there's no sense in your running up more of a phone bill on my account. Just make sure you're on hand when I get there, Dawn Kailey."

"I will," I promised and hung up.

I didn't go back to see Iris for almost a week, figuring that she and Lucy needed all the time together they could get. And, to be honest, I was scared of what changes might be waiting for me. But I knew, too, that I couldn't let her go into that good night without a word.

Lucy answered the door. She was tall and thin, with her father's blue-gray eyes. *Iris's eye color, too,* I thought, and that made it seem as though she really *was* Iris's daughter. She had picked up Iris's unusually firm handshake and low, warm voice, too.

"Mum has told me all about you," she said. Her face, like her voice, was very expressive and animated, making her seem younger than she was. "I'm glad that you could be here with her all these months." She smiled sadly, her hands going through the motions of making an invisible cat's-cradle. "I guess I'm having a bad attack of the 'guilts' right now because I wasn't."

"But she *wanted* you to have that chance—she told me so." Lucy's face lightened, and her eyes lost a little of the "guilts." I handed her Iris's address book, which I'd stuffed in my gray patchwork hobo bag. "How is she?"

"Weak—very weak. The pain must be tremendous, but she won't take any medication. She says she's afraid it—it'll keep her here longer, and she doesn't want that." Lucy's voice broke, and she turned away, tightening her hold on the faded little book until I was sure its edges must be cutting into her hands. "Excuse me—she's the only mother I've ever really known, and I just can't believe it's really happening."

"Neither can I." My own voice was heading for a free-fall.

Lucy set the address book down on the spool-legged table next to her and wiped her eyes. "She's very weak, like I said, so I'm afraid you'll only be able to stay a few minutes." She managed a smile, and—well, forget the color—the *expression* in her eyes was so very much Iris's, I smiled, too, in spite of the tears I could feel welling up in mine. Nurture had definitely won out over nature in Lucy's case. "But you can always come back, Dawn—you know that."

"A few minutes are enough," I choked, and headed down the hall toward Iris's bedroom.

I had only been in there a few times before, when Iris had asked me to fetch a book, an old photo, or some curio whose story she wanted to share with me. It was a comfortable room, its walls painted coral like the inside of a pink roller shell. In fact, I kinda felt like I *was* inside a shell, the way the morning light filtered through the lace curtains, dancing on the wooden floor, coaxing rainbows from my little crystal leaf, which was hanging in the window facing her bed.

And there were the books. Crammed into the built-in bookcase, piled on her bedside table, and practically spilling over onto the floor. Wherever Iris was, books would not be far behind. I sat down on the little cricket chair by her bedside.

"I like your leaf," she said suddenly. "The rainbows entertain me, especially now that I'm too tired to read much on my own."

"I'm glad."

"And I'm glad to have been part of your writing," she told me, reaching up to stroke my hair, her eyes shimmering.

I gave her my best smile, water-logged though it was. "I haven't done that much."

"No. But you will." The lines of her face softened, and there was a very, very faint wash of color in her cheeks, which would've thrilled me if some instinct hadn't told me this was her final flickering, that last eerie heart-piercing incandescence before the flame went out. "I think you're wonderful."

"I think it's always been a mutual admiration society." I rose from her bedside and forced the next words out. "I won't be back unless you need me." I bent down and, cupping her pointed face gently in my hands, kissed her good-bye.

Lucy met me at the end of the hallway with a large cardboard box in her arms. "Mum wanted you to have this. She said you'd know what to do with it, being a writer. It's got all her war memorabilia and a few books and other things in it."

I hesitated. "Are you sure?"

"Very sure. Of course, there's one condition"—she smiled—"and that's that you have to send me a copy of the book when it comes out."

195

I took the box from her. "You sound pretty certain I'll be able to pull it off."

"Mum is never wrong about people—I learned that long ago." We stood there for a while, silent and awkward in our shared grief. Finally, Lucy shook herself. "Well, I should go see if she needs anything. You'll be back?"

"Not unless she needs me," I replied, falling back on my words to Iris. "But I'll want to know when—when she goes."

Lucy nodded. "You and Mary will be the first ones I call. Your number's in Mum's address book, isn't it?"

"Yes." I'd come across it while making my phone calls, written in Iris's spidery but elegant script.

She suddenly took a gander at the carton I was holding and gasped. "Oh, my God, I didn't think! You can't possibly manage the door with that great thing in your arms. Hold on a sec—"

"I'll get it," Mary said. It was as though she'd materialized out of dust motes and muted sunshine. "You go see to Iris."

Lucy left, and Mary and I made our silent trek to the back door. "I'll miss our luncheons," I said lamely.

"So will I," she whispered, opening the door. Her hand lingered on the knob. "You know, it meant a lot to Iris that you kept coming the way you did. It gave her something to look forward to."

"Me, too." If my voice had been lame before, it was utterly broken now. I leaned over the top of my keepsake box as best I could and kissed her on the cheek.

I stumbled out into the yard and walked over to my car, blinking against the brightness of the day. I popped the hatchback open and placed the box carefully inside; then my curiosity took hold of me, and I pulled apart the flaps.

It was all there: the letters, Jerry's drawings—even that first clever caricature on the back of a very yellowed envelope—the spur, the box he'd picked up for her at the *estaminet,* the old photos of him and Daniel Blaine, and even May's robin. The framed traveler's joy print that had caught my eye that first day. Some of what I knew were her favorite Goudge novels and—I smiled—*My Lady of Cleves.* And an odd oblong, knobby tissue-swathed package that looked like a miniature mummy. I carefully undid its wrappings. There lay the wooden statuette of St. Dorothea, a tad more weather-beaten but her faded blue eyes just as steadfast and comforting.

But how had she gotten there? I wondered, turning her over in my hands. Iris had made no mention of ever having brought the saint back with her; indeed, I had never seen her anywhere in the house. Dorothea's presence in the carton was something of a loose end.

A car pulled up behind me, startling me out of my reverie. A wiry brown-haired man, who looked to be my own age, give or take a year or two, got out and tried to help someone out of the back seat, only to get a cane waved at him for his trouble. The cane touched ground and was followed by a pair of trousered legs and a second cane. An elderly man with gold-rimmed glasses slowly emerged. I looked from one face to the other and gasped: the resemblance between the two was so uncanny, I knew I could only be looking at grandfather and grandson. Or, rather, Tim Skinner Past and Present.

Tim Skinner Past saw me first. "There's a good-looking girl looking at me," he chuckled. He made his way over to me surprisingly quickly, considering his infirmities, his grandson following close behind.

"You must be the Dawn-girl," Tim greeted me. "Tim Skinner at your service. I'd shake hands, but I can't let go of these damned canes for the life of me. Grayson, you do it for me. This is my older grandson—Colin's the one you spoke to on the phone—and a pretty decent one, though he's a bit full of himself and thinks he knows everything."

"Like grandfather, like grandson?" I remarked, shaking hands with Grayson. I looked into his eyes and instantly felt as though I knew him and not just because he resembled the Tim of Iris's story.

"Ha! Full marks," chortled Tim. He whistled as he took in the open box in the back of my car and the wooden statuette in my hands. "Iris's war chest," he said softly. "And St. Dorothea."

"Do you know how she got here?" I asked.

"Stole her," Tim replied unabashedly. "I knew she'd come to signify a lot to Iris, but I also knew that she wouldn't feel right about taking the old girl herself. So I liberated her myself when I left the hospital a few days later. Of course, St. Dorothea and I had a few adventures first, so it was a while before she reached the States. You should've seen Iris's face—it was a study, all right."

He grinned at the memory; then his face dimmed like a sad old Cheshire cat's. "I'll just pop in now, and if she's not up for visitors just yet, I can have a good catch-up with Lucy. Never had much use for her old man, but she's a different story, Lucy is, and she does Iris proud." He started up the sunken stone walkway, then turned. "Dawn-girl?"

"Yes?"

"Seems to me I recall Iris mentioning a visiting writer of sorts during our conversations. You wouldn't happen to be she, would you?"

"Well, I do some freelancing for various publications but—"

"No 'buts.' If Iris said you're a writer, you're a writer. She wouldn't have given her war chest to just anybody." The fire was back in him now—in the way he held his head, in his voice, and in those fey blue-green eyes of his. "Be that as it 'wither' we need to talk, the three of us here."

"The *three* of us?" I was barely sure of my own part in all this, never mind Grayson's.

Tim chuckled. "Grayson's just started up his own publishing company. Small but select, as we used to say. And he's looking for new authors, aren't you, boy?"

"Definitely." Grayson produced a business card out of his breast pocket, rather like a magician pulling a rabbit out of his hat, and handed it to me. "I'm particularly interested in historical novels—ones that really carry you back to the time and place like Thomas Costain or Anya Seton used to write."

"You've been raiding Iris's library," I laughed.

He grinned, and again, I had that powerful sense of being at home with him. "You betcha. Since I was a kid—Granddad's, too. And if you're going to be writing their story, I want in on that." He paused. "You *are* going to be writing it, aren't you? It's one helluva story."

"Yes," I said, and this time, I knew I would.

"Great. Well, I'd better head inside before Gladly, my old cross-eyed bear, gets mad at me."

"'Cross-eyed bear'?"

Grayson laughed. "It's from an old hymn we used to sing in church—'Gladly the cross I bear.' Well, apparently, generations of kids have heard it as 'Gladly the cross-eyed bear.' I just happen to think Granddad here makes a damn fine cross-eyed bear." But he said it affectionately.

"And the bear says it's time we got a move on," Tim said, nudging Grayson with one of his canes. "Quit your flirting—Iris is waiting."

"Yes, Gladly." Grayson shook my hand again. "We'll talk. And soon."

I watched him walk to the house with his grandfather; then, once Mary had let them in, I turned back to my treasures. I wrapped Dorothea up in her tissue and placed her gently back in the box. I tucked the carton's flaps back into place and closed the hatchback's door. My busywork done, I leaned against my car, the sadness seeping into me as I tried to imagine my world without Iris.

Suddenly, a bone-chilling wind sprang out of nowhere, blowing my hair every which way. I wrapped my arms against my chest. A sweater-jacket really wasn't warm enough for this time of year, I chided myself. I walked around to the front of my car and froze.

There, near the slope where the woods began, right by Iris's favorite white birch, sat a cat, watching me solemnly. Small with silver flecks scattered like snowflakes against the black night of his fur and silver "specs" around those glowing eyes that held mine fast. Slowly, he bowed his bullet-shaped head, then bounded up the slope into the woods, a black streak blurring first to gray, then turning to the pure white-gold of morning light among the still-leafless trees . . . The tears rained down my face freely then. "Traveler's joy, Iris," I murmured. "Traveler's joy."

ABOUT THE AUTHOR

T. J. Banks is the author of *Catsong*, *Souleiado*, and *Houdini*, a novel for young adults which the late writer and activist Cleveland Amory enthusiastically branded "a winner." *Catsong*, a collection of her best cat stories, was the winner of the 2007 Merial Human-Animal Bond Award. A Contributing Editor to *laJoie*, she has received writing awards from the Cat Writers' Association (CWA), *ByLine*, and *The Writing Self*. She has worked as a stringer for the Associated Press and as an instructor for the Writer's Digest School.